JUST ONE DANCE

Praise for Jenny Frame

Longing for You

"Jenny Frame knocks it out of the park once again with this fantastic sequel to *Hunger For You*. She can keep the pages turning with a delicious mix of intrigue and romance."—*Rainbow Literary Society*

Hunger for You

"I loved this book. Paranormal stuff like vampires and werewolves are my go-to sins. This book had literally everything I needed: chemistry between the leads, hot love scenes (phew), drama, angst, romance (oh my, the romance) and strong supporting characters."—*The Reading Doc*

The Duchess and the Dreamer

"We thoroughly enjoyed the whole romance-the-disbelieving-duchess with gallantry, unwavering care, and grand gestures. Since this is very firmly in the butch-femme zone, it appealed to that part of our traditionally-conditioned-typecasting mindset that all the wooing and work is done by Evan without throwing even a small fit at any point. We liked the fact that Clementine has layers and depth. She has her own personal and personality hurdles that make her behaviour understandable and create the right opportunities for Evan to play the romantic knight convincingly…We definitely recommend this one to anyone looking for a feel-good mushy romance."—*Best Lesfic Reviews*

"There are a whole range of things I like about Jenny Frame's aristocratic heroines: they have plausible histories to account for them holding titles in their own right; they're in touch with reality and not necessarily super-rich, certainly not through inheritance; and they find themselves paired with perfectly contrasting co-heroines…Clementine and Evan are excellently depicted, and I love the butch:femme dynamic they have going on, as well as their individual abilities to stick to their principles but also to compromise with each other when necessary."
—*The Good, The Bad and The Unread*

Still Not Over You

"*Still Not Over You* is a wonderful second-chance romance anthology that makes you believe in love again. And you would certainly be missing out if you have not read *My Forever Girl*, because it truly is everything."—*SymRoute*

Someone to Love

"One of the author's best works to date—both Trent and Wendy were so well developed they came alive. I could really picture them and they jumped off the pages. They had fantastic chemistry, and their sexual dynamic was deliciously well written. The supporting characters and the storyline about Alice's trauma was also sensitively written and well handled."—*Melina Bickard, Librarian, Waterloo Library (UK)*

Wooing the Farmer

"The chemistry between the two MCs had us hooked right away. We also absolutely loved the seemingly ditzy femme with an ambition of steel but really a vulnerable girl. The sex scenes are great. Definitely recommended."—*Reviewer@large*

"This is the book we Axedale fanatics have been waiting for…Jenny Frame writes the most amazing characters and this whole series is a masterpiece. But where she excels is in writing butch lesbians. Every time I read a Jenny Frame book I think it's the best ever, but time and again she surprises me. She has surpassed herself with *Wooing the Farmer*."—*Kitty Kat's Book Review Blog*

Royal Court

"The author creates two very relatable characters…Quincy's quietude and mental torture are offset by Holly's openness and lust for life. Holly's determination and tenacity in trying to reach Quincy are total wish-fulfilment of a person like that. The chemistry and attraction is excellently built."—*Best Lesbian Erotica*

"[A] butch/femme romance that packs a punch."—*Les Rêveur*

"There were unbelievably hot sex scenes as I have come to expect and look forward to in Jenny Frame's books. Passions slowly rise until you feel the characters may burst!…Royal Court is wonderful and I highly recommend it."—*Kitty Kat's Book Review Blog*

Royal Court "was a fun, light-hearted book with a very endearing romance."—*Leanne Chew, Librarian, Parnell Library (Auckland, NZ)*

Charming the Vicar

"Chances are, you've never read or become captivated by a romance like *Charming the Vicar*. While books featuring people of the cloth aren't unusual, Bridget is no ordinary vicar—a lesbian with a history of kink...Surrounded by mostly supportive villagers, Bridget and Finn balance love and faith in a story that affirms both can exist for anyone, regardless of sexual identity."—*RT Book Reviews*

"The sex scenes were some of the sexiest, most intimate and quite frankly, sensual I have read in a while. Jenny Frame had me hooked and I reread a few scenes because I felt like I needed to experience the intense intimacy between Finn and Bridget again. The devotion they showed to one another during these sex scenes but also in the intimate moments was gripping and for lack of a better word, carnal."—*Les Rêveur*

"The sexual chemistry between [Finn and Bridge] is unbelievably hot. It is sexy, lustful and with more than a hint of kink. The scenes between them are highly erotic—and not just the sex scenes. The tension is ramped up so well that I felt the characters would explode if they did not get relief!...An excellent book set in the most wonderful village—a place I hope to return to very soon!"—*Kitty Kat's Book Reviews*

"This is Frame's best character work to date. They are layered and flawed and yet relatable...Frame really pushed herself with *Charming the Vicar* and it totally paid off...I also appreciate that even though she regularly writes butch/femme characters, no two pairings are the same."—*The Lesbian Review*

Unexpected

"If you enjoy contemporary romances, *Unexpected* is a great choice. The character work is excellent, the plotting and pacing are well done, and it's just a sweet, warm read...Definitely pick this book up when you're looking for your next comfort read, because it's sure to put a smile on your face by the time you get to that happy ending."—*Curve*

"*Unexpected* by Jenny Frame is a charming butch/femme romance that is perfect for anyone who wants to feel the magic of overcoming adversity and finding true love. I love the way Jenny Frame writes.

I have yet to discover an author who writes like her. Her voice is strong and unique and gives a freshness to the lesbian fiction sector."
—*The Lesbian Review*

Royal Rebel

"Frame's stories are easy to follow and really engaging. She stands head and shoulders above a number of the romance authors and it's easy to see why she is quickly making a name for herself in lesfic romance."—*The Lesbian Review*

Courting the Countess

"I love Frame's romances. They are well paced, filled with beautiful character moments and a wonderful set of side characters who ultimately end up winning your heart...I love Jenny Frame's butch/femme dynamic; she gets it so right for a romance."—*The Lesbian Review*

"I loved, loved, loved this book. I didn't expect to get so involved in the story but I couldn't help but fall in love with Annie and Harry...The love scenes were beautifully written and very sexy. I found the whole book romantic and ultimately joyful and I had a lump in my throat on more than one occasion. A wonderful book that certainly stirred my emotions."—*Kitty Kat's Book Reviews*

"*Courting The Countess* has an historical feel in a present day world, a thought provoking tale filled with raw emotions throughout. [Frame] has a magical way of pulling you in, making you feel every emotion her characters experience."—*Lunar Rainbow Reviewz*

"I didn't want to put the book down and I didn't. Harry and Annie are two amazingly written characters that bring life to the pages as they find love and adventures in Harry's home. This is a great read, and you will enjoy it immensely if you give it a try!"—*Fantastic Book Reviews*

A Royal Romance

"*A Royal Romance* was a guilty pleasure read for me. It was just fun to see the relationship develop between George and Bea, to see George's life as queen and Bea's as a commoner. It was also refreshing to see that both of their families were encouraging, even when Bea doubted that things could work between them because of their class differences...*A Royal Romance* left me wanting a sequel, and romances don't usually do that to me."—*Leeanna.ME Mostly a Book Blog*

By the Author

A Royal Romance

Courting the Countess

Dapper

Royal Rebel

Unexpected

Charming the Vicar

Royal Court

Wooing the Farmer

Someone to Love

The Duchess and the Dreamer

Royal Family

Home Is Where the Heart Is

Sweet Surprise

Royal Exposé

A Haven for the Wanderer

Just One Dance

Wild for You

Hunger for You

Longing for You

Dying for You

Wolfgang County Series

Heart of the Pack

Soul of the Pack

Blood of the Pack

Visit us at www.boldstrokesbooks.com

JUST ONE DANCE

by
Jenny Frame

2023

JUST ONE DANCE

ISBN 13: 978-1-63679-457-0

This Trade Paperback Original Is Published By
Bold Strokes Books, Inc.
P.O. Box 249
Valley Falls, NY 12185

First Edition: June 2023

CREDITS
EDITOR: RUTH STERNGLANTZ
PRODUCTION DESIGN: STACIA SEAMAN
COVER DESIGN BY JEANINE HENNING

Acknowledgments

Firstly, thanks to Ruth for helping me be the best writer I can be. Thanks to Rad, Sandy, and all the BSB staff for all their hard work and for making BSB the best environment for authors to thrive.

Also huge thanks to Lou, Barney, and my family for all their support.

To Lou—My very own Mr Darcy
XX

CHAPTER ONE

Despite being in a crowded office, Taylor Sparks was entirely in a world of her own, as was often the case. She worked for a marketing company that mostly dealt in household goods. At the moment, she and her team were working on a new breakfast cereal campaign, and to say her heart wasn't in it was an understatement.

Taylor had finished the work she needed to do this morning an hour ago, and since then her mind had flitted from one idea to the next. She tapped her pen incessantly on her notepad and drummed the fingers on her other hand. These stims helped quiet her ADHD symptoms.

Her notepad that was largely filled with hearts, arrows piercing hearts, and more hearts. Anyone who saw her scribbles would think her hopelessly in love, but in fact the opposite was true.

At twenty-six Taylor'd had her heart broken—the last time, a year ago. But that didn't discourage her from being in love with love. She was quite sure and quite determined to find it someday. That was something she knew for certain. Taylor would never give up on love.

Taylor's phone beeped and knocked her out of her daydream. It was a notification from a dating app that she should have deleted by now. She should have known better, but she opened it and saw a nice-looking woman, whose profile described her as: *Up for a laugh, and looking for no-strings fun.*

She sighed and closed the app, then finally deleted it. Taylor wanted *strings*, many strings, love, and a committed relationship. It's what she'd daydreamed about her whole life. How could you find something so pure and beautiful on a dating app?

How could you judge a person based on a brief profile and a quick appraisal of their looks? The person you swiped left on could be the love of your life if you had only got to know them the old-fashioned way—the very old-fashioned way.

Brilliant, thought Taylor. The perfect line for an advert. She wrote it down. *Fall in love the old-fashioned way—the very old-fashioned way.*

Taylor got a text from her friend Margo: *You ready for lunch?*

Lunchtime finally. Taylor hated to be sitting this long, just one of the ways this job was killing her. She liked to be on her feet, moving, putting her energy into something she enjoyed, not breakfast cereal campaigns.

She shut down her computer and grabbed her handbag before texting back, *On my way.*

Margo worked for a different company but in the same building as Taylor, so they always met up for lunch. They'd first met when their companies teamed up for a joint charity event. Both Taylor and Margo were on the event committee, got on like a house on fire, and became friends ever since.

Margo was the head of the editing team in her company's publishing business and loved her job. Taylor envied her in that.

Taylor travelled down in the busy lift until she reached the Garden Cafe's floor. They were lucky to have this place in the building. There was greenery everywhere, making it a change from her grey, dreary office, and the food was excellent. As nice as it was, Taylor couldn't bear to sit down indoors, so they often got sandwiches to go and walked over to the park, even when it was a frosty December day like today. They were fortunate that their building was minutes from Green Park, lucky indeed in the built-up centre of London.

Both of them liked to get exercise during lunchtime, so they only sat to eat and then went for a brisk walk. The only weather they didn't venture out in was rain and snow, but today was dry and crisp.

Taylor heard her name called and saw Margo catching up with her.

"Hi, Margo."

"Hey. Let's get some food before our favourite picnic bench at the park is gone."

They purchased their food and made their way out onto the busy London streets.

"Good morning?" Taylor asked.

"Yes, excellent," Margo said. "I'm working with a new young author. That's always the most exciting bit for me, the start of a literary journey. How was yours?"

Taylor sighed. "Boring as usual. I was working on this new cereal brand. I was finished in a few hours and spent the rest of the time itching for the clock to go round."

"You're wasted in that company, Taylor. You're one of the best marketing people I've seen. Come and work for us. I know it's not your own business that you dreamed of, but at least it's a creative business, not cereal and washing powder brand campaigns. My publisher is crying out for someone like you."

Margo wasn't kidding. Working with books and authors would be more interesting than what she was currently doing, but Taylor was frightened she would get comfortable and not push herself to start the business that was her dream, the project that she had been planning for the past six months.

"I think I need to be this bored at work to keep pushing myself. How else will I keep the hunger to open my own business?"

They walked in through the park gates and made their way over to the picnic bench they liked best. It was situated most beautifully next to a lake, where they could watch the water.

"How did your meeting go with the investor you lined up?" Margo asked.

"Not so good. They made me feel like I was wasting their time. If I'd gone to them with an online business model, it would have been looked at differently."

"And your business is more unique than that."

"It certainly is. But I won't let myself be downhearted. The Regency Romance Club can be a success. I know it can."

"With your energy behind it, Sparkle, I know it can," Margo said.

Taylor laughed at the use of the nickname her friends gave her. "I just know there is a market out there for finding love in a more traditional way."

"I know what you mean. I did the whole online dating thing for the longest time, and I met some odd people. You can't judge a book by its cover, and I include my little girl's father in that."

Taylor smiled broadly. "Then you met the most interesting, sweetest man ever."

"That I would have swiped past if I saw him on a dating app."

Josh Webb—three-time gold medal winning Olympic snowboarder and adrenaline junky—would never have made a match on any app with Margo, a decade older than him and the well-respected senior editor at one of the world's biggest publishers.

But when Margo's company was publishing Josh's autobiography, the two of them, who were like chalk and cheese, fell hopelessly in love.

"You see? That's exactly what I want to replicate in the Regency Romance Club. To bring people together who wouldn't normally meet and give them the social environment to get to know the people under the surface."

"I know. That's what's missing from today's dating game. When I met Josh, I judged him. I thought he was an egomaniac man-child, but once I saw underneath, he was so much more. I mean, he is still a man-child, but his personality keeps me young and reminds me not to be so serious. I perish to think what would have happened if I hadn't met him. My little Clara wouldn't have the perfect stepfather, or the little sister who came along quite quickly after Josh and I got to know each other better."

"You saw beyond the cover. That's what I want my clients to experience."

They finished their sandwiches and began a brisk walk around the small circuit they could fit in before the end of lunch break.

Taylor took a big lungful of cold air. "I don't know what I'd do if I couldn't get out to walk at lunchtime."

"You certainly keep me fit. I can hardly keep up with you," Margo said.

Taylor looked to her side and saw Margo struggling to keep up. She immediately slowed down.

She loved walking and hiking, just like some of Jane Austen's heroines. It calmed her unquiet mind. "I can't bear being stuck in the office for too long. I need to be out in the fresh air. I'm going to come unglued if I stay in this nine-to-five rat race."

"Let me ask Josh if he's got any contacts, investors we could introduce you to." Through his sponsorships, Josh probably did meet many companies and businesspeople.

"Okay, thanks. It's worth a try, but don't worry about it over Christmas. We both need a break."

"I know. Josh goes all over the world so much, and it'll be nice to have him in the same place for a while," Margo said.

"Are you still going to Switzerland in the New Year for the snowboarding?" Taylor asked.

"Oh yes. Clara and her dad can play in the snow to their hearts' content, and I can enjoy the spa." Margo smiled. "Are your mum and dad having the whole family?"

"Yes. The invasion, as Mum likes to call it. She loves every minute of it, though. My three brothers, partners, wives, husbands, and children. It will be a madhouse."

"I don't know how you survive it."

"I love it—Christmas and the family invading, although you have to be able to outshout everyone to be heard at any point. My brothers and their spouses rely on me to keep the kids occupied, since I never can sit still anyway."

Margo laughed. "You must be exhausted by the time you get back to work."

"Not me. I get tired when I stop doing anything. I've got to be on the go."

"Don't I know it?" Margo stopped to catch her breath. "Can we head back before my lack of fitness makes me faint?"

"Sure." Taylor laughed. Her mum was always telling her to slow down life, or she might miss it.

"Let's go then. A boring afternoon awaits."

❖

The china on the tea tray rattled as Jaq Bailey shouldered her way through her study door. She put the tray on her desk, and the cup and spoon rattled against each other again, the only sound, apart from the clock ticking, in this empty room.

Bailey used a spoon to give the teapot one last stir and then lifted the tea strainer to pour out the loose-leaf tea. Others would think having a proper cup of tea, made in a teapot, with real tea leaves a complete waste of time—not for Bailey, though.

The art of making a real pot of tea brought calm to her mind, always had. The time it took to prepare everything and wait for it to brew made you slow down, and so made your mind slow down.

She poured the tea through a strainer into a bone china cup that sat on a matching saucer until the cup was a few inches from full. Bailey liked her tea without milk, a trait inherited from her mother, so she only needed to add one spoonful of sugar with her silver spoon and the tea was ready.

The tea set, as well as the way Bailey took her tea, was passed on from her mother. She stirred the cup and then tapped the spoon three times on the edge of the cup, an essential part of the meditative process, and carried her cup and saucer over to the window.

Bailey needed the meditation more than ever today. It was a day when large numbers of the population were blissfully happy, and she was anything but. Christmas Day. She took a sip of her tea and looked out onto the cold and frosty scene before her.

Children were running around the street with bikes and new toys, while parents looked on beaming with pride, terrified that their precious little one would fall off their new bike or scooter or many other kinds of wheeled toys. Bailey had hoped it would rain so that she would be spared this nausea-inducing happiness before her.

It was one of the hazards of living in such a family-friendly area. This old nineteenth-century house had been in her family for a couple of generations, and the houses that lined each side of the road, with their large rooms and ever larger gardens to the rear, attracted middle class families who wanted room to grow and a safe area to play in.

Unfortunately for Bailey, the thought of moving was too big a change for her. She liked things to be unchanging. There was safety in that, and after the few years she'd had, the main thing Bailey wanted was the safety of sameness.

She took another sip and a bite from the biscuit lying on the edge of her saucer. The adults were no better, either following their children around with their phones videoing them, or walking along with garishly wrapped presents in bags or Christmas bottle bags with cascading ribbons hanging from them.

They were clearly either delivering presents or on their way to Christmas lunch with family or friends.

She couldn't blame the children for buying into the Christmas myth of happiness and joy, but the adults had no such excuse. They knew life was not like the Christmas myth they perpetuated in their children, going into debt each year to finance greed for items that would be thrown away and forgotten by the next Christmas and pretending to enjoy being in their families' company for a whole day, stuffing themselves with food to the point of feeling sick.

At least she didn't have any family left to invite her to lunch any more. Not that she would have gone, but it saved her making any excuses.

"Enough of this. Please, God, bring them rain."

She put her tea on her desk and went over to tend the open fire.

Bailey picked up the poker and agitated the wood that was nearly burned down, then added a few more logs.

"Why couldn't it rain?" Bailey asked.

Rain suited her mood, since it had rained in her soul for the last few years, not that she'd been the life of the party before her life changed forever, before Ellis.

Live the life you want to live. Live it to the fullest, Bailey. Ellis's words were a constant in her mind.

Bailey's best friend in the world had died two years ago, and it had broken Bailey. No matter Ellis's wishes and advice to her for after she passed on, Bailey didn't take it.

She didn't want to take the advice—she wanted to live with the pain and misery, because she deserved it. So a Christmas Day in a big empty lonely house suited her mood. Before she thought of any more memories, she went over to her desk to finish her tea and restart work.

Dr. Jaq Bailey was a professor of early modern history and had taught at Cambridge University until her friend's tragic death. When Ellis passed away, she took a year-long sabbatical, but that time had come and gone, and the sabbatical had been extended and extended, and she'd retreated into herself at home.

Unable to face teaching her students, all she did was write popular history books. It was something she had done throughout her teaching career, as her time allowed. Now it was all she had or wanted.

Once she sat down, Bailey refilled her teacup and got back to her manuscript. She loved writing big biographies, but she also loved writing smaller books, introductions to historical figures and periods of time. For the last five years Bailey had been writing a pocket guide to history series for her publisher.

They had become hugely popular, and she had been commissioned to write more and more volumes. If there was something that gave Bailey satisfaction in her life now, it was the thought of someone reading through these pocket guides and being inspired to do more in-depth reading on the subject.

Bailey believed history should be widely studied by all, from crusty old professors to a teenager first diving in to one of her books and becoming hooked. It was that passion that first drove her into teaching, but now that passion was only met through the solitude of her writing.

The manuscript she was working on at the moment was on the Wars of the Roses, one of her favourite subjects—she had completed her PhD on that period—and the beginning of the Tudor era. It was a long, complicated period of time to disseminate into a short pocket guide, but it was a challenge that Bailey enjoyed—well, had enjoyed. She hadn't enjoyed anything these past few years.

She looked at her writing pad, and there was a note she wanted to highlight for later in the chapter that she was working on. When she opened her desk drawer, Bailey's breath caught in her throat. In there was a framed picture of Ellis.

Bailey forgot she had put the photo in here the other day when she couldn't bear to look at it any more. The guilt and the pain were too much for her to look in her eyes.

She had let her down so badly. Ellis had loved her in every way possible—she had Bailey on a pedestal since they were youngsters, so Ellis had admitted the day they had gone out to celebrate Ellis's forty-second birthday.

Having just split up with a girlfriend, Ellis had been feeling raw and unloved. She had reminded Bailey that they had made a pact to get married if they were both single by the time they were forty. It was a promise they had made to each other that Bailey never thought would come to pass, as Ellis was everything anyone would want in a partner—she was beautiful, with the most kind and loving personality.

When Bailey had made the pact, she'd been sure Ellis would be snapped up well before she turned forty. But Ellis had dated very little, and nothing seemed to stick. Bailey, on the other hand, had never felt the need for a relationship, or believed that long-term relationships were healthy.

Her parents hadn't shown her a positive model for them, and really Bailey didn't think she needed what they had. She had everything she needed to make her life content—her dream job, a good life of friends and colleagues at Cambridge, and she had her beloved best friend, Ellis. Bailey truly did love her, but as a deep friendship, not a romantic love.

When Ellis reminded her of their pact, Bailey didn't have an argument against it. Ellis was forty-two and clearly needing that kind of permanence with someone, and Bailey supposed they could help each other through life by marrying, so she agreed.

When almost in Ellis's next breath she admitted being in love with Bailey since they'd first met, Bailey again found herself agreeing with her friend, and her friend became her wife. They had three years together before Ellis was hit by a drunk driver and died from her injuries. Bailey had been the best spouse she could be, but there was one thing Bailey couldn't do and that was be in love with her.

She had lied to her friend to make her happy, and it tortured her. Especially at the end.

Bailey heard Ellis's words in her mind. The ones that tortured her.

"I know you never were in love with me. I was selfish in a time when I needed to believe you loved me like I loved you."

"No, don't talk like that, Ellis," Bailey said.

"I have to because I want you to find happiness when I'm gone. Promise me you will find a woman your heart yearns for. You have been the best friend in the world, giving up your freedom and your chance at true love to make your friend happy—you deserve happiness. Promise me you will find her."

Ellis became weaker and weaker that night, and she kept asking for Bailey's promise. In the end she gave it but didn't mean a word. Bailey would never be happy again, she was convinced of that in her grief, and was determined that if she couldn't love Ellis the way she deserved, that she would not find love with anyone.

Bailey slammed the drawer shut. Why couldn't she be there for Ellis the way she needed her?

Guilt tortured her soul. Bailey had been meant to pick Ellis up from the train station that evening of the accident, but Bailey had been swamped with work and asked if Ellis could get a taxi home.

Instead of that, Ellis walked, since it was a warm summer's night. If Bailey had ever met anyone in her life who deserved her love and attention, it was Ellis, and Bailey had failed on both counts.

Bailey should have left her desk and gone to pick up Ellis, and she should have loved her. Now all she could do was cope badly with the guilt.

Bailey had never been a believer in long-term love, relationships, and romance. And after the hurt, guilt, and shame she'd been through, there was no way she could ever fall in love with a woman now.

Bailey sat in her office chair and let her head fall back. She closed her eyes and tried to focus on the ticking of the grandfather clock in the far corner of the room. Her mind started to quiet. That was the way Bailey liked it. Quiet and solitude were the only things Bailey wanted in her life now. Quiet, solitude, and peace.

CHAPTER TWO

The Sparks family home was full of noise, chaos, and laughter on Christmas Day. Chief mischief-maker was Taylor. Since five o'clock that morning, Taylor, her niece Ruby, her two nephews Aaron and Jaden, and her parents' pet dog, Hunter the Labrador, had been running riot. They'd been playing with toys, eating chocolate for breakfast, and generally annoying all the adults, of which Taylor didn't really consider herself one.

She was the fun auntie, and she loved it. Taylor had Jaden on her back whilst they chased Ruby, Aaron, and Hunter.

"We're going to get you," Taylor shouted.

Jaden had the new lightsabre that he'd gotten from Santa, which he was whooshing about as they went. All was going well until she heard a crash behind them. They froze. Taylor put Jaden on the floor and turned around to find a picture frame, face down on a side table with bits of glass all around it.

Shit.

She lifted it up and more glass fell out. Typical, it had to be her mums' favourite photo. It was a picture taken on their first date. This was going to be difficult to explain. Taylor turned back to the kids so they could get their story straight, and they were nowhere to be seen, and Hunter was gone too.

"Traitors. They've scarpered."

"Tay-Tay." That was her mama's voice.

Uh-oh.

"Yeah?"

"Can you come here please?"

Taylor sighed and trudged through to the living room. She found an unusual scene. Her mum Kel, her mama Vicky, her oldest brother Thomas and his wife, Gianna, Luke her middle brother, and finally Edward, Taylor's youngest brother, and his husband Max, were all sitting on the couch and in armchairs, looking like they were about to start an intervention.

The kids were sitting by the Christmas tree with the dog, trying to look like the best-behaved kids ever. Taylor gave Ruby, the oldest, a glare.

"Am I in trouble?"

"Yes, the worst, Sparkle." Eddie giggled.

"Ed," Kel said, "quiet."

Vicky smiled sweetly, "Sit down, Tay. There's something we'd like to talk to you about. Kel?"

Her mum sat forward in her seat and clasped her hands. "We've all been impressed by the hard work you've put in on your dating business idea. Your business plan is excellent and all your own work, but you've had trouble getting investors to bite."

"We all think they are fools," Luke said.

Gianna sat back and crossed her legs. "Clearly no imagination."

"So," Kel said, "we would like to become your investors."

Taylor's mouth dropped. "What?"

Kel turned to Thomas. "Tommy, you're the lawyer, hand over our investment."

Tommy brought out an envelope and handed it over to Taylor. "You deserve it, Sparkle."

Taylor opened the envelope and found the family had pledged to fund her start-up. "I…I don't know what to say."

"We all chipped in," Vicky said. "We are all so proud of you. Family hug, everyone."

Taylor jumped up and down excitedly and ran in to hug them all. "Thank you, thank you, thank you."

This might not be the time to mention the broken frame. Give it a few hours…

Taylor sat cross-legged on her bed and typed out a text message to Margo. *Merry Christmas! I got the investment!!! All systems go now come January. xx*

When she sent the message, she felt her stomach flip with uneasiness. It had been doing so all evening, after coming down from the excitement of her gift.

Her mind was going a million miles an hour with everything she would have to do now, the first being giving up her job. It was a scary thing to do, but she just wouldn't have the time to manage all the business without devoting this upcoming year to it totally.

Taylor's thoughts were interrupted by a knock at her bedroom door.

"Come in."

"Hey."

It was her brother Eddie. He was dressed for bed too in boxers and a T-shirt. He jumped on the bed beside her.

"We just got Jaden to sleep, so I thought I'd see how my baby sister is."

Taylor smiled. Eddie was the sibling she had the deepest connection with, perhaps because they were both gay, and maybe because they were closest in age. He could always put a smile on her face.

"I'm okay."

"Have you had a good Christmas Day?" Eddie smiled.

"The best. I couldn't have asked for a better one. I'm really lucky to have the best family."

Eddie had a smug smile on his face. "Yes, you are, Tay. Very lucky to have us."

They laughed, and Eddie gave her a gentle shove. "We are lucky to have you. Imagine if you'd have been another boy. Four boys in one family? Mama would have killed us by now. Mind you, you sometimes were the ringleader of our wildest adventures."

Eddie wasn't wrong. As the baby of the family she tended to get away with things a lot easier than her brothers, and so she got into a lot of mischief.

"Remember our yearly hunt for Christmas presents?"

Eddie laughed. "It was our yearly battle with Mama."

Every year Taylor had led Eddie on a hunt through the house—from the basement, to the bedrooms, to the large attic space—to try to find where their mums had hidden that year's Christmas gifts.

"And Mama always won. We never found them once. I don't know how she did it," Taylor said.

Taylor giggled. "I know. She is a wily woman, but you know, I think we would have been disappointed if we'd found them."

"Yeah, it was the hunt that was the exciting part," Eddie said.

As their laughter subsided, Eddie asked, "Are you all right? You've seemed quiet this evening. Is it the business? You know I'll support you in every way we can, not just the money."

"I know that. It's just kind of hit me that it's real, now. When I was planning and trying to raise money, it was something that was happening in the future, now I have to set everything in motion in January. To resign from my job will be a huge step, a leap of faith, and what if it doesn't take off? I'll be left without a job."

"All businesses start with a leap of faith. I felt the exact same thing when I started my business. But I had the support of a big loving family to fall back on. Just like you do. If you need to, you can always come and work for me."

Eddie owned a successful web design business, which he and his husband ran together. He'd started it just after he left university and now had fifty employees.

"You would?" Taylor said.

"Of course I would—in fact I was going to ask you about doing some freelance work for me anyway."

"You were?" Taylor said with surprise.

"Yes, we're starting a new advertisement campaign, and the pitches we've had from some of the big companies haven't exactly impressed us. Your ideas are always so innovative."

"I'll be happy to help. It'll give me something to fall back on while I get the Regency Romance Club off the ground." Taylor threw her arms around her brother and squeezed him in a hug. "Thank you so much, Ed."

"Don't thank me. You're my baby sister. I'm always going to look after you—we all are. So, tell me. What's first for you to do in January, apart from binning your boring job."

"I was going to ask you to redesign my website, for one," Taylor said.

"No problem at all. I'll make it professional with all the bells and whistles."

"Thanks. I've got a waiting list, so I'm hopeful they will be my first paid-up members. I'm limiting the first season to queer Regency fans. Just to see how everything works out. If it does, then second season I can include everyone."

Eddie touched his chest. "If I wasn't a happily married man, I'd love to take part. It sounds so romantic. What about the venues?"

"Luckily, thinking I'd already have had investment before now, I'd made contact with a couple of stately homes for the spring and summer balls I'd planned. About ninety-nine per cent of the stately homes that cater for events are booked up years in advance for weddings and parties. One I like hadn't done events before but were quite up for talking about it."

"Sounds good for starters then," Eddie said.

"I need a historian. That's a big thing. I want them to give me historical advice, and when the group go to the stately homes for the weekend, I want the historian to give a talk on the history of the home and the Regency period," Taylor said.

"Have you anyone in mind?"

"No, but Margo says she might have a few ideas. I'll get in touch with her soon. She's on a skiing holiday just now."

"Lucky her. That sounds like a lot of fun at Christmas. Oh, wait—she's married to that gorgeous snowboarding champion, isn't she?"

"That's the one." Taylor smiled.

"There's someone that can make any man's or woman's heart melt."

"Don't let your husband hear that."

"Max knows I only have eyes for him, but there's no harm in the odd glance now and then." Eddie grinned.

Taylor sighed. "I wish I had your luck with love. But it'll be fun concentrating on finding love for my club members for the next year."

"Don't write off the year, Tay. You never know when love will jump up and bite you."

"I've been waiting and waiting for it to do that, and I've been left disappointed, so I'm going to give dating a rest. It'll do me good."

"Hmm." Eddie didn't seem convinced. "I know. Why don't we go and have one of our famous Christmas dinner leftovers sandwiches."

"Yes! I love Christmas dinner food—even better, leftover food stuffed between two hunks of bread with mayonnaise. Beautiful."

"You have an addiction to sandwiches, baby sister. Let's go quickly, in case the others have had the same idea."

They ran at top speed out of the bedroom and down the stairs.

CHAPTER THREE

Thankfully—for Bailey—the Christmas period was now at an end. The first week into January brought wind and rain, which suited her mood.

She was busy with her manuscript and eating a sandwich while she worked, when a video call alert popped on her screen over her document. It was her editor, Margo. They had a good working relationship and were friendly, as far as Bailey ever allowed herself to be friendly.

Bailey answered, and Margo's smiling face appeared on screen.

"Margo, hello."

"Hi Bailey. How's things?"

Margo knew not to ask if she'd had a lovely Christmas. She knew Bailey's wife had died and was sensitive to it.

"I am fine, and the manuscript is going well," Bailey said.

"Glad to hear it. I'm not phoning you about the book today. I have a proposition for you."

"Oh?" Bailey was intrigued.

"One thing first. Promise you'll hear me out till the end? Don't just dismiss it straight away."

Now Bailey started to worry that the proposition was going to be something she didn't like. "Okay. I will."

"Right." Margo cleared her throat. "I have a friend that's starting a new business. It's taking groups of people away for the weekend, people who share a love for the Regency period. They'll be going to and staying at some of our great stately homes for the weekend. They'll enjoy some country pursuits that they might have done had they lived during the Regency, and learn more about the period. That's where you come in."

Groups of people were the last thing she wanted to be around, so it would be a no from her, but she had promised to listen and so let Margo continue.

"My friend Taylor, who's opening this new business, wants a historian to work with her on the project—research the great estates and give a talk at each weekend."

To soften her refusal Bailey said, "I'm an expert on the early modern period—it's stretching it to include the Regency."

"Bailey, you are the most well-read person I know. You're an expert on British history. That's why we have you writing the pocket guides to British history, and may I remind you that you did write one about the Regency period."

She was caught out there. Bailey *had* written that and had more than a passing interest in the Regency. She had no excuse. It would have to be a straight refusal.

"I'm sorry, Margo. It's not something I'd be interested in."

Margo's shoulders dropped in disappointment, and she sighed. "Give it a chance, Bailey. My friend is a young woman, just starting up in business. I think you'd be a great fit with her, with your experience and knowledge. It would also be good for you, I think. Think of it as some pleasant weekend breaks."

Nothing filled her with more horror than being around happy groups of people. "Margo, I appreciate your offer, but no. I simply want to be left alone to write my books."

"At least meet Taylor, for a coffee or something. I want her to get the best start for her business. She's important to me, and I'd trust you to help her."

Taylor. Sounded like one of her students at university.

"I'd see it as a personal favour," Margo added.

Oh no. Margo had to say that, didn't she. When Ellis died, Margo covered for her and protected her from those above at the publisher who were expecting her manuscripts on her usual schedule.

When Bailey couldn't even bear to open the computer, Margo was there for her. Bailey closed her eyes and tried to find a way out of her predicament. Short of pretending that the signal had gone down, she was stuck. Even more guilt piled on top of her.

She took a deep breath. "I'll meet her for coffee, but I'm not promising anything. Maybe I can give her some advice."

Margo smiled brightly. "Thank you, Bailey. I really appreciate it. I'll email you with the details. Bye."

When the call ended, Bailey put her head in her hands. "Why did I have to say yes?" A young woman with lots of exciting ideas for a new business was the worst kind of coffee appointment she could think of. Too late now.

❖

Taylor was so excited. Jaq Bailey had agreed to meet with her. When Margo had told her that a well-respected historian had agreed to meet her, she was so happy. Taylor immediately bought some of her audiobooks and found some lectures and interviews she had given on YouTube.

The audiobook played now from her bedroom speaker as she got dressed. Well, she was still undressed and agonizing over which outfit to wear. She had five different choices laid out on the bed.

She picked up what she called her serious business suit, with a short skirt, ivory silk blouse, and matching jacket. This was what she had worn to meet potential investors.

"But she's not an investor. That's too formal. It's just a coffee date...I mean, appointment."

Taylor sat down on the bed and closed her eyes, listening to Dr. Bailey's audiobook on the Regency.

Luckily for Taylor, Dr. Bailey narrated her own book, so she got to listen and, in some way, get to know her. Her voice was what had caught Taylor's attention straight away. It was deep, honeyed, and authoritative. She could imagine Dr. Bailey's lectures were popular.

Then she found a couple of online lectures and got to put a face to Dr. Bailey's voice, and it couldn't have been better. Margo had told her that Dr. Bailey was gay, which fitted in well for the first season of their club, as it was to be people from the gay community. But even if she hadn't told her, Taylor could have guessed in a second when she saw her.

Dr. Bailey had gay vibes bouncing off her. She was a masculine-presenting woman with slightly greying short dark hair and a calm and confident persona.

She had that sexy older woman thing going on, Taylor thought to herself.

Taylor felt butterflies at the thought of meeting her. She didn't want to look or sound like a silly young girl in front of this impressive, learned woman.

"What will I wear?"

She picked up her phone and FaceTimed her brother. "Hello?"

Taylor could see he was in his kitchen and holding little Jaden. He must have been working from home today.

"Hi Ed, hi little Jay. Ed, I've got a fashion emergency. I don't know what to wear for my coffee date, um, appointment, I mean."

Why did she keep saying that?

"Is it to meet your super serious crusty old professor?"

Taylor laughed. "It is to meet the professor, but she's not crusty—she's gay with that sexy older woman thing going on."

"I see your problem. Let me see your choices."

Taylor panned the camera over the bed.

"Hmm." Taylor could hear Eddie pondering. "You don't want to be too serious, but I'd go with a skirt or dress for sure, to show off those gorgeous legs of yours."

"It's not a date, Ed," Taylor said.

"You can't go meeting a sexy professor looking like a plain Jane. Come on now. I'd say the flowing blue dress. It's beautiful on you, and it's not too formal, but just well-dressed enough and sexy."

"Yeah, you're right," Taylor said.

"I'm always right when it comes to fashion. What time's your date?" Eddie asked.

"My *appointment*'s in an hour and a half, and I haven't even got my make-up on. I better run. Thanks, Ed."

"Any time, honey."

She put down her phone and started to dash about the room getting dressed and finally started to put on her make-up.

"Why do I always have to run late? I'm never going to make it."

❖

It took a lot for Bailey to come out to meet someone new, or anyone at all. Luckily it was only a couple of Tube stops to the coffee shop where she was to meet this young woman. What a colossal waste of time. There was no question—she wouldn't take part in this project. It was only a meeting to repay a favour to Margo.

She had planned to perhaps give her some advice on some other historians who could help, but that was it. Then Bailey could get home as soon as possible, lock her front door, and keep the world outside.

Bailey put on her jacket and made sure she had her phone before leaving the house. It was only a two minute walk to the Tube station, so she had plenty of time. That was one thing she couldn't stand, lateness—the height of bad manners.

She made her way down the street and into the station. It wasn't long till the train arrived, and Bailey stood near the door so she could get off quickly and be on her way.

After a few stops she got off and went in search of the local Starbucks. It wasn't where Bailey would have picked, she preferred the smaller, independent coffee shops, but this was where Taylor Sparks wanted to meet, according to Margo.

When she'd read the young woman's name, she'd immediately pictured someone overenthusiastic, who would have too much energy for her.

Bailey was twenty minutes early when she arrived at Starbucks, so she went ahead and ordered a coffee and sat down at a table facing the door. She hoped she could try to spot Taylor Sparks as soon as she came through the door.

She waited and waited. It was now fifteen minutes past their appointment time and Bailey's annoyance grew with each minute she was kept waiting.

What a waste of her time.

❖

Taylor jogged down the road as quickly as she could in heels and carrying her laptop bag and handbag. She'd been running late and decided to jump on the bus that was passing, rather than go the longer walk to the Tube, but that had been a mistake. The bus broke down, and Taylor had to walk the rest of the way.

Thankfully she was now nearing Starbucks, and she prayed that Dr. Bailey was still there. She stopped when she got a few paces from the door of the coffee shop. She was so nervous.

Everything she had read or watched told her Dr. Bailey would be a perfect fit for the Regency Romance Club. Taylor had to get her on board if she was still there.

She took a deep breath and walked through the door. Taylor scanned the tables and saw Dr. Bailey sitting right in front, glowering at her. She must have guessed who she was.

Dr. Bailey was just as good-looking in the flesh as she had been in her video lectures, but she was going to have to placate her.

Taylor put on her best smile and walked slowly over to Dr. Bailey. For her part Dr. Bailey never took her steady eyes off her. As Taylor approached, she felt it was a bit like being called to the headmistress's office, and it made her shiver.

"Dr. Bailey, I'm so sorry for keeping you waiting. I was running late, and then my bus broke down."

Shit why did she say she was already late? She could have blamed it all on the bus.

"You're here now, I suppose," Bailey said.

Oh, frosty. "I'll just grab a coffee, and I'll be right with you—can I get you something else? Tea? Coffee?"

"A black coffee please."

"Okay. Two ticks."

When Taylor got to the counter, she was relieved to be out of Dr. Bailey's icy stare. Maybe her second coffee would thaw her out a bit.

When she got back to the table, Taylor handed over the black coffee and then offered her hand in greeting.

"I'm Taylor, and it's so nice to meet you, Dr. Bailey."

"Call me Bailey."

Bailey did shake her hand but still looked grumpy. She was going to have to hope some of her Taylor Sparks sparkle would make Bailey more open to her.

While she got out her iPad for her presentation, she reiterated, "I'm really sorry—again—that I was late, Bailey. What time did you arrive?"

"Twenty minutes early. I'm always on time."

Wow. She was annoyed. Best just to get on with it. "Did Margo tell you about my business?"

"Just that you wanted to take groups of people away for weekends at great estates and let them enjoy Regency pursuits."

Okay, nothing about dating then. Did Margo think it would put Dr. Grumpy off? It probably would.

Once she had set up her slides, Taylor started with a brief introduction.

"Hi, I'm Taylor Sparks. After graduating from university I began working in the marketing business, but I've always wanted to start my own business, and I saw the way to do it was by using my passion as inspiration."

"And what was that?"

She wasn't expecting an interruption.

"My passion is Regency romance, and especially Jane Austen. Now if you'll just let me explain..."

Bailey nodded, sat back in her chair, and crossed her legs. To Taylor her attitude looked like *Impress me if you can.*

So Taylor would do just that.

Bailey vowed to keep tight-lipped. No doubt she wouldn't like what was coming, but she had promised to listen. Taylor started to talk, but Bailey had already checked out on her actual words. She watched Taylor speak animatedly and full of energy. Too much energy for Bailey. She was a beautiful young woman, though, with gorgeous dark hair that curled and cascaded over her shoulders and green eyes that shone with excitement and energy. Then she heard one word that knocked her from her appreciative gaze.

Dating.

Bailey was sure she heard her say *dating.*

"Could you repeat that last part please?" Bailey said.

Taylor put her hands on her hips and sighed. Bailey thought she realized that Bailey hadn't been listening fully.

"Today in the dating world, you take a quick glance at someone's picture and swipe left or right. You cannot judge people like that. Who knows? The person you have swiped away could be the person of your dreams."

"This is a dating company?" Bailey said with disbelief in her voice.

"A multiplatform dating club."

"I thought this was to do with the Regency period. Taking groups of people away to large estates to experience the world of the Regency."

"It is if you'll just let me finish my pitch." This was harder than a protentional investor meeting. "Could you just let me finish?"

Bailey sat back after indicating with her hand for Taylor to continue. Dear God, she was being asked to work for a dating website.

Taylor continued, "Some of the many things I love about Regency romance are the rules of courtship. The introductions, the conversations, the balls, the country pursuits, getting to know each other slowly. Now we do it backwards. We jump into bed and then try to get to know someone's mind, their personality, their beliefs, if we even do that. Sometimes sleeping with someone extinguishes a fire that might have been natured and grown even hotter and brighter—"

Taylor's words were said with such passion, that it felt like she was longing for that fire, a fire that she'd never found, and Bailey's body reacted to it. A heavy beat started inside her and shocked Bailey. She hadn't felt it in such a long time, and it made her angry.

Why, she couldn't process at the moment, but she felt it all the same. Taylor was too young—she didn't know her age, but too young for her at forty-five years old.

She had to get out of here.

"—if the pair had taken the time to get to know each other. My job is to give people that chance. So the business is this. A season's membership with the Regency Romance Club gives you two weekends at different stately homes, over a six month membership. Over the weekend the clients will get lectures about the particular house, its history—that's where you come in. They also get to take part in Regency pursuits together, like riding, fencing, and needlework, all to help the group get to know each other and for each one to possibly form an attachment. The weekends will culminate in a grand ball where they will take part in dancing and everything that a ball entails. Romance will hopefully blossom."

Bailey wanted to stop Taylor and leave, but Taylor was so full of excitement relaying her idea that she couldn't. So she sat and waited. What a ridiculous view of the Regency Tylor had.

Taylor's slides moved on to a group of happy Regency dancers, some in fine costumes and some in military uniform.

"They will also attend dancing classes with a group of Regency dance reenactors, so the club members will be able to fully take part in the ball. This is more than dating, Dr. Bailey, it's a social and entertainment club, where you can learn about the past, and for two weekends leave the modern world behind. Thank you for listening."

Taylor closed up her iPad and took a sip of her coffee. The high of her excitement was soon dashed as she looked across the table to Bailey's steady gaze. She looked stern, almost annoyed.

"If you have any questions, I'd be happy to take them." Bailey's stare was making her uneasy.

After a few moments Bailey said, "Do you know what the life expectancy of someone in the poorest parts of Liverpool and London was during the Regency?"

Taylor was not expecting that question. "I—I'm sorry. I don't know."

"Twelve years old. Can you imagine the level of poverty there was to yield such a life expectancy? The misery those poor children must have endured makes me shudder."

Taylor didn't have a clue how to answer. Why was Bailey asking this? "I understand there was shocking poverty but—"

Bailey leaned forward and kept her gaze on Taylor. "How about this question? What was the age of some of the youngest children used in coal mining during the Regency?"

"I'm sorry, no."

"Three years old. I'll repeat that. Three years old. Their parents took them down into the deep black pit to keep the rats from eating the rest of the family's meagre rations. A bit older, they were then expected to haul coal."

"I didn't know that, and it's very shocking, but why are you asking me these questions?"

"Because as much of an exemplary writer as Jane Austen was, it was only the one percent of Regency society that she was writing about. The rest of society experienced poverty, pain, depravity—that was what the majority felt."

"I'm not trying to dismiss—"

But Bailey didn't let her finish. "The past is not a place to be used as some kind of fun park, for people trying to find a date. The past is to be documented and studied so that we can learn from them and learn more about ourselves. I'm a serious historian, Ms. Sparks. I'm not here to help people with too much spare cash to have a fun weekend in the country. Treat the past with some respect."

Taylor froze. She didn't know what to say to that.

Bailey drank the last of her coffee and stood. "I'm sorry to have wasted your time, Ms. Sparks. I only came as a courtesy to Margo. Let me give you some advice. You're a young woman, and I'm sure love like you see in *Pride and Prejudice* or *Sense and Sensibility* seems like something real and something to dream of, but believe me, love like that does not exist. You'll find that out as you get older. Goodbye."

Then she walked away. It was only when Bailey left the coffee shop that Taylor got her voice back.

"Of all the condescending, arrogant, superior, egotistical…"

Her furious response was interrupted by a waitress who had come to clear Bailey's cup. The waitress looked at her as if she was the weirdest customer she'd had this week.

Tylor felt the need to cover for her outburst. "We had an argument over the proper way to make coffee."

The woman nodded and smiled as if she had lost the plot and cleared the dishes, getting away as quickly as she could.

"Fool! Why did I even say anything?"

She packed up her things and left Starbucks as quickly as she could.

❖

There was lots of work Taylor should be doing, but after her turbulent meeting with Dr. Bailey, everything that was said kept playing over and over in her mind. She was equally angry at Dr. Bailey's arrogant, snooty attitude, and questioning herself and her plans. Was her idea stupid? Was it wrong to glorify a period in time that had so many societal problems?

There was one thing Taylor did know Bailey was wrong about, and that was love. That kind of undying love, pure love, did exist, even though she hadn't found it yet.

Taylor felt deep down in her soul that this was true. She'd also grown up with it. Her two mums shared a love that was special, had overcome obstacles, and created a loving family of four children.

She needed to speak to her mums, especially Kel. Whereas both her mums always made her believe in going after her dreams, Kel would also be realistic and not sugar-coat the truth.

Taylor made her way to the nearest Tube station. The family business was housed in a large industrial warehouse around twenty minutes away by Tube, and then a ten minute walk. The walk would help clear her mind. Taylor hated journeys by car or public transport as a rule because she hated to be seated for such a prolonged period of time. But her Tube journey went by extremely quickly, due to all the thoughts whirling around in her head.

A few minutes into her walk to the warehouse, a large van stopped beside her. It was a Sparks fruit and vegetable delivery van.

The driver put down the window and said, "Jump in, Taylor. I'll give you a lift."

Taylor sighed inwardly. She was looking forward to her walk, hoping it would sort out her head, but she couldn't be rude. So Taylor smiled and got into the van.

"Thanks, Mike."

They arrived in no time and pulled through the security gates.

The van stopped at the front of the huge series of warehouses that made up Sparks Fruit and Veg.

"I'll drop you off here, Taylor," Mike said. "I need to go to dispatch at the back."

"Thank you, Mike."

Taylor walked towards the first warehouse, where the staff made up the boxes or pallets for delivery. The business supplied a supermarket chain, restaurants, and other shops.

Vans and lorries brought the produce in from farmers all over the UK and from the docks where produce came in from all over the world.

Taylor was greeted by the staff as she walked through the open warehouse doors and into the main packing area. Her mums' office was at the back of this building.

She waved and smiled at the staff as she walked through. Taylor had always been a favourite of the staff here. She had been coming here since she was a little girl, and she had got to know the majority of the staff over the years.

Unlike a lot of businesses, Sparks retained staff loyalty because of the way Taylor's mums ran it, so a good number had seen her grow up through her visits to the warehouse.

To new visitors the warehouse could be a loud, daunting place, but not to Taylor. She had loved it as a child and still did. Against each wall of the space were pallets stacked high to the roof, and down below were packing areas where staff used a tablet screen to check the orders and box them up.

There was a constant flow of people moving pallets from the shelves over to the packing tables, and then from there out back to dispatch. Taylor was quite sure she'd got in everyone's way when she visited as a child, but they never said anything and were fond and extremely kind to her.

She saw her favourite lady, who was a packing manager, giving instructions to another employee.

"Hi, Mattie."

A huge smile came to her face. "My little Taylor."

"That's me." Taylor smiled.

"How are you, honey?"

"I'm doing well. I just started my own business."

"Well done. If you're anything like your mums, it'll be a huge success."

"Are they up in the office?" Taylor asked.

"Your mum Kel is, but your other mum is out on business with your brother."

"Thanks, Mattie. It's good to see you."

She gave Mattie a kiss and made her way over to the back of the warehouse, then climbed up some metal steps to the office. She peeked through the window and saw her mum, sitting on the edge of her desk in her usual jeans and sleeveless bodywarmer, looking at the whiteboard on the wall, and tapping a pen against her lips.

Organization was Kel's strength. She kept on top of all the many different supply chains she dealt with, supply chains that spread all over the world. Her mama Vicky was quite different. She was an excellent communicator who had an abundance of empathy, a brilliant foil for Kel, who was blunt and a bit brash sometimes, but never to her family.

The business was a true family affair. Her brother Luke was a lawyer, and he dealt with all the Sparks business affairs from his office in London. Then there was Thomas, who after university began working as assistant manager to Kel. And even though Eddie had his own software design company, he designed the computer systems, app, and website for the Sparks company.

It was only Taylor who worked outside the family business, but her mums had often told her they hoped she would come to work with them eventually, with her marketing knowledge.

Although Taylor had always liked working here—as kids they'd all worked part-time with the company when they were old enough—she wanted to spread her wings a bit and see what the working world was like outside her comfort zone. It turned out it was extremely boring outside her comfort zone, but now Taylor had her own business and would pour her energies into that.

Taylor walked in and said, "Hi Mum."

Kel looked surprised. "I thought you were meeting your prof today."

"I was, but we finished, and I wanted to come and talk to you."

"I'm always happy to have my Princess Sparkle come talk to me." Kel stood and opened up her arms. "Hugs and kisses please?"

Taylor went to her mum's arms without hesitation. This was the side to Kel that she didn't show to the outside world, and that made Taylor feel so loved.

Kel hugged her tightly and Taylor pushed her nose into her chest.

She inhaled the reassuring scent of her mum's favourite cologne. It always made her feel so much love.

Taylor pulled out of the hug and said, "Where's Mama?"

"Out with your brother schmoozing clients."

Taylor chuckled. "You say that with such disgust, Mum."

Kel walked around her desk and sat down. "I hate all that. Ingratiating yourself and laughing at their jokes. If it were me, I'd say—do you want to buy my fruit and veg? Yes? Well how much, and here's the price. End of."

"Thank goodness you met Mama when you did," Taylor joked.

"Don't I know it. I was twenty when I was looking for my first space to store my produce, and full of bullshit, drive, and arrogance. I was used to demanding what I wanted, but that didn't help get me some of the supply contracts I wanted. I couldn't help it. You had to grow up tough where I came from."

All the children loved the story of their mothers meeting. Her mama worked for a letting agent who was trying to rent out space in a new building. Kel ran her dad's fruit stall since she was sixteen. She had to grow up quickly when her dad became unable and unwilling to keep the business afloat. Kel was a brilliant businesswoman, and leaving school at sixteen with no further education, it was all through her own intelligence and ability. Kel saw her future in becoming a fruit and vegetable supplier, and she needed space to begin that dream.

Her mama, with her charm and warmth, was met by an arrogant, cocky, and dismissive woman. Mama gave Kel a piece of her mind and stormed out of the meeting.

Kel was annoyed...and entranced. Despite the bad meeting, Kel was determined to see her again, and although it took a month, she did eventually get a date, and it changed their lives. They fell in love, and in about six months, Mama came to work with Kel. The rest was history.

"Our business wouldn't be anywhere near as successful without your wonderful mother. So I let her do her thing, and I play to my strengths. What did you want to talk about?"

Taylor looked down at her lap. How could she describe it? "I've lost confidence, and I need to know I'm doing the right thing."

"Lost confidence in what?" Kel asked.

"The business—I mean, is it just a silly immature notion?"

"Is this the Taylor Sparks that I know? The one who's dreamed about your idea for the last two or three years?"

"It's just doubts. I don't know, is it silly?" Taylor asked. "I know you'll tell me the truth."

"You didn't have these doubts yesterday, so what happened?"

"I met the historian I want to work with this morning. My friend Margo recommended them to me."

"What did they say to you?" Kel said sternly.

Taylor could tell her mum's protective hackles were up.

"Her name's Dr. Bailey. She studied and taught early modern history at Cambridge. She said…a lot. I'm still trying to process it. Mainly that I was using the past as a playground for overindulged people with too much money, and a dating club made a mockery of the poor from that time."

"Absolute bollocks. You're not a historical re-enactment society, where every detail has to be bang on about the past. You're taking people to the world of Jane Austen and giving them some historical background from a historian as you go. What more does Doctor Hoity-Toity want?"

Taylor smiled. Her mum wasn't much impressed with titles like doctor. She was a bit of a downward snob, as she always felt people looked down on her for her humble background.

"Do you truly think my idea is good? You don't think I'm playing with the lives of people in the past?" Taylor asked.

"Would we all have given you the start-up money you needed if we didn't think it was good? And like I said, you're trying to make a historian part of the experience, so your clients can learn about the other side of the Regency. The poor, the needy. You've got it covered."

"Thanks, Mum. I really needed that. I was not prepared for her objections."

"Get a new historian, maybe from a college or more down-to-earth university than Cambridge. Someone who isn't so up their own arse," Kel said.

In Taylor's head she could hear her mama saying, *Bottom or backside, Kel.*

They always sparred over Kel's more industrial language.

"I could get someone else, but I really wanted her." Taylor thought about that spark she felt, that shiver that Bailey's voice and presence gave her, but she dismissed that to the back of her mind quickly. "The group I've put together for my first season intake is queer. Dr. Bailey's gay, so she would fit perfectly."

"Did she tell you she was gay?" Kel asked.

"No, but you could tell from a hundred feet away."

Kel raised an eyebrow and smiled. "Is that why you want her in the business?"

"No, no, not at all." Taylor felt her cheeks heat up. "She's forty-five—she wouldn't look at me."

"If you think a forty-five year old wouldn't look at a twenty-six year old, then me and your mama have failed you. But if she did look at my princess in that way, I'd have to kill her," Kel joked.

"It's nothing like that. It's money, Mum. Dr. Bailey is an extremely popular historical author. Her name on my club would bring gravitas and popularity to it. She'd be a big pull."

"Well, if you really want her, then I'd say don't let a first meeting put you off. Look at me and your mama. You're a persistent girl. Get back in contact with her and give her more well thought out responses to what she said this morning."

"How should I do that? Phone her?"

"Why not email her first. Tell her you were glad to meet her and then give her your responses. If she doesn't email you back, then phone her. Be persistent, and in the end, if you don't get her to at least talk to you, then she isn't worth bothering about. Move on and find an even better historian."

Taylor was full of enthusiasm again. She could see a path forward and was determined to make her plan work.

"Thank you, Mum. You always know the right thing to say."

Taylor hurried around the desk and put her arms around Kel's neck from behind and kissed her head. "I love you, Mum."

"I love you too."

At that moment her mama and her brother walked into the office.

"What's all these loving cuddles about?" Vicky asked.

Kel put on a cheesy smile and said, "I'm brilliant."

"So you always tell me."

❖

Bailey's steak was sizzling away nicely in the griddle pan, and she checked the oven to see if her roasted vine tomatoes were ready, and they were. She lifted them out, ready to adorn her steak.

Steak with chunky chips, onion, and red wine gravy was Bailey's favourite meal, and today she felt like she needed it. Her meeting with Margo's friend was playing over in her mind.

Was she too hard on her?

The idea of a Regency dating game was ridiculous, but had she explained it in too harsh a way?

Bailey plated up her meal and took it to her kitchen table. Before sitting down Bailey poured herself a glass of red wine. Everything was as she liked it—quiet solitude, with classical music playing from the kitchen speaker, her favourite meal, and a glass of red wine.

She hadn't always been a decent cook, but she had to learn after Ellis died. She wasn't the best chef in the world, but she could do quite a few dishes that were very tasty, steak being one.

Bailey sat down, swirled the red wine around her glass, and took a sip. Delicious.

As she started to eat, Bailey's thoughts returned to Taylor Sparks. She felt bad. She should have let her down easily.

But as much as Taylor's idea was simple frivolity, it was the other physical sensation that both shocked and angered her. She reacted to the heat she felt in her body when she met Taylor and listened to her speak. Taylor was a beautiful young woman, but Bailey had been around other beautiful women before, and she'd felt nothing. Bailey was dead inside.

The last time Bailey had felt anything approaching this was over three years ago, when she had a casual fling with a colleague she had met at a historical conference. But a week later Ellis told Bailey her news.

Bailey dropped her cutlery on her plate and took a large gulp of her red wine. The guilt that was always swimming around in the background crashed over her mind and body, because she had never felt that for Ellis.

They had a sex life after they got together, and she tried her very hardest to make Ellis feel loved, but Bailey didn't feel the passion that Ellis did. Bailey tried to give her everything she wanted and to make Ellis's life the happiest she could have.

Little did Bailey know that Ellis knew of her deception all along, and the night she died, she made Bailey promise that she would find love and a happy relationship once she was gone.

Of course she didn't and wouldn't keep that promise. Bailey was going to punish herself for not being able to shower romantic love and attraction on Ellis, her wife.

Why now feel something? For someone she'd met for less than an hour. She couldn't eat any more. Just as she was about to clear her dinner away, her phone beeped.

She picked it up and saw it was an email from Taylor Sparks. That was strange—she was just thinking about Taylor. Bailey expected the message would express annoyance or anger towards her, given their meeting yesterday.

Bailey opened the email. It wasn't what she was expecting.

Hi Dr. Bailey,
I wanted to thank you for meeting me yesterday. I appreciate your points of view, and it's completely up to you not to be involved in my project. But I wondered if I might contact you from time to time, just to clarify a few historical points? If not, it was nice meeting you anyway, and I will be careful about my historical accuracy and try to explain to my clients the inequality between both ends of Regency society.
Taylor

Why was she being cordial?

And here she was feeling she had been a little harsh on the young woman—well to be frank, she had been—and yet Taylor had the generosity to write her such a pleasant email. Bailey pulled over her iPad and started typing a reply.

Dear Ms. Sparks,
Thanks for your kind email...

What next? What would she answer to Taylor's request? She knew straight away.

I would be happy to fill you in on any question you might have. I'm always happy to help anyone learn more about the past.
Yours sincerely,
Jaq Bailey

She pressed send and it was off. Now at least she could go to bed without feeling bad about Taylor Sparks. At least that was one thing.

Bailey cleared up her dishes and went back through to her study to work on her book.

CHAPTER FOUR

Taylor meandered along, walking at a slow pace, only she wasn't outside at the park or even at the gym. She was in her flat on her walking desk, one of her best purchases ever.

She resented the time that she had to sit still at a desk when all she wanted to do was move. When Taylor saw the walking desk advertised online, she just had to have it. Now all her planning, all her work, she could do on the move. It was brilliant.

Taylor was in good spirits today. When she got home last night from visiting her parents, she sent an email, just as her mum had advised, telling Bailey that she enjoyed meeting her.

She was positivity personified and decided to try to get Bailey to agree to help her business in a small way. Taylor asked if she could email Bailey to clarify some historical information. To her great amazement, Bailey did email her back and said she would fact-check some things for her.

This was just a first step. She was going to build up the email correspondence and hope that she could build a rapport with Bailey, with hopes that she could persuade her to work for Taylor's company.

Taylor had her laptop on the desk as well as her iPad, so she had all her plans at her fingertips.

She opened her email on her iPad and found quite a few messages waiting for her. Two were from the people confirming their participation in her first season. She could have sold her club membership twice over, but she could only have so many in the group or it would become unruly and unmanageable.

But perhaps, if her business was a reasonable success, she could take on more staff and run two groups of Regency Romantics. As it was she could only afford one part-time employee. Her young cousin Gracie was at university and agreed to work part-time for the extra money, but for the rest, Taylor would juggle and keep everything ticking along.

The second email was from the venue of the first spring ball, Fairydean Castle, confirming the provisional booking was now official. Fairydean Castle was on the Scottish border and had centuries of great history as it was fought over by the Scots and the English.

Taylor's plan was to have the first weekend ball at a Scottish location, then move down into England, and finish off in the south of England. It would give her clients a broad experience of the history of Britain's greatest stately homes. The history of the homes was just as important to the experience as the Regency aspect.

When Taylor started looking for a venue in Scotland, she wanted something old, something truly special. Fairydean Castle was that. What could be more romantic than a castle?

Taylor opened up her Fairydean Castle folder to look at her notes on the place. She had just done a very quick internet search for her early research, but she would need a hell of a lot more for the actual weekend.

"I need my historian."

Margo had offered to ask a few of the other historians contracted with her publisher if they'd like to work with her, and it might come to that, but she wanted Bailey.

She had felt a connection with Bailey, and her gut told her that it had to be her.

Taylor scrolled through her information. "But how will I coax you out to play, Dr. Bailey?"

Bad history. That was it. If there was one thing she'd picked up on from their strained first meeting, it was that bad history aggravated her.

And she'd spotted exactly the kind of tourist-type history she was sure would annoy Bailey.

Taylor clicked the link in her notes, and she was taken to a website: *Myths and Legends of Britain.*

She scrolled down the page of monsters, evil creatures, and ancient Celtic myths until she found the Woman in the Casket of Fairydean Castle.

A rather gruesome myth, it told the story of a medieval couple having fun and playing hide-and-seek. The girl chose to hide in the casket that had held her marriage dowry of plate, money, and jewels. The girl waited and waited, and waited until, giving up on her groom, she decided to get out, only to find the casket spring didn't allow her to open it from the inside. She was trapped. The girl screamed and clawed at the inside of the casket, but no one thought to look in the casket in a storage room next to the girl's bedroom. It was empty of her dowry and therefore was not checked.

Her groom, after frantically searching the castle and grounds, eventually thought his bride had got cold feet. Years later the casket was opened and a skeleton was found, and scratch marks were gouged into the casket lid.

Taylor shivered and tried not to think of the claustrophobia too deeply. She could maybe bait Bailey if she presented this as fact and threw in another few titbits.

She took a drink from her water bottle and started to type out an email to Bailey. Taylor spoke out loud as she typed. "Hi Dr. Bailey. I hope you are having a super day."

Bailey would probably hate that. She wasn't the most cheerful of people.

I hope you don't mind, but I'd like to take you up on your offer of help. I haven't managed to get a historian willing to work with me, so I'll be giving the talks to my clients at the weekend Regency retreats. I have been doing my research and wanted to run a couple of historical events past you—

Taylor was interrupted by a FaceTime call. It was Margo. "Hi Tay. How are you enjoying being your own boss?"

"Hi, I love it. Missing our lunchtime talks, though," Taylor said.

"Tell me about it. Without you to make me walk at lunchtime, I'm going to put on weight. I see you're keeping walking."

Taylor grabbed the chance to share her enthusiasm. "You like it?" Taylor held out her arms, indicating the treadmill desk.

"It looks exhausting. How anyone could type and walk at the same time beats me."

"Got to keep moving. You promise we'll meet up every couple of weeks for a girls' night, because I'll miss you."

"I can't wait. A nice little wine bar and a good gossip. So, on to business. I had been talking about your new venture to a friend, who happens to be a colleague of Zee Osman. Have you heard of her?"

"Zee Osman..." Taylor thought for a minute, then snapped her fingers. "Doesn't she present the history documentaries on the History Channel?"

"That's her. She presents *Day in the Life*, where she spends the day as a historical character to understand how they really lived."

"Oh yeah, I remember her dressing up as King Charles I and Oliver Cromwell for the English Civil War."

"It's a popular show," Margo said, "and she writes extremely popular history books."

"Do you publish them?" Taylor asked.

"No, we have put several offers to her, but she's self-published and does really well with that, by all accounts."

"She heard about my Regency Romantics from your friend?"

"Yes, she was intrigued by it and would like to write a piece for a magazine or newspaper column on your new venture. Zee contributes to quite a few publications. It would be good for publicity."

"Sounds great. Have you got her details? I'll give her a call."

"I'm emailing them to you right now. Are you any further forward with Bailey?" Margo asked.

"Step by step. We've opened a line of communication, let's say. Bailey's willing to look over my research, and I'm hoping to annoy her until she agrees to be my historian."

Margo laughed. "You've set your heart on her then? Bailey's an extremely accomplished historian, and no pushover either."

"Neither am I, and I'm determined," Taylor said.

"It would do her good, and I told her as much. She's not taught in a few years, and she has a talent for it. I've been to a few of her lectures for her new book launches. But there is one thing."

"What?"

"She doesn't like Zee Osmond at all," Margo said.

Taylor was surprised they even knew each other. "Why?"

"They have a professional rivalry, you could say. Bailey doesn't appreciate Zee's kind of history. Zee tries to make history big, loud, and sexy, and Bailey cares about well-reasoned, thoroughly researched history. To me both have their place, but Bailey wouldn't agree."

Yes, yes. Now there's something she could work with. Taylor smiled. "Thanks for that, Margo. That's super useful."

"No problem. I better get on. Speak to you soon?"

"Yeah, thanks, Margo."

Taylor ended the call and clicked her email back onto her screen. Her mind was firing with ideas. She could definitely use this rivalry with Zee Osman to coax Bailey out. She started to add that Zee would like to be involved in her project, but then deleted what she had written.

"Don't play your hand too soon, Taylor."

Instead, she asked Bailey about the woman in the casket story, and some other details about Fairydean Castle, and pressed send.

"Fingers crossed this will get her interested."

Taylor's doorbell rang. She got off her treadmill desk and answered the door. It was Gracie. She was laden down with bags and a tray with two cups of coffee.

"Sorry I'm late. The bus never came, then the Tube was packed—"

"Don't worry about it, Gracie." Taylor took the coffee from her and led her to the couch area of her open plan flat.

"Thank you, but don't just let me off because I'm your little cousin. I'm here as your employee."

Taylor laughed and gave her a gentle shove. "Shut up, silly. Besides, you brought me coffee. How could I be angry?"

Gracie lifted up one of the bags she had brought and grinned. "I brought pastries too."

Taylor took the bag and looked inside. "Maple-walnut pastry, my favourite. You keep this up and you'll be employee of the month in no time."

They each took a pastry, and Tylor hummed with delight. "Perfect."

She then sipped the black coffee Gracie had brought. The bitterness of the drink suited the sweet pastry.

"Hmm. This is the perfect pick-me-up. Thanks, Gracie."

"Not a problem. So, who am I up against to get employee of the month?"

Taylor put her finger on her chin, pretending to think hard. "Um… Alexa, Siri, all vitally important to Regency Romantics."

Gracie played along. "Well, I can see that. No one can fault their work effort."

Taylor sat back in her chair and pulled her legs up under her. "Exactly, where would I be without them? Alexa puts the lights on and plays me music, and there isn't a single word in the dictionary that Siri can't spell. You know what my spelling is like. Indispensable, you see?"

"They're my superiors then?" Gracie joked.

"Of course. Siri is supervisor, and Alexa is office manager, I think. You've got a lot of catching up to do."

Gracie put her cup down on the coffee table. "What needs doing then?"

"If you check your email, I've made a list for this week. But basically, we need to make up the welcome packs to mail out to our Romantics—"

Gracie interrupted, "Aww, is that what we're calling our clients?"

Taylor smiled. "Yes, I thought it was cute. The packs will have all the info they need plus some merch I had made. It's all in the spare room."

"Sounds good. Oh, I wanted to ask, when I'm helping you be hostess with the mostest at the ball, do I get to dress up?"

"Of course, and you can choose any costume that best fits you. I want to emphasize that to our groups—they get to choose how to express themselves, especially with our first queer group. As long as it's from the period, they can be a military officer, a clergyman, a gentleman, or a lady in a ballgown. Anything goes."

"That's cool. You get to experience history as it should have been, not how it was," Gracie said.

"Exactly." Taylor clapped her hands together excitedly. "We are going to have so much fun."

❖

Bailey was standing in a queue at the checkout of her local store. Frustratingly the line wasn't moving at all. The person at the till was having trouble with their credit card. The people behind and in front were sighing and tutting, the British way to quietly show displeasure.

It didn't bother Bailey. She was in no rush. She had nowhere to be and no one to miss her, so she just stood quietly and stared out of the windows beyond the till.

Bailey preferred to shop daily for dinner, as it was the only time she got out of the house really. The supermarket's sights and sounds melted away, until she saw Ellis's face. Bailey knew Ellis would be mightily disappointed with her.

She wasn't enjoying life and finding someone to truly love, as she'd promised Ellis she would. Instead, she was here on her one daily outing, buying enough food for one.

The crash of a broken bottle brought her back into the moment. She saw staff with mops and buckets hurrying to the next till to clean up. Bailey just happened to glance to the side and saw a man in the adjacent queue staring at her.

She was used to that sort of thing. Even in this more enlightened age, people sometimes weren't used to a gender nonconforming person like her. Staring didn't bother her, but then he uttered the awful line, "Cheer up. It might never happen."

What was this obsession some men had about women being cheerful? Bailey gave him a dark glare and said, "What if it's already happened?"

He immediately put his head down.

Fool.

Her phone beeped with an email. She found herself smiling when she saw it was from Taylor Sparks.

She was persistent.

Bailey scanned the email quickly and shook her head. "Not the body in a casket myth. Dear God."

She was itching to get home and give Taylor a full reply. She couldn't let her peddle bad history. Taylor was an enthusiastic young woman, and as much as she couldn't be her historian, she could at least give her some well-researched information to get her started.

When she finally got to the top of the queue, Bailey paid for her food quickly, before hurrying home. She put her food away in record time and made her way to her office with some urgency.

She woke her computer and opened her email. Bailey started to type quickly but stopped almost as quickly as started.

"No, no, that's too blunt." Many times during their lifelong friendship, Ellis had told her to go more softly.

Bailey could hear her voice clearly. *You're not going into battle, Bailey. Calm your approach and you will get a better response. Just try it. For me.*

But Bailey found it hard. She was so passionate about her subject— or she had been. Since Ellis died, Bailey hadn't had the interest to keep up with new books, research, or even get worked up about opposing ideas.

The only reason she was writing her current book was through obligation.

Bailey worried that she'd never get the passion back. Was this the end of her career? She reread the email that Taylor had sent, and something sparked inside her.

She began to write on the notepad at the side of her computer.

Fairydean.

Then she started to sketch out some bullet points. She knew that

Fairydean had been a player in the Wars of the Roses, despite being in Scotland, and she would have evidence in her extensive files.

It would take some deeper research to find out Fairydean's history in the Regency.

Bailey stopped writing and looked down at her notes. This felt fresh, and she experienced energy that she hadn't felt in so long. Certainly not when she was plodding away at her book.

Maybe she could help Taylor in some way…

Bailey started to type and then stopped halfway. "This is for a dating club. What are you doing?"

She sat back in her chair and drummed her fingers on the desk. Bailey didn't understand why she was so torn. She owed Taylor nothing.

"But she's Margo's friend. Maybe I could help a little more."

It was decided. Bailey's fingers raced over the keys and she pressed send.

❖

Taylor was kneeling by the coffee table writing out the first invitations to the spring ball, while Gracie made up the welcome packs across from her.

"This is really hard."

Taylor was trying to handwrite the invitations in the Regency style, using a quill and inkpot.

"Don't ask me," Gracie said. "My handwriting is atrocious."

Beside Taylor there were many scrunched up pieces of parchment, and wax and a seal to give the invite that authentic feel.

Taylor heard her email chime and when she saw who it was, she felt a wave of excitement.

"Yes, yes, yes. I knew she'd bite."

"Who'd bite, and bite what?" Gracie asked.

"You know the historian I had a meeting with?" Taylor said.

"The one that turned you down?"

"That's her. She's going to do the research and write the lecture for Fairydean Castle." Taylor held up her arms and danced, swaying and clicking her fingers.

"Who gives the lecture then?" Gracie asked.

"She thinks I will, but she is."

"Does she know that?"

"No, not yet. Dr. Bailey didn't want anything to do with the project, but now she's writing the whole lecture. I asked for some advice on the history of Fairydean. I threw in some bad history, knowing she couldn't resist putting me right, and tomorrow I'll bring out the big guns."

"Who or what is that?"

"Remember the journalist who is coming to visit us? My friend Margo tells me that Dr. Bailey and Zee Osman clash in a big way. I thought some professional rivalry might inspire Bailey to help us."

"Maybe you could ask Zee Osman, if Dr. Bailey won't do it?" Gracie said.

"No, I'm sure I can get Bailey."

"Why do you want Dr. Bailey so much?"

Taylor was momentarily flustered by that question, but there was no smile or cheeky grin from Gracie, so she must have meant it in all innocence.

"Dr. Bailey is one of the most respected historians in the country. She would bring a lot of prestige to our company."

Taylor thought about their coffee shop meeting. She remembered the excitement she felt when Bailey was right across the table from her. She'd sat back, legs crossed, and holding her gaze with her steady eyes.

Bailey had an ease of confidence that only age could bring. It made Taylor's heart flutter. If Bailey had a girlfriend, partner, or wife, they were very lucky.

"Fingers crossed then."

"What?"

Gracie had caught her lost in her thoughts.

"For getting Dr. Bailey."

"Oh yeah. Gotcha. But no luck needed. I have a good feeling she's going to give in."

Taylor started to write the invitation again and immediately smudged it. "Oh my God. This is so frustrating."

She balled up the paper and threw it to the side. "This paper is too expensive to be wasting it."

"I don't have a steady hand. I got an F in art at school."

"That's it." Taylor snapped her fingers. "Eddie. He is great at art. I don't know why I never thought of him before."

"You think he'll do it?" Gracie asked.

"My big brothers would do anything for me, and anyway he's part of the team."

"How so?"

"Ed agreed to play the host with me at the weekend balls. I needed someone to welcome our guests with me—you'll be busy making sure everything is in place and ready, and Ed jumped at the chance to dress up like a gentleman dandy."

"It's going to be such good fun," Gracie said.

"I hope so."

CHAPTER FIVE

Taylor loved Wednesday nights. She got to eat her mama's delicious dinner and get both mums all to herself. Her brothers came for Sunday lunch, but as she was the only single one, and the rest were busy with their spouses and kids, Taylor got to be spoiled on her own.

Taylor was sitting at the kitchen table while Vicky cooked on her big kitchen range, while Kel got them some drinks.

It was a large kitchen. When her parents redecorated a few years ago, they knocked through to a room adjacent to make the space bigger. While the kitchen was Vicky's pride and joy, Kel's pride was the whole house.

They moved into this large Victorian town house, in a leafy suburb of London, when Taylor was a little girl. For Kel, building the business to a point where she could move her family here was a source of huge pride.

Unlike Taylor's grandpa, who died while Kel was still a teenager, Kel's work ethic was amazing. So much so that Vicky had a hard time getting her to relax and enjoy their time together, away from the business.

Kel had a wine fridge and one for bottles of lager and beer. She stood beside them, then looked over to Taylor.

"Are you staying tonight, or do you want a lift home?"

Sometimes Taylor would spend the night and stay in her old bedroom. It let Kel have a drink if she wanted to. She had given up offering to get the bus or the Tube home. Her mums wouldn't let her get public transport on her own at night.

Even when she was out with friends, if Taylor wasn't sharing a taxi home with them, Kel would drive into the town and drop her off home. They had always been extremely protective, but especially after her brother Ed had gotten beaten up after leaving a gay club. Since then they had been extra cautious.

"I'll stay. Why not?"

"Excellent," Kel said.

Vicky came over from the cooking range and hugged Taylor around the neck. "My baby's staying."

She smothered her in kisses and Taylor laughed. "Stop it, Mama."

"Don't strangle her, Vic."

"I miss my baby."

She gave her one last kiss and went back to finish dinner. Kel brought over two bottles from the fridge.

"Sparkling rosé for your mama, a nice bottle of red for me, and your strange watermelon thing for you."

"Ooh, lovely," Taylor said.

Taylor's drink of choice was a sweet alcopop called Weird Watermelon.

Kel popped open the rosé and started to pour it into a glass. "How's your first week of working for yourself going?"

"It's so good. I'm not bored, and I'm not stuck at a desk," Taylor said.

Vicky took the glass of rosé from Kel and said, "You're just like your mum. She could have never worked behind a desk."

Kel shivered. "It's bad enough when I have work on that bloody computer at work. Luckily your brother and mama are there to do the heavy lifting on that score."

That was very true. Kel was always at her happiest working down on the packing floor or helping dispatch.

Some days Taylor felt she was most like Kel, and some days Vicky. All she knew for sure was that she was the best of both of them.

"I'm plating up," Vicky said.

That was a cue for Kel to go over and help.

"It smells amazing, Mama." It was her favourite—roast chicken, roast potatoes, and all the trimmings.

Kel brought over a large tray laden with the roast potatoes and dishes of broccoli, green beans, and carrots. One of the perks of owning a family fruit and vegetable business was always having the best and freshest veg.

As kids they didn't appreciate this fact, but as they grew up, they finally started to get on board.

Vicky followed behind with the gravy, and Kel said, "Sit down, baby. I'll get the plates."

Once they were finally settled and eating, Vicky said, "Tell us what you've been doing your first week, and how is Gracie getting on?"

Gracie's mum was Vicky's sister, and they were close.

"Gracie is great—so helpful and good company. We've been making up the welcome pack for my Romantics."

"Is that what you're calling your clients?" Vicky said. "That's sweet."

Kel just rolled her eyes and shook her head.

"Yeah, I thought it was cute. They'll be sent out with the invitations. They're being written on parchment with quill, ink, seal, and everything. I wanted to make them authentic."

"What's it like writing with a quill?" Kel asked.

"Hard to not make it look like a big mess. I tried it and gave up, but Ed's going to do them for me."

"He'll do a lovely job," Vicky said.

Taylor took a mouthful of food and remembered she'd forgotten to tell her parents about Zee Osman.

"Oh, I forgot to say. Margo called me to let me know a freelance writer and historian would like to write a story on my new venture."

Vicky face lit up with smiles. She was always so enthusiastic about anything her children did.

"Who is it? Do we know of them?"

"Yeah, it's Zee Osman, the woman that does the historical TV shows. You know, it's all sex and scandal?"

"Oh yes. I've seen some of them, although it was a bit too bloodthirsty for me," Vicky said.

"She's coming to the flat tomorrow to have a meeting about it."

"Good publicity," Kel said. "What about your professor? Any luck persuading her to come on board?"

Taylor smiled. "Yeah, I've got her to the point where she's researching the lecture for my first venue, Fairydean Castle."

"Are you going to give it yourself?" Kel asked.

"No, Dr. Bailey is. I'm working on her."

"Just don't work on her too much. She's a lot older than you."

"How old?" Vicky asked. "Is she gay?"

Before Taylor could answer, Kel said, "In her middle forties, much nearer to our age than Taylor's."

Taylor hadn't thought about it that way. Vicky was fifty and Kel was fifty-three. She looked at her mums and saw them as coming from a much older generation, but when she had gazed at Bailey in that coffee shop, her age signalled an air of authority, worldliness, and sexiness. But she wasn't going to tell her mum that.

"Age is just a number, Mum."

"Age has different expectations."

Vicky said, "She's looking for a historian, not a girlfriend, certainly not in our age bracket."

"Thank you, Mama. As I was saying, I'd like Dr. Bailey for the gravitas she would bring."

Kel stayed surprisingly quiet. Had she noticed some sort of interest or excitement when they had talked at her office?

"What's the difference between them? They're both historians," Vicky said.

"If Zee is cable TV, then Dr. Bailey is BBC serious documentaries. She's done quite a few of those. I've got one of her audiobooks on the Regency period too."

"Sounds like an interesting person," Vicky said.

She is, Taylor thought with excitement.

Later that night, Taylor had retreated to her old bedroom to catch up with some work. She had her laptop, iPad, and notepad all laid out on her bed, while *Sense and Sensibility* played on the TV in the background. Eddie had texted earlier to tell her that the website was finally up. It looked better than she could have hoped.

There were figures wearing gentleman's and lady's Regency wear, but they were all androgynous, so that you couldn't gender them. It was so important to Taylor to have her Romantics adopt the role and wear the clothes they wanted.

The chatroom looked great. Really easy to use and fun. She sent the link to Gracie and they both signed up. The Romantics would all be encouraged to take a pseudonym to suit the time. Gracie chose Lady Woods, her surname being Woods, and Taylor chose to keep it simple like her heroine Miss Elizabeth Bennet, with a simple Miss Sparks.

"It will be so good if I can get Bailey." Taylor sighed.

On a whim she paused *Sense and Sensibility* and instead put on Bailey's audiobook. Bailey's voice gave her shivers. She fell back on the bed and closed her eyes, letting Bailey's voice wash over her.

"If only she wasn't so grumpy."

While she continued to listen, she heard a beep from her phone. Taylor got up from the bed and opened her email. One had just arrived from Dr. Bailey. "I was just thinking about you."

Her excitement dwindled when she read the message. Bailey had just written to say she would have information for her lecture very soon.

Taylor replied quickly, *There's no rush. We have plenty of time before the spring ball.* She also added, *How are you today?*

She was hoping to start a more personal conversation, but all she got in response was, *I am very well, thank you.*

"God. I need to find a way to shake that stiffness out of you."

Taylor smiled when she closed her eyes and pictured Bailey giving a lecture, but there was only Taylor in the lecture hall.

Taylor got up and walked over to Bailey in the hall.
"Can I help you, Ms. Sparks?"
"Oh, very much so."

Taylor sat up quickly. "No, no, not appropriate."

She switched *Sense and Sensibility* back on because Bailey's voice was far too distracting.

Taylor's phone beeped again. It was Bailey. *How are you today? How is the business going so far?*

She smiled. "I'm in."

CHAPTER SIX

The next day Taylor and Gracie were busy at work in Taylor's flat. There was so much to do but Taylor was enjoying every minute of it.

"That's all the welcome packs ready, except for the invitations."

"When do you think Ed will have them finished?" Gracie asked.

"Over the weekend, he said. I'll pick them up from his house, and then, all being well, we can post the welcome packs on Monday."

"It'll really feel like we're getting somewhere then."

"Yeah, it really will. Let's put these packs in the spare room for now."

They both carried boxes of the welcome packs through to the spare room. Taylor heard her email beep, and as soon as she put her box on the floor she checked her phone.

She hoped it would be Bailey again, and it was. Since last night they had been messaging backwards and forwards, and Bailey was becoming friendlier every time. Taylor was sure there was more to the haughty, patronizing, serious person underneath the persona that she met. It was nothing more than a hunch, and Bailey's emails were starting to bear that out.

From the stiff emails to the slightly less stiff emails, Bailey was warming to her—Taylor knew it.

The doorbell chimed. "That'll be Zee."

"Yes," Gracie said, "I can't wait to meet her. So sexy."

"You think?" Taylor said as they walked to the door.

"Oh yeah. They call her the rock star of history."

Taylor buzzed Zee in. She knew Zee from TV but had seen only snippets of her shows. They weren't really about her era of history. But Taylor was looking forward to meeting her.

There was a knock at the door, and Taylor quickly opened it. *Wow* was all that she could think.

Zee leaned against the doorway dressed in a slim-fitted black leather jacket, jeans, and black T-shirt. Around her neck was a thick silver necklace, and she had a chunky skull ring on her middle finger.

This was a historian?

"Hi, I'm Zee Osmand. We had an appointment?"

Taylor gave herself a shake. "Yes, of course. Hi, come in." She led Zee to the couch and said, "Take a seat. Can I take your jacket?"

"Yeah, thanks," Zee said.

Zee put her laptop bag down on the coffee table. She took off her jacket to reveal two full sleeve tattoos on her arms.

Wow. Zee Osman really was something. No wonder TV audiences liked her. She certainly would make history sexy.

Between the tattoos and her hair she was one good looking package. Zee's hair was naturally dark brown and shaved on the back and sides, and the top was longer and dyed blonde. Zee had it carefully combed to the back.

"Gracie, can you hang up Zee's coat for me?"

Gracie was mesmerized with Zee, it seemed, so Taylor elbowed her. "Can you take Zee's jacket?"

"What? Oh yes, of course."

"Can I get you a drink, Zee? Tea, coffee, or a soft drink?"

"Coffee would be great. Black and two sugars, please." Zee flashed a gleaming smile that Taylor was sure disarmed most.

Taylor started to make coffee in her espresso machine. As she waited, she looked over at Zee, who had brought out an iPad and was soon typing away on it. Gracie came up beside Taylor and whispered, "She is gorgeous, isn't she?"

Taylor watched her run a comb through her already perfectly styled hair.

"I think she knows it too. Here, you take her coffee, and I'll make ours."

"But what will I talk about when you're not there?"

"Anything, just be yourself."

Gracie was most definitely a fan already. Then Taylor remembered she hadn't read Bailey's email. It had been forgotten when rock-and-roll historian had arrived. She quickly scanned it and was happy to see that Bailey suggested having a meeting about what she had found.

A Zoom meeting? That was a huge step forward. Maybe it would be a good time to drop in her news about Zee.

Here's hoping that Bailey would have enough professional rivalry that she'd want to do the lectures herself. She quickly typed out: *Tonight sometime? I'm in a meeting this afternoon.*

She sent it off and finished off the coffees for herself and Gracie and took them over to the couch.

"Thanks for agreeing to meet me," Zee said. "As soon as I heard your story, I knew I had to meet you."

"Thank you for being interested. We're just at the beginning of this dream, and there's a long way and a lot of hard work to do."

Zee brought her iPad onto her lap. "To start, can I just ask you some questions and find out a little bit more about you and the company?"

"Fire away."

"Gracie tells me that you are in love with love. Is that what inspired you to become involved in the dating business?"

In love with love? How embarrassing.

Taylor gave Gracie a sharp look. "I wouldn't go that far, but I am a romantic. My parents are an extremely loving couple, and I suppose that rubbed off on me, and then I fell in love with Jane Austen, and I was hooked."

"Why do you think the Regency period can help us with relationships in the modern day?"

"Well, I think to teach us to slow down, mainly. I think dating has been reduced to looking at a picture on an app, and swiping left or right. I feel that people could be missing out on the person of their dreams."

Zee smiled at her, and Taylor noticed what deep brown eyes she had. They were warm, open, and *gorgeous*, as Gracie would say.

"Yeah, you're right," Zee said. "People are a lot deeper than they might show on the outside."

"It's not to say that people in the Regency always knew each other well—marriages were often made for money and titles. They also got married a lot more quickly than we would today, but at least they had a chance. They danced together, played cards, took part in country pursuits like riding and shooting, and very basically walked together a lot."

Zee kept her eyes locked on Taylor. "Have you met your love by walking and dancing?"

Taylor sensed that this was not a prepared question. Zee had a definite twinkle in her eye. "No, I'm single at the moment."

Zee held her gaze and said, "I'm sure anyone would be happy to walk and dance with you, Taylor."

She was so confident. How Taylor wished she could feel confident where love was concerned.

There was a silence before Zee said, "You work out of your flat?"

"Yes, just me and Gracie. Gracie is my younger cousin," Taylor said.

"Two beautiful women in the one family." Zee smiled and Gracie blushed.

She's cheeky. I'll give her that.

"Tell me how the club operates," Zee asked.

"At first we are signing up members for a six-month package. It might become more in the future if the business is successful enough. My Romantics get three balls for that membership—two weekend private balls and one public assembly. The assembly rooms were places where local people could intermingle, and the only requirement for attendance was that you could afford the ticket. The assembly is a one night dance, but the other two are weekend stays in country houses, where the Romantics can enjoy all the Regency pursuits we've talked about. In between we meet up for dance and etiquette classes."

"Sounds like lots of fun. Are there any special rules that your Romantics must keep to? Some from the Regency period?"

"Yes, if two people take a shine to each other, they are to refrain from close physical encounters during our weekends away, and even between the weekends. It would make the purpose of the club redundant. If you want to play by twenty-first century rules and jump into bed, then there isn't much point in going back in time to a different era. The point is to get to know each without the pressures of sex getting in the way."

Zee's eyes widened. "But that would be pretty hard to keep to."

"I think it will only make it more special when that moment comes around eventually," Taylor said.

Zee smiled. "I suppose. Now I have a proposal for you. I'd like to write an article about your new venture for some of the magazines or Sunday papers I work for."

"What would it involve?" Taylor asked.

"I would come to your weekends, some of your dance classes, and just shadow you in the background. Take some notes, take some pictures with your clients' permission, and build an article over that time. It would be good for publicity to get your story out there."

This was really exciting. It would do Taylor the world of good to have her business out there in the media.

"I think that would be an excellent idea. We might ask you to dress up so that you don't look out of place."

"I would be more than happy to don a top hat and tails and carry a cane, Miss Sparks."

"Excellent. Oh, I forgot to mention—we'll have a historian at each weekend to discuss the history of the house we're at and the period," Taylor said.

"Oh? Who have you got?" Zee asked.

"Dr. Jaq Bailey. Do you know her?"

Zee burst out laughing. "Know her? Yeah, I know her. We aren't the best of friends."

"Why?"

"A professional rivalry. Let's leave it at that. You could have chosen someone with a bit more charisma. History to Bailey is factual, boring, no colour, no adding excitement so that it jumps out of the dull history books. I would have done it for you if you hadn't already asked her."

Taylor hoped she hadn't gone too far out on a limb. She had gambled that she could get Bailey, and now if she couldn't, Taylor couldn't ask Zee because it would look as if she was second choice.

"I thought her skills would bring a lot to the weekends."

"I'm surprised that Bailey is even doing it. She's been absent from her teaching post at Cambridge a long while now. She doesn't come to any of the professional meetings either."

That surprised Taylor. "Do you know why?"

"No, I don't. She's become somewhat of a recluse now, so I'm told," Zee said.

Why? That was strange. There was so much going on under Bailey's surface.

❖

That evening Bailey was in her office waiting for Taylor to join her in a Zoom meeting. Why she had suggested a video call, she had no idea. Things were getting a bit too familiar.

Familiar? They had only exchanged emails, and this was only a Zoom meeting.

She had them every other week with Margo. But this felt different somehow.

Suddenly, Taylor's smiling face filled the screen. "Bailey? Hi, how are you this lovely evening?"

"I'm fine, thank you."

"Sorry I was a few minutes late. I was just clearing up the dinner things. Have you eaten yet?"

"Yes, I had a sandwich," Bailey said.

"Just a sandwich? That's not enough for a busy historian."

"It was enough for me. Sometimes I can't be bothered cooking, just for one person," Bailey said.

"I love cooking. It's the whole experience—listening to my favourite radio station and singing while chopping my onions, to dancing while I stir my stir-fry." Taylor laughed.

Bailey only gave her a small smile. "You sound like you amuse yourself."

"I do, yes. I hate to be idle. I have ADHD, so I have to keep busy."

"That must make some things difficult for you. Wait, are you moving?"

Taylor smiled. "Yeah, it's a treadmill desk. I can't bear sitting down at a desk, so this is a godsend."

"You like walking, then?"

"I do. I don't enjoy the gym, so I get all my exercise walking or jogging outdoors. Do you exercise?"

"I have gym equipment in my large shed outside. I lift weights to de-stress, but I hate cardio."

"Excellent. You said you had some good information about Fairydean?"

"Yes, there is a lot of history there, and even better social history."

"Oh, now I'm excited. Tell me a few things you've learned," Taylor said.

"There's a lot, but just as an overview—there's been a settlement there since Roman Britain. And when the Romans left abruptly, the Anglo-Saxons and then the Normans used it. It was an excellent defensive castle on the border between Scotland and England, where there were constant raids. It was a lawless place to live. Oh, and I checked out your story about the casket woman. It is a generic story in the North of England—it's like the green or white lady ghost at every large house or country estate."

"That's right. They all have them, don't they? You know, Fairydean also mentioned having green and white ghosts. Good for publicity, I suppose."

"Exactly. Now, coming into the Regency period—the castle had major refurbishing work to make it a nicer place to live when the family's fortune quadrupled, due to the fourth duke's investment in the cloth-making and coal-mining industries. The fifth duke was a social campaigner and didn't allow small children down into the mines, and he insisted that school age children attend school. He paid the parents to send their children to school so they would not be tempted to send them out to work in defiance of his rule."

"That is amazing. What a nice guy," Taylor said.

Bailey couldn't stop herself from smiling at that comment. "I suppose he was. That's just scraping the surface, a few days of research. I'm sure there'll be a lot more interesting information for you and your…what is it you call them?"

"My Romantics." Taylor smiled.

"Your Romantics, of course. I think they'll enjoy your speech."

Taylor slowed the pace of her treadmill a little. Now she would need to bring up Zee Osmond.

"A historian—a writer, and broadcaster—came to visit me today. They want to write an article about my Regency Romance Club."

"Who's the historian?" Bailey asked.

"Zee Osman."

Bailey's eyes went wide. "Zee Osman? She is not an historian."

"No?"

"No. She writes books and documentaries with no training at all. No PhD, no master's, not even a basic degree in history."

"Why is she so popular, and why do TV companies give her the documentaries then?" Taylor asked.

"Because her books are exceedingly popular. She writes history in such a populist, sensationalist way, that it comes across as historical soap opera."

Wow, she hadn't expected Bailey to be this against Zee.

"Oh. Well, it'll be good publicity for my company. I thought it was a good idea."

She watched Bailey take a breath. "Yes, of course. It's your company. It has nothing to do with me anyway."

Taylor stayed silent while she considered whether to drop in her final play to get Bailey to be her resident historian.

What the hell. It was now or never. "Um…she offered to be my historian if I couldn't get one to present for me."

Anger was shimmering in Bailey's blue eyes. "I thought you were going to give the lecture if I did the research for you," Bailey said.

"My guests are paying for a professional. I still would like to use your research."

"What? No chance am I having that imposter parroting my research. Either you want my information for yourself, or you use Zee Osman. The choice is yours."

Taylor opened her mouth to reply, but Bailey had cut off from the video.

"Of all the…bloody cheek. Fine then. I'll do it on my own."

❖

Bailey lay in bed that night unable to sleep. A million thoughts were whizzing around in her mind. She was angry, angry that Taylor would use that joker and imagine Bailey would let her use her research.

But Taylor was a young woman, just starting out in the business world. She would assume that someone who had been on TV, presenting herself as a historian, would in fact be one.

It wasn't that Zee had no university affiliation. Bailey knew a few others like Zee, but they treated history with respect. Zee looked for all the salacious evidence and blew it up until that's all that was left.

Bailey turned on her side and wondered *What would Ellis say?*

Exactly the same thing as Ellis had said every other time Bailey had asked that question. *Help the young woman. Get out there and become part of life again.*

"What if I don't want to?"

All Bailey had wanted to do since Ellis died was stay away from everyone and punish herself for not being everything that Ellis needed.

"This is ridiculous."

Bailey got up and went downstairs to get a drink. By the time she wakened up a bit, she realized she was really hungry too.

"Taylor was right. I didn't eat enough at dinner."

Taylor was such a sweet girl. Bailey regretted the anger she had shown on their Zoom meeting earlier. Taylor didn't know what kind of person Zee was. It wasn't her fault.

Bailey made a sandwich, then sat down and began to eat.

Her life had been quiet and solitary a few weeks ago. Now she couldn't sleep for worrying about Taylor and her new venture, and the influence of her professional rival, Zee Osman.

What should she do? Leave Taylor to Zee Osman and her crackpot ideas? Zee was already going to be there for her article, influencing from the sidelines.

Bailey held her head in her hands. The season was only three balls, two in the country houses. She could give her talk and just enjoy some quiet time at the country houses, reading and enjoying the history, while the others took part in their country pursuits.

But she'd have to see that fool Zee, and these people using history as a plaything. Bailey was being torn both ways. She didn't want to come out of her quiet cocoon and face the loud, brash world out there.

"I'll sleep on it. If I can sleep, that is."

Bailey finished her sandwich and tidied up before going back to bed.

CHAPTER SEVEN

The next Monday Taylor was visiting her brother Eddie and brother-in-law Max. She had to pick up the invitations Eddie was writing for her, and they invited her to stay for dinner.

She was standing in their kitchen holding her little nephew Jaden, while the two dads cooked dinner.

"He loves Auntie Tay," Max said. "He's always so content with you."

Taylor gave Jaden a kiss on his head. "He knows who loves him."

At one year old, Jaden was into everything and didn't often tolerate being held up in someone's arms. But he was enjoying his cuddle with Taylor.

"We'll need to put him to bed soon, and then we can eat dinner," Eddie said.

Taylor inhaled and said, "Something smells good."

"Pesto pasta and cheesy garlic bread," Max said, giving a spoonful of the contents of one of his pots a taste.

Taylor's mouth started to water. "Hmm, that will be so good."

Max put his spoon down and gave Eddie a kiss. "I'll go and put little one down to bed, and you can talk to your sister."

"Thanks, sweetheart."

After another kiss from Taylor and one from Eddie, Max whisked Jaden off upstairs to bed. Taylor moved beside Eddie at the cooker and started to stir the pot Max had been in charge of.

"Thanks for writing out those invites for me. You've done an amazing job," Taylor said.

"No problem. I enjoyed it, actually. It must have been a skill Regency kids learned from very early on. It's not easy to write in that long flowing script with a quill."

"Yeah, I found out it was hard the moment I started writing with it. Oh, and the website you made me is just beautiful."

Eddie grinned. "What are big brothers for? Have you managed to get your sexy historian on board yet?"

"I never said she was sexy," Taylor said.

"Your eyes did."

Taylor gave Eddie a playful shove. "Stop it. As a matter of fact I'm still working on it, but I'm confident I'll do it."

"How are you going to manage that? You said she was so set against it," Eddie said.

"I'm using my feminine wiles," Taylor joked.

Eddie opened his eyes widely at her.

"Not that way, dope. I'm using psychology." Taylor pointed to her head.

"You're using mind games on a mature professor of history?" Eddie asked with incredulity.

"Everyone has something that can be used to help them see things from your point of view," Taylor said.

"And what was the professor's?"

"Professional jealousy. Granted, the last time we spoke she cut me off, but I'll get there." Taylor smiled.

At that point Max walked back into the kitchen and said, "You two must have mastered that skill together because Ed can manipulate the hell out of me."

"Shut up, you. Start plating up and we can eat. I'm starving," Eddie said.

Between them they brought all the food over to the kitchen table. Eddie switched on the baby monitor in case Jaden needed them.

Taylor tore off some cheesy garlic. "This is so good. You need to give me the recipe."

"It's really easy," Max said. "I'll email you later with it."

They began to eat, and Max poured out some wine for them all.

Eddie asked, "How's everything else going with the business? No problems?"

"No, quite the opposite. You know the TV history woman, Zee Osman. Gay, butch, good-looking?"

"I love her," Eddie said. "*The history, the scandal, the sex...* She always says that at the beginning of each show."

"That's her. She heard about me through a friend of a friend and asked to meet me. She wants to write a story on the business for the

Sunday papers, history magazines, something like that. That's how I'm going to get Bailey, actually. She can't stand Zee's kind of sensationalist history. I told Bailey I'd have to use Zee if she wouldn't help me, so that's going to fester in her brain until she agrees to do it," Taylor said.

"That's amazing," Eddie said.

"I know. Bailey doing my history stuff and Zee following the events and reporting on what we do will deliver the club excellent PR."

Eddie pointed a fork at his sister. "You are so going to fall for her. Zee, I mean. Sexy Prof will be forgotten when Zee is around."

"Ed, I'm running a business. I don't intend to fall in love with anyone."

"You so will," Eddie said. "Dressing up in the Regency costumes, dancing at the balls—you are going to be lost in the whole romance of the occasion and fall in love."

"I'm there to help other people fall in love," Taylor said.

"You never know," Max said. "The person of your dreams might be one of your Romantics."

"Or Zee Osman," Eddie added.

"Oh no. Definitely not. That would be totally unprofessional, and besides, I'll be run off my feet making sure everything is right."

"We'll see." Eddie winked. "In Regency terms, Zee Osman is a rake, and there's nothing sexier than a bad girl or boy. Your Sexy Prof sounds more like your boring but reliable gentleman. Which one will win your heart?"

"Neither," Taylor said, "now stop it."

❖

"Why don't we send out for lunch. I'm so hungry," Gracie said as they travelled up in the lift to Taylor's flat.

"Good shout. That was a long morning."

This morning they had visited a costumier who made costumes for TV and theatre and struck a deal for them to supply bespoke costumes for the Romantics and come to Fairydean Castle to fit them.

Then it was on to meet Mr. Bamber, or Major Bamber as he liked to be called. Mr. Bamber led a Regency dance troupe that worked as extras for TV and film and gave demonstrations at historic homes and palaces. Mr. Bamber and his dancers would be giving the Romantics dance lessons and be taking part in the balls to lead the dances.

Everything appeared to be going well.

When they emerged from the lift, Taylor was shocked to see Bailey standing by her front door.

"Dr. Bailey—how can I help you?"

Taylor couldn't help but sound deliberately frosty. Bailey had thrown a strop and hung up on her.

"I wondered if I could talk to you."

"If you like."

Gracie, clearly thinking on her feet, said, "Why don't I go to the sandwich shop and get us something for lunch?"

"Perfect. Thank you, Gracie." Taylor unlocked the door and walked through. "Come in and take a seat."

"Thank you."

"Can I get you a drink? Bottle of water, tea?"

"Water would be great, thanks."

Taylor got a couple of bottles from the fridge and brought them over to the sitting area. "Here you go. Were you waiting long?"

"Not too long. Have you had a busy morning?" Bailey asked.

"Yeah, I was meeting with the costume suppliers and the dance troupe that are going to help us with the balls," Taylor said.

"Everyone will have a lot of fun dressing up in period clothing, I'd imagine."

"Yes, they will, and they'll have the freedom to choose how to express themselves. The first group of Romantics are a queer group, and I want them to choose whatever suits their gender identity."

"That's very admirable. It lets people become involved with a community and culture that wouldn't have welcomed them at the time," Bailey said.

"Exactly, but that's not why you're here. How can I help?"

Bailey cleared her throat. "I wanted to come and apologize for my behaviour the last time we talked. It was unacceptable, and I should have never hung up on you."

"Margo told me you don't get along that well with Zee, but I didn't think you'd hate her that much."

Bailey sighed. "I don't hate her. Her type of history riles me up, but it wasn't about that."

"What was it about?"

"I haven't taught in two years, and to be honest, your offer came at a time when I should have been getting back out there, but I just wanted the solitude of my library and writing my books. But when I offered to do research for you and write a lecture, I felt the old buzz of writing a lesson plan and giving a lecture. But I was fighting myself. One part wanted to do it and the other wanted to stay well clear," Bailey said.

"I thought you said a learned historian like you wouldn't lower yourself to work with a dating business?" Taylor said.

"I didn't say it quite like that."

"*Using history as a plaything* is a phrase I seem to remember."

"That could still be true. It was right to think so when I first met you, but now, through our emails back and forth, I believe you have good intentions," Bailey said.

"I'm so glad you have judged me favourably, oh mighty arbiter of history," Taylor snarked.

Bailey sighed and stood up. "I came to apologize, not to be made fun of."

It had obviously been a mistake to come here. She should have stuck to her instincts and stayed at home.

"Sit down. I'm only having a laugh with you."

"You accept my apology then?"

"Of course I do. Sit down," Taylor said.

Bailey was relieved. She'd been unsure her good intentions would be accepted by Taylor. In fact, by the time she was travelling to Taylor's flat, she was questioning apologizing at all.

If Bailey had just left things the way they were, Taylor would have got on with her business, and Bailey could have retreated into her quiet world again. But something inside was pushing her to become involved in Taylor's plan, something that hadn't been there every time she had been offered a new lecture, or an interview with a history podcaster.

"I'm glad we cleared the air."

Taylor gave her a warm genuine smile. Since Bailey had first met Taylor, it struck her how happy, positive, and full of life Taylor was. Even now when she could have refused her apology or drawn it out, she'd accepted, and her smiles and good nature shone through.

She reminded her of Ellis.

Bailey had always been standoffish, bad-tempered, solitary, and negative, and she didn't suffer fools gladly, but Ellis—from when they'd first met at Cambridge as students—had infected her with a positive attitude, with a belief in brighter tomorrows.

This was what had been bothering her since she'd ended the Zoom with Taylor. She was such a young, positive person, untouched by the harsh realities of the world, and her memories of Ellis were prodding her to help her.

"Are you sure you wouldn't like tea or coffee? It won't take a minute," Taylor said.

"No, no. Please sit. There was something else I wanted to talk to you about."

This was the moment, and there would be no turning back if she said it. Her thoughts had been going back and forth all morning, but now she had to make up her mind. Should she offer or not?

"What was it you wanted to talk about?" Taylor prompted.

Bailey cleared her throat. "I want to offer my services as your historian, unless you've already asked Zee Osman."

Taylor jumped up and threw her arms around Bailey. "That's wonderful. Thank you."

Bailey stiffened, but then the scent of Taylor's perfume filled her nostrils, and she pulled back in fright.

She smelled so good.

Bailey couldn't tell if Taylor realized she'd pulled away, but she just kept smiling so happily.

"It'll be so great. I can't wait for your first lecture. We'll make such a good team."

"I hope that my lectures will be of interest to your clients," Bailey said.

"My Romantics will love you."

Her Romantics? Bailey was starting to regret this already.

"What is the timetable, and what will you need from me?"

"I'll email you all the precise details, but first of all I'd like you to join me in a few weeks when I go to Fairydean. We'll have a look around and a run-through of events. Then I've booked a room in a private members' club to have a welcome meeting for my Romantics. Could you say a few words about the Regency period we'll all be stepping into? Just an introduction?"

"Of course. I will look forward to visiting Fairydean. Researching it has been an interesting experience. It played a part in the Wars of the Roses. That and the Tudors are my specialist interests."

"I'm glad you'll enjoy it too. Wait—you haven't even asked about your fee yet. My brother's a lawyer and is going to handle contracts for me."

"Don't worry about it. My travel expenses will be enough," Bailey said.

Taylor's shock was plain on her face. "What? You can't be serious. I'll pay your standard fee for your lectures and your weekends with us and your travel expenses."

"I'm not doing this for the money, Taylor, and I don't need the money. Please just accept my help."

"I couldn't possibly. Bailey—"

It was at that that Gracie arrived back with lunch. "Hi, I got extra sandwiches so Dr. Bailey could have lunch with us."

"Excellent idea, Gracie. Bailey, will you stay?"

Bailey was already on her feet. She had done what she came for and didn't want to become any more involved. "Thank you, but no. I have to go."

Bailey was at the door, and Taylor was still protesting. "Could you not stay for even half an hour and have lunch?"

She had to get out of there. "Sorry, no," Bailey said. "I have to get going. Goodbye."

"I'll be in touch with all the details then."

Eventually Bailey got out of the flat and into the safety of the lift. She let out a breath. "Why am I doing this? I could be at home in my library."

Bailey was regretting this hugely, but something inside made her do it, and she didn't know why.

CHAPTER EIGHT

Two weeks passed from the day of Taylor's last meeting with Bailey, and the day had finally come for their visit to Fairydean. This didn't feel like work—it felt like a road trip. Taylor rushed to the train platform at London's King's Cross Station to start the journey. Gracie was staying at base camp today and doing some errands, so it was just her and Bailey.

This commuter train would take them to the Scottish borders, and then tonight the sleeper train would bring them back to London. She had thought about staying overnight in a hotel, but she was eager to be home and back to work the next day.

The platform was busy with travellers and difficult to pass through.

This was going to be awkward. Yesterday she had emailed Bailey and asked if she would wear period dress at the event weekends. She'd had no response. This wasn't like Bailey. Every email or text she had sent got a timely reply, but this time she had nothing back. Ignored, essentially.

Taylor quickly messaged Bailey and asked if she was on the train yet. She got the reply quickly. *Yes. Last carriage.*

Very blunt and to the point. She wondered if that was because Bailey was angry or if she was always like that.

Taylor arrived at the last carriage and saw Bailey sitting there, waiting for her. She smiled and waved to Bailey. She didn't wave back, but she got up, stone-faced, and walked to the train door immediately.

This didn't bode well.

Bailey took Taylor's bag and walked back to her seat to stow the bag away overhead.

"Thanks," Taylor said as she walked behind. "I thought I might be late. What time did you get here?"

"On time," Bailey said. She sat back down and picked up her book from the table without saying another word. This must have been about the costume because Bailey had been fine with her up until yesterday. I mean she was a woman of few words at the best of times, and a bit grumpy, but she was purposely annoying her.

Taylor just decided to carry on as if everything was fine. "This is going to be fun. A historical road trip together—well rail trip but fun all the same."

Bailey never even raised her eyes from her book. Taylor sighed. Then she remembered she had something in her handbag that might tempt Bailey. She brought out three different kinds of sweets and placed them on the table between them.

"Would you like some travelling sweets? I've got mint humbugs, fruit sherbets, and toffee."

Again, Bailey never looked up but this time said, "No, thank you."

Taylor's shoulders slumped. The train started to pull away from the platform, and they were on their way.

Silence hung heavily between them, and Taylor hated silences. She would much rather they'd be screaming at each other in argument than silence, so she was obliged to fill it.

"You know, they're there any time you fancy a few. When I was a child, my mum always had travelling sweets for when we'd go on day trips."

Nothing. Nothing from Bailey. Not a word, not a raising of her eyes. Nothing.

She looked at the book Bailey was reading. *The Battle of Bosworth: Hour by Hour*.

"What's your book about?"

Bailey had no choice but to look up this time. "The Battle of Bosworth, as you see."

Taylor's temper broke. "Look, this is ludicrous. What's wrong? Is it about the costume thing?"

Bailey slammed her book down on the table. "Do you think? I'm already stepping out on a professional limb to help with what is essentially a dating agency, and now you ask me to dress up like a fool?"

Taylor was shocked. She couldn't believe this was the same person who had come to apologize to her.

"This is not a dating agency, and what do you mean out on a limb?"

"If my colleagues knew I was involved in this, I'd be a laughing stock, far less strutting about in a fancy dress costume."

"I don't understand. You came to apologize to me," Taylor said.

"I apologized for hanging up on you and being rude. Not anything else. I'm doing this for Margo as a favour, nothing more."

Taylor didn't quite know what to say to that. "Fine, if that's the way you want it to be."

Great. A bad-tempered historian. Just what she needed.

Every time Bailey read a paragraph, she was jolted from her place, deep into the last battle in the Wars of the Roses, by Taylor drumming her fingers on the table, shifting in her seat, and crinkling her sweet papers.

She lowered her book. "Could you be a little quieter please?"

"Sorry, I have ADHD. I hate sitting this long."

"There's quite some time to go yet," Bailey said.

Taylor sighed. "I know. I'll go and buy some coffee at the food place further down the train. It'll give me a walk. Do you want some coffee?"

"Yes, thank you. Black, please."

She nodded and shot out of her seat as quickly as she could.

Now that Bailey knew Taylor had ADHD, she could see the signs clearly. Walking desk, talking constantly, fidgeting, acting impulsively.

Bailey lay in bed last night thinking about Taylor and her energy, her obvious impulsiveness. These could be assets if channelled in the right way—perhaps she could advise and mentor in some way through this project. But then she remembered the last minute email about wearing a ridiculous costume, and her anger diminished her enthusiasm to help.

Taylor returned with the drinks. "Here we go. One black coffee."

She handed it to Bailey, and Bailey tried to hand over some money for it.

"It's okay. You can get the next."

"I'll buy lunch," Bailey said firmly.

Taylor raised a quizzical eyebrow. "Oh, will you?"

"Yes, I will," Bailey said firmly. She took a sip of her coffee and lowered her eyes to her book again.

Before long all she could hear was the *crunch, crunch* of Taylor eating her boiled sweets, a hard candy with sherbet inside.

Valiantly Bailey held off for as long she could before it got on her last nerve. "My God," Bailey shouted, before bringing her voice down. "Can you not eat one sweet without crunching?"

Taylor looked confused. "It's a boiled sweet. You're meant to crunch them."

"No, you are meant to suck them, to savour each one till it disappears in your mouth. Have you never heard of delayed gratification?"

Taylor's cheeks had a pinch of red to them, and her eyes flitted everywhere except to Bailey's own.

"Nobody does that," Taylor said. "They're crunchy for a reason, and delayed gratification isn't something I'm used to or like. Why delay pleasure?"

This conversation had gone in a completely unexpected direction. Bailey couldn't help it, but she experienced stirrings in her body that she thought long dead.

"Because the longer you delay, the more pleasure and intensity you receive. Call it the concept of the boiled sweet."

"The concept of the boiled sweet?" Taylor laughed.

On impulse Bailey reached over and grabbed the bag of sweets. "How about a challenge?"

"What kind of challenge?" Taylor asked.

Bailey reached inside the bag and got out two sweets. She placed one in front of Taylor and one in front of herself.

"The challenge is to see if you can keep it in your mouth as long as me—and don't crunch."

"Easy." Taylor picked up the sweet and quickly unwrapped it before popping it in her mouth.

Bailey did the same and placed the sweet in her mouth. She sat back in her seat and crossed her legs. "Easy, you say?"

"Yes, easy."

Whereas Bailey relaxed and calm, Taylor was taut and trying very hard to be nonchalant about the whole thing.

Bailey didn't pick up her book. She kept her eyes fixed on Taylor.

"I could do this all day," Taylor said as she sucked on the sweet.

Bailey could only smile at that statement. The concentration and frustration on Taylor's face were hilarious. She had her hands clasped together so tightly her knuckles were white, and her face was tense and frowning.

It had only been a minute, and it was giving Bailey pleasure to draw it out.

"Come on, Taylor. It's not that hard. Roll the sweet around your mouth, taste it fully. Enjoy the experience."

"Can we just stop this now? It's silly."

"You can stop any time you like." Bailey leaned forward and said, "You just have to give in and ask—" Bailey had to stop herself from finishing that sentence. This simple game to annoy Taylor and show how impulsive she was had turned into something Bailey was not expecting.

The blush on Taylor's cheeks, the parting of her lips, and her tongue slowing wetting her bottom lip had sparked a burning heat inside Bailey. It was a shock to her and something she didn't want to continue or examine.

"There, you happy now?" Taylor's heart was beating fast, and she couldn't stand the tension any more. She crunched her sweet and ate it quickly. "What does that prove?"

"That you lose and have no self-control, obviously. So now, if you could keep the noise down so I can read my book..."

Taylor's frustration was turning to annoyance. "This silly game was your idea, you know. Read your stuffy old book. I'll be glad if we can say as little as possible."

Taylor turned to the window and put her earphones in, hoping the music would make her journey more peaceful.

She put on her favourite love playlist and gazed out the window at the passing scenery, but her mind kept returning to the person sitting across from her and the game they had just played.

From the first moment they had started that silly game, Bailey's calm confidence caused a visceral reaction in her. Taylor shivered thinking about it, how her hunger built until she couldn't stand it any more and munched the sweet.

It had been a raw reaction. How could a competition over the correct way to eat a sweet make her body go loopy?

She closed her eyes and hoped the music and the soft rocking of the train would make her go to sleep. Then she wouldn't have to engage in conversation. Even with her eyes closed, her mind's eye could still see Bailey sitting across from her, reading her boring book.

Get out of my head.

Before long she drifted off to sleep.

CHAPTER NINE

Taylor gathered up the rubbish she had created from sandwiches and sweets and put it in the bin next to the seat. A short sleep and a few hours of boredom later, they were nearing the train station at Fairydean.

Since their strange game earlier in the journey, Bailey hadn't said a thing to her apart from *yes* or *no* as Taylor was trying to make conversation. She really was antisocial and clearly found more pleasure in a book than in human beings.

She wished Zee could have come with them. She would have entertained Taylor the whole journey. Unfortunately, she'd had another appointment today.

"Bailey? We're almost there."

Bailey looked up and out the window. "Yes."

Then she packed away her book in her case, stood up, and brought down Taylor's overnight bag. Taylor was ready to take it, but Bailey just walked to the door of the train.

The train slowed as it pulled into the station, and Taylor hurried along to the door.

"I'll take my bag."

"I've got it," Bailey said firmly.

"Excuse me—"

Taylor was about to reprimand Bailey for assuming that she couldn't carry her own bag when the train doors opened.

She followed Bailey out onto the planform and looked around. It appeared as if they were the only ones who were getting off at this station. It was a tiny station with no staff and no taxis.

"If we walk out to the front of the station, I'll call Lady Catherine. She said she would send someone to pick us up."

"It's very…rural," Bailey said.

It was true. All they could hear was the baaing of sheep, and all they could smell was the scent of manure.

"You say that as if it's a bad thing," Taylor replied.

"I'm more of a city person myself."

There was a bench at the front of the station. Bailey sat, but Taylor stayed on her feet. She couldn't bear to sit any longer. She had to move about, or she would scream.

Taylor took out her mobile and placed a call. "Lady Catherine? It's Taylor Sparks...Yes, we're here...That's very kind, thank you."

Once she hung up, Taylor said, "She's sending someone to get us."

"How did you organize this?" Bailey asked. "I mean, Fairydean Castle doesn't open to the public and doesn't cater for weddings or parties."

"I loved the look of the place, and I emailed. Then we spoke over the phone, and I could tell how excited Lady Catherine was. She's on her own, I believe. She offered to put us up for the night, but I told her we had to get back to London quickly."

"She seems open and kind," Bailey said.

"She's quite the character, going by my phone calls."

"How are you going to get your clients down here? It'll be tricky to get a whole load of people up to the house."

"It's Romantics, not clients, and I've hired a bus company to bring everyone down. That means that we can pick up any Romantics that live outside London."

They waited for about fifteen minutes before Taylor spotted a green Land Rover coming their way. A grey-haired man got out of it.

"Ms. Sparks?"

"Yes, that's me, and this is my colleague, Dr. Bailey."

"I'm Jamie, Lady Catherine's gamekeeper and gardener. Pleased to meet you both. Jump in, and I'll get your bags."

Taylor handed over her bag and headed for the front seat, but Bailey was already holding open the back seat door for her.

She got in reluctantly. Bailey was so, so...carrying her bag, holding doors, insisting on buying lunch...so *annoying*.

Jamie got in and smiled. "Anything you need, just let me know. Her Ladyship is very excited about your visit. We don't get too many people out here, and she loves company."

"I can't wait to meet her," Taylor said.

They set off, and Taylor was loving the scenery. "You live in a beautiful part of the world, Jamie."

"We like to think so. I've got a cottage on the estate, and I feel very lucky," Jamie said.

"My colleague here isn't so impressed. She's a *city person*."

"I can appreciate the scenery," Bailey said. "I just meant I don't like to be cut off from the things I need to do my work—internet, phone signals, things like that."

"The internet can be patchy, to be fair," Jamie said, "but we get by."

They were soon pulling through the gates to the Fairydean estate. Taylor squealed when she saw the house.

"Oh God, it's gorgeous and so romantic."

"Yes, what a fine house," Bailey said, in agreement.

Going by Bailey's standards, that was positively glowing praise. The tyres crunched on the gravel as Jamie drove the Land Rover to the front entrance. It was only seconds before a woman appeared and walked down the entrance steps.

"Is that—?"

"That's Lady Catherine, my dear, and the kindest woman I've ever met. Eccentric old bird, but kind."

Taylor had gotten the impression over the phone that she was quite the character.

Just as she was about to open her door, it was opened by Bailey. She frowned at her. "I can open a door, you know."

For someone who hardly opened their mouth in general conversation, Bailey appeared to anticipate her every move.

Lady Catherine came down the final few steps with her arms open wide. She was an unusual sight. She was taller than your average woman, with collar-length salt-and-pepper hair and a pair of small round spectacles on her nose. "Come ye in, come ye in."

"Lady Catherine," Taylor said, "it's so nice to meet you in person at last."

Lady Catherine grasped her hand and shook it vigorously. "Delighted to have you here."

Taylor turned to Bailey and said, "This is my historical advisor, Dr. Bailey."

Bailey stepped forward and took Lady Catherine's hand. "Dr. Herbert, it's a pleasure to meet you. I've read some of your excellent work on our native wildflowers and how vital they are to our insect species."

Taylor looked at Bailey with surprise. Where did that come from? *Why didn't you tell me she was a professor?*

She was quite annoyed.

"Thank you, Dr. Bailey. You are too kind. What is your specialty, Professor?"

"Early modern history. End of the Wars of the Roses through the beginnings of the Tudor period are where I'm most comfortable."

"Wonderful. An extremely interesting period. Do come in, both of you."

They walked into the entrance hall and Taylor gasped. "This is beautiful, Lady Catherine."

The hall was cosier than some of the huge rooms in bigger stately homes. A dark wood covered the walls and matched the staircase in front of them. Tapestries covered some of the wooden walls, as well as paintings, presumably of Lady Catherine's family.

But the most spectacular and atmospheric display covered the wall at the half landing on the stairs.

A flourish of spears made the shape of a half circle, and around and below them were swords, axes, maces, and other deadly weapons. It gave the house a sense of history straight away.

A man in a butler's outfit came out from one of the side corridors to greet them.

"This is Parrot. He'll look after you for the weekend of your ball," Lady Catherine said.

He turned to greet Taylor. "Hello, ma'am."

Taylor looked at Bailey and tried to stop herself from laughing. "Hello, Mr. Parrot."

"Now come on through. I'm sure you're anxious to see the ballroom, and then we can have tea." Lady Catherine carried on walking and called out, "Parrot, can you organize some tea for us, and some of Mrs. Parrot's cakes. Thank you."

"Yes, ma'am."

As she and Bailey followed Lady Catherine, they shared a look, and Bailey actually smiled, which was a welcome sight.

They walked into the ballroom, and Taylor had an intake of breath. The large room had classical figures and scenes painted across the ceiling and two of the walls. The paintings were highlighted by gold paint at every ceiling cornice, and there were wood frames between paintings.

"Will this do?" Lady Catherine asked.

"Do? It's out of this world. It's everything I could have dreamed of."

Bailey was walking around with her head craned to the ceiling too. "It's exquisite."

"Thank you. I'm so delighted that it's going to be used as it was intended. I was delighted when I got your message, asking to use the house. Let's have tea, and you can tell me all about your plans," Lady Catherine said.

❖

"I cannot thank you enough," Taylor said. "I couldn't have hoped for a better house for my Regency weekend."

Bailey was happy to see Taylor so happy, so excited. There was such a sparkle in her eyes when she smiled. Miss Sparks's name really did suit her.

"Not at all, my dear. The Regency period was certainly when Fairydean was at its height."

Bailey took a sip of tea and said, "I've been doing research on your ancestors, the 4th Earl and Countess. They appear to have been a great driving force in the abolitionist movement."

"Indeed. At a time when many great estates were built on the slave trade, the Herberts were fighting against it. There's a great deal of history for you to impart to your— What did you call them, my dear?"

"Romantics," Taylor said.

"Romantics. That's it. Tell me, Dr. Bailey, are you a romantic yourself?" Lady Catherine asked.

"I believe that the love of friends and family binds us together as family units, but romantic love? I have never been that way inclined. Perhaps it works for some, but most often it is infatuation or lust."

Taylor looked at her with narrowed eyes.

"Ah, you have a sceptic here, Taylor. Perhaps your group of Romantics can change her mind."

"I doubt that, Lady Catherine. She seems determined to be displeased with my whole concept."

It was just a job. Why did Taylor insist on believing in her quest for love? Bailey tried to remember that Taylor was young, with a head and a heart full of dreams and possibilities. Perhaps one day she'd learn how complicated and hurtful love, or lack of it, could be.

She decided to change the subject. "You're going on a research mission, I believe, while Taylor's group is here."

"Yes, two weeks to Dorset. I'm cataloguing the wildflowers of Britain. I find the untamed beauty of wildflowers to be much more pleasurable than carefully cultured plants and flowers," Lady Catherine said.

Taylor put down her teacup. "I've seen on the internet that you have beautiful gardens."

Lady Catherine pulled her glasses down her nose and asked, "Fairydean is on the internet?"

Taylor nodded enthusiastically. "Yes, some lovely photos of your gardens."

"Well, well. I'm glad people think the garden is worth looking at. I plan to give the house to the National Trust after I've kicked the bucket, so a lot of people will be able to share in the house and gardens."

"Really? That's a lovely thing to do," Taylor said.

"Well, I have no family to leave it to. They will be no more Earls and Countesses of Fairydean, but I hope that the history and beauty will live on with those that visit here."

Bailey smiled. She liked Lady Catherine. She was an eccentric lady, but in such a charming and endearing way.

Lady Catherine poured out some more tea and said, "If you've any questions about the place, fire away."

Straight away Taylor said, "Can you tell me about the lady trapped in the trunk?"

This was Bailey's time to exit. She had told Taylor it was just a myth.

"Well—" Lady Catherine started to say.

"Excuse me, Lady Catherine," Bailey said. "Would you mind if I went to look at your wonderful library? I've heard you have many rare books."

"Of course. It's straight across the entrance hall. You can't miss it."

"Thank you. Excuse me."

Bailey left the room with Lady Catherine saying, "Everyone thinks the lady in the chest is a myth, but—"

Bailey sighed. Now Taylor would take it as fact.

She walked across the hall until she came to two very old looking wooden doors. Bailey pushed them open and entered the library.

Bailey was overawed. "Wonderful."

She walked in with her necked craned high. The library was over two levels. The second floor was accessed by a spiral staircase, and on the ceiling was another painted fresco.

It was a large library full of leather-bound books, a wealth of knowledge that Bailey could spend months lost in. She used a lot of online resources for her own work, intermixed with trips to the British Library for original sources, but nothing could replace the thrill, the smell of well-read and -worn books.

She ran her hand along their leather spines. It was a pity she and Taylor were spending such a short time here. She looked through the titles—works by Sir Walter Scott and Dickens, histories of Britain, and many botanic titles, no doubt enjoyed by Lady Catherine. But of course they would be back here soon for a whole weekend.

It wouldn't be so bad after all. Bailey could give her lecture and then escape to this library and enjoy time with these precious books. That thought made her much more cheerful about the whole thing.

She caught sight of a large old book sitting open on a lectern, on a long library table. Bailey walked over and scanned the text. It was an early translation of *Malleus Maleficarum*, or *The Hammer of Witches*, the standard medieval text on witchcraft, printed in the early modern era.

"This is exquisite," Bailey said in astonishment.

She read down the page it was open to and was anxious to flick through the pages, but without permission she wouldn't do it. She couldn't tell the state of the volume just by sight, and it might be vulnerable to damage.

"I'll need to remember to get clearance from Lady Catherine next time."

There were few things that could get her excited like leafing through some old text.

The sound of laughter made Bailey look up. Through the library window, she saw Taylor and Lady Catherine, walking arm and arm through the garden. She found herself walking over to the window to get a better view.

The two women appeared to be getting on well. She and Taylor had different outlooks on life and held differing opinions, but Bailey found Taylor's laughter and optimism made her feel lighter in some way. Reminded her of a different time when she herself had optimism and excitement about the journey of life.

Bailey thought back to what had happened on the train. It was a strange sensation to feel need again, and she didn't want it. That side of life was gone for her, because of the grief that she felt, and by design.

She couldn't help but smile as she watched Taylor walk by. Then she remembered that she had no right to smile. Bailey had promised herself that she would never smile again.

❖

"Are you sure we're not driving you off?" Taylor asked as they walked around the gardens.

"No, I assure you it's not putting me out. I was planning a weekend away in Dorset. Your request just pushed me to make plans."

"It's a lovely part of the world," Taylor said. "Where exactly are you going?"

"A little village called Rosebrook. It's an eco-village, and they've planted fields of wildflowers for the bee population there. They've chosen to try to encourage rare wildflowers, and I'm going to consult and study."

Taylor stopped by the fountain as they came upon it. "Rosebrook. That rings a bell from when I was trying to research stately homes I could use."

"Yes, I'm sure it does. It's a beautiful home, I'm led to believe, but it was rebuilt in the 1920s, so it wouldn't have suited your purpose."

Taylor nodded. "That must have been why I didn't go any further with it."

There had been something bothering Taylor, and it felt like the right moment to bring it up.

"Lady Catherine?"

Lady Catherine looped Taylor's arm through hers. "Yes, my dear."

"You've given me your beautiful home at such a low price. It's a fraction of what the other house has cost me to hire. Are you sure—"

"Now now"—Lady Catherine patted her hand—"none of that, none of that. I'm fortunate in that I don't need the money. Not a lot of landowners of these great houses are in that position these days. I'm delighted to help a young woman trying make her way in life. I only really charged you anything to give Mr. and Mrs. Parrott a bonus for the extra work they and the daily staff will do. They can clean, help hand out drinks, anything you need."

"They won't be annoyed at all these extra people to look after?"

"They'll be delighted with the extra money. One more thing,

Jamie will be doing your clay pigeon shooting for you. He wondered if you would like his son to do some falconry with your guests."

"Really?" Taylor said excitedly. "I tried to find a falconer, but there were very few and all booked up."

"Sam has his own business, touring around National Trust houses, medieval fairs, things like that. You'll find him very reasonably priced since I've recommended you."

"Honestly, Lady Catherine, you are too kind."

"Not a bit of it. I'll give you his card, and you can phone him. Sam's expecting your call. Now let me introduce you to Mrs. Parrot."

After visiting Mrs. Parrot, Taylor left Lady Catherine and made her way to the library in search of Bailey. She rubbed her hands together with glee. Things couldn't have gone better with Mrs. Parrot, and she couldn't wait to tell Bailey.

She opened the door and saw that Bailey was so engrossed in a book, she didn't notice Taylor coming in. Bailey was sitting in a leather armchair, holding her chin thoughtfully as she read.

There was something really sexy about an intelligent woman—an intelligent *older* woman like Bailey. She looked so calm and controlled, and that was such an attractive quality in Taylor's eyes.

Bailey had made her opinion on love clear, but she wondered if that was always the case. Had Bailey been in a long-term relationship and been hurt, or had she always avoided romance?

Bailey suddenly looked up and caught her looking. "Have you finished talking about women in chests?"

"Yes, thank you. Honestly it might be a myth, but you're no fun."

Bailey shut the book she was reading and stood to put it back. "That is generally how I am seen."

Taylor was certain there was a fun layer underneath that melancholy exterior. Maybe she would manage to find it while they were working together.

"Come and see this."

Taylor walked over and saw that Bailey had pulled out an old-looking book.

"It's a first edition *Pride and Prejudice*. Rare editions of all of Austen's works are here."

"Wow." Taylor took it and leafed through its pages carefully. "It's beautiful. I've never read Jane Austen, you know," Taylor admitted.

Bailey did a double take. "Excuse me? You love Jane Austen. Isn't she the whole reason you started this business, the reason we are here?"

Taylor felt embarrassed now. She always did when she explained this. "I...I can't read. I mean, of course I can read, but it's my ADHD, you see. I have problems with focusing, memory and retention, processing information."

"Of course," Bailey said, "I've encountered many students over my career with similar problems. How did you manage at school and university?"

"With great difficulty. I would use the voice function on my iPad and Kindle for uni, and I watched the TV adaptations and films first. Now I get audiobooks and listen while I'm cleaning, travelling, or going to sleep at night."

"I admire the way you cope with it and got to where you are today," Bailey said.

"Do you?" Taylor met Bailey's eyes.

Neither broke the other's gaze, and Taylor found herself falling slowly into Bailey's blue eyes. They got closer and closer. Taylor's heart was beating fast, but then Bailey cleared her throat and moved away quickly. She put the book away and an awkward silence was left.

They'd nearly... How did that happen?

This, along with the incident on the train, made Taylor realize she had a crush— No, no, it wasn't anything like that. Bailey was bad-tempered, antisocial, and moody. She liked positive upbeat people.

The silence was deafening, and Taylor had to fill it. "Lady Catherine was telling me about the name of the house."

Bailey turned around. "Oh? Fairydean?"

"Yes. Apparently, the original house was built on fairy land."

Bailey raised an eyebrow. "Fairy land?"

"Yes, land of the fairies? Anyway, they started causing mischief, and Lady Catherine's ancestor agreed to let the fairies have free run of the house and gardens, and the ancestor promised to put out an offering of food every full moon. Lady Catherine still does it."

"What nonsense. I wonder why a woman of science like Lady Catherine would carry on such silliness."

"It's a tradition—and let me show you this." Taylor started scanning the library walls.

"What are you doing?" Bailey asked.

"Looking for something. Ah, there it is."

Taylor waved Bailey over.

She pointed to an archway chiselled and painted into the skirting board. "It's a fairy door. Lady Catherine's ancestors promised to put a door in every room, so they could easily move through the house."

"How do they go through solid wood?"

Taylor smiled. "Magic, of course."

"Dear God." Bailey sighed then looked at her watch. "We better be making tracks if we want to get the connecting train to Carlisle."

"No need. Lady Catherine has invited us to dinner, and Jamie will drive us to the station."

"That's kind of her."

"I think she likes the company. I've more to tell you, but I'll talk to you later on the train."

CHAPTER TEN

Bailey hung up her suit jacket on the coat hanger provided in her sleeper room. This was a much more civilized way to travel home, and she was glad Taylor had suggested it. The first-class room had a couch that converted to a single bed, a toilet, and a shower, and all the amenities you needed to charge your devices.

There was a club lounge where you could have drinks and nibbles. She had promised she would meet Taylor for a drink later. She took her shoes off and lay down on the bed to check some emails and read before she met Taylor.

She thought back to the moment in the library where she had momentarily fallen into Tylor's soft gaze. The two things she could remember vividly were Taylor's perfume and her eyes. It was the same scent she had noticed every time they'd been together. It filled her nostrils and intoxicated her. Then there were Taylor's green eyes. They were verdant, alive, and so full of promise. Was it that hope, that promise that attracted her so much?

Bailey didn't know enough about Taylor's background, but she felt she saw a soul unburdened by the harsh realities of life.

Bailey would be glad when they arrived home. Apart from video calls, they wouldn't have to see each other until they came to Fairydean for the first weekend.

By that time, Bailey would have calmed whatever was attracting her to Taylor. She was sure.

❖

Tylor made her way to the club lounge. She'd had a shower in her cabin and felt so much better for it. She saw Bailey as soon as she walked into the lounge, and for a change she wasn't reading—she was writing on her laptop.

Bailey looked up and caught her gaze, and Taylor felt excitement in her stomach. Bailey stood as she approached.

"Evening. Everything okay in your cabin?"

"Yes, thanks. It's a great way to travel."

"Can I get you a drink?" Bailey asked.

Taylor smiled. "Yes, that would be lovely."

She opened the menu on the table and read through the selections while Bailey signalled for one of the train staff.

"What can I get you?"

"I'll have a Auchentoshan malt with ice please, and my friend will have a…?"

"Weird watermelon, please," Taylor said.

By the look on Bailey's face, she hadn't heard of that drink before.

"Would you like anything to eat?" the staff member asked. "Nuts, olives, sandwiches?"

"Taylor?"

"Some nuts and olives would be lovely." Taylor smiled.

Bailey packed up her laptop and put the case to the side. She wasn't going to be rude and continue working.

"What were you working on?"

"Just some notes for my book."

"I hope that helping me isn't taking you away from your work," Taylor said.

"Not at all." That was partially true. She was going to be writing up to her deadline, but what was new?

The drinks arrived. Bailey's was simply whiskey with ice, but Taylor's watermelon drink came in a tall bulbous glass with a straw, a cocktail umbrella, and fruit on a toothpick. Bailey didn't think drinks garnished like that had made it past the eighties.

"Oh, that's so nice. Thank you," Taylor said to the server.

"My pleasure. We like to make an effort."

Once he left Bailey asked, "What is a Weird watermelon?"

Taylor took a sip through her straw and shivered slightly. "That's so good. It's from a range of drinks. Weird kiwi, Weird mango, Weird tropical. The *weird* bit is that there's a fizzy sherbet taste to it. It's an alcopop aimed at women, university students, and—controversially—teenagers."

Suddenly the gulf of a generational age gap opened between them, in Bailey's mind anyway.

"Sounds delightful," Bailey said sarcastically.

"This from someone drinking whiskey? Here, have a try."

"What a kind offer, but no."

Taylor moved her glass over to Bailey. "Go on, grumpy. Have a go. If you do, I'll try your horrible whiskey. I've never tried a drop in my life, but I'm willing to try something new."

Bailey sighed, lifted the glass, and took a sip. Her tastebuds were first assaulted by the intense taste of sweetness, and then the sour flavour of a fizzy sherbet.

"Oh my God. That must have ten spoonsful of sugar in it."

Taylor just laughed.

"It tastes like I've drunk a sweet shop."

"That's the point. It's for people who don't like the taste of alcohol. Gimme yours then."

Taylor held out her hand and flexed her fingers. Bailey sighed and handed it over. How had her life come to this? Swapping drinks with a young woman on the Caledonian Sleeper.

Taylor swirled it around and sniffed it suspiciously.

"Don't spill any—that's eleven pounds a glass."

"Is it? My Weird watermelon is only three pounds a bottle. I'm a cheap date." Taylor laughed.

"That will never be true, or it shouldn't be," Bailey said firmly.

Taylor's laughter stopped straight away, and her eyes locked with Bailey's. "No?"

"No, whoever is lucky enough to take you out should treat you like a—" Bailey stopped herself from going too far. "Very well. Should treat you very well."

Taylor locked eyes with her and said nothing, but the space between them felt intense. Bailey had to force herself to look away. She busied herself with her iPad and hoped that Taylor would look away.

"Okay, bottoms up," Taylor said.

Bailey looked up as Taylor took a sip of her whiskey. The face she made was reminiscent of a toddler trying a Brussels sprout.

Then Taylor exclaimed, "Argh! That is disgusting. How can anyone drink that?"

Bailey laughed and took her glass back. "It's an acquired taste."

Taylor took a big gulp of her drink and said, "Who would want to acquire it?"

"Old people like me," Bailey said.

"You're not old."

"Compared to you, I am."

Bailey thought she should remind Taylor of their respective ages. Bailey could cope with her attraction to Taylor much better if Taylor didn't gaze at her with the same sparks of attraction.

"You're only as old as you feel."

Bailey didn't reply to that. She wanted the subject to change.

Taylor cleared her throat and said, "I think we should discuss the elephant in the room."

What? The sexual tension?

"What elephant?"

"You dressing in period costume."

Bailey was so relieved. This topic she could handle. "You know how I feel about it."

Taylor popped a few of the nuts in her mouth. She had to word this carefully if she was to get what she wanted.

"I know, but think about what I'm trying to do. I want my Romantics to lose themselves in the period. They're paying to take part in a time-travel mission, going back in time and becoming part of the Regency period. Imagine they're taking part in shooting, fencing, or poetry reading. They are immersed in the Regency world—then you come out to give your talk in normal clothes, and the illusion is shattered."

Bailey took a sip of her drink and sighed.

Taylor knew she was wavering. "Please, Bailey. It would make me so happy."

"Fine, I'll do it, but I'm not dancing." Bailey pointed her finger towards Taylor to emphasize the point.

Taylor clapped her hands. "Thank you, thank you."

The dance was an argument for another day, but Taylor wanted Bailey to dance and enjoy the ball. She was sure Bailey would like it once she was part of it.

"I'll take you to the costumer to measure you up myself. They are coming to the dance lessons, but I think you would appreciate more privacy," Taylor said.

"Thank you. I would."

They both remained silent for the next few minutes, both looking out the train window into the gloom of a darkening sky.

Then Bailey broke the silence. "What are your mum and dad like? What do they do for a living?"

Taylor chuckled. People always made that assumption. "It's mum and mum, actually."

"What? Really? I'm sorry."

"It's okay. People always assume that. It's the way our brains are culturally wired. Mum and Mama work for the family business— fruit and vegetable suppliers. They supply the best restaurants all over London."

"Oh, excellent. Did they start it together?"

"Mum took over my granddad's fruit and veg stall when she was sixteen and built the business up to one that supplies the UK and Europe. Mama joined when they became an item."

Bailey smiled. "You sound very proud. They must be nice people."

"They are. The best. Mum, Mama, and my brothers all came together to give me the last bit of capital I needed to start my business."

"You have a kind and loving family."

"The best."

"Tell me about your siblings?" Bailey asked.

"Three big brothers, Luke, Thomas, and Eddie. Thomas is married to Gianna, and they have two kids, Ruby and Aaron. Luke has a girlfriend called Jess, and Eddie is married to Max. They have one boy called Jaden."

"Three big brothers. That's a big family. What was that like growing up?" Bailey asked.

"It gave me a lot of confidence, I suppose, because I always felt I had a safety net behind me. What about you?"

"Family? There's just me. My parents were older when they had me. They'd never planned to have any children. I was quite the surprise. My mother thought she was going through the menopause."

Taylor laughed. "Sorry, that's quite funny. I bet they were pleased when you arrived."

Bailey screwed up her face. "*Pleased* is a strong word. They got used to me. We didn't spend much time together. Mother and Father both were professors at Oxford. Mother, chemistry, and Father, physics. I had a nanny and then was sent off to boarding school at eight."

"Eight? That's awful," Taylor said.

Bailey shrugged. "They did their best. It was the way they were brought up. Mother and Father weren't the most emotional of people. I don't even think they loved each other in the conventional sense. They greatly respected each other's work."

Bailey had never had an experience of warm family or love as far as she'd known.

"So how and why Cambridge if your parents were at Oxford?"

"A small act of rebellion. They weren't best pleased. But I wanted to be somewhere I'd be judged for me, not for who my parents were."

"I can see that."

Taylor was silent for a few seconds. "All this money my family has given me—I get nervous and worried I'll let them down."

"How could you think that? I'm sure they're very proud of you."

"I know they are, but if this doesn't go well, I'll lose my family's money."

"You won't let them down. You're a dedicated hard worker."

"But you've said yourself that you think this is a silly idea, playing with history and its people," Taylor said.

"You don't want to listen to me. I am an eternal pessimist. From knowing you better now, I know you have the skills to make this business work."

"Thank you. That means a lot, coming from you. I don't think you give out positive opinions very often." Taylor smiled.

Bailey matched that smile. "You are probably right."

They chatted a while longer, but Taylor was getting tired. She yawned and stretched her arms. "I think I need my bed."

"Of course, I'll walk you to your cabin, then come back and finish up some of my work," Bailey said.

"It's fine, I can make my way back. You carry on with your work."

Bailey clearly didn't listen and stood and extended her hand for Taylor to take.

"You are extremely polite."

"One tries," Bailey said with a twinkling smile.

Taylor took Bailey's hand and felt the warmth from Bailey's hand travel to hers and into her body.

She felt safe. Bailey made her feel safe. That was something she hadn't felt from someone outside her family before. It was strange.

Bailey walked her along the corridor to the end where her cabin was. "Well, this is me," Taylor said.

They both stood awkwardly, the tension building between them.

"Thank you for a lovely day. It was fun spending it together. It didn't turn out as bad as you thought it was going to be, did it?"

Bailey gave her a lopsided smile. "No, it wasn't."

Before Taylor could change her mind, she stood on tip toe and kissed Bailey on the cheek, then went in her room and shut the door.

CHAPTER ELEVEN

Taylor emptied her bags from the boot of her mum's car. She'd asked to borrow it since she had so much to transport to the hotel for the Romantics' open evening. Gracie couldn't come with her tonight. She worked part-time at a bar, and she'd traded an awful lot of shifts already to help Taylor. Taylor told her that she would be fine.

But in truth, Taylor was nervous. It was the first time she was coming face to face with all the new members of the Regency Romance Club. She had to convey the magic of the period and fulfil these people's dreams, and it was a lot of pressure.

"Taylor?"

She turned around and saw Zee. She was looking gorgeous tonight in black jeans and a simple white T-shirt, with a black leather jacket. Her camera was slung over her shoulder.

"Hi, Zee." Taylor put down one of her heavy bags and took a deep breath.

"Hello, beautiful," Zee said, "are you nervous?"

"Yes. It's a big night."

"It'll be fantastic. How about we go for drinks after this?"

"Yeah, that would be great." Zee actually asked her out? Gracie would be jealous.

"Excellent. I'll go inside and get the lay of the land and take some shots of the room." Zee walked away and up the front doorstep.

Taylor looked down at all the bags she had to take in, and then considered the two free hands that Zee'd had. "She could have offered."

Taylor shut the boot of the car, so that the remaining bags would be safe till she came back out, and walked up the stairs and into the hotel. The receptionist smiled at her, as she'd already been in to check in and make sure the function room was in order.

When she walked in, she saw Zee walking around taking shots and Bailey sitting next to the large smart board the hotel had provided, looking at her MacBook.

Had Bailey sneaked in past her without saying anything? Bailey spotted her and immediately got up and hurried over to her.

"Let me get those." Bailey took all the bags.

"Did you sneak in? I never saw you," Taylor asked.

"No, I didn't know you were here, or I would have come to help you. There's a side entrance down the alley at the side where you can go straight into the bar."

"You've been here before then."

"Once or twice. Have you got more bags outside?" Bailey asked.

"Yes, lots."

"I'll take these and put them beside the smart board, and I'll meet you back outside."

Taylor sighed. "Thanks, I could do with the help."

Bailey walked back to where she had been sitting and put the bags down. She could feel the presence of Zee beside her and hear the click of her camera.

"It won't work, you know."

"What do you mean?" Bailey asked.

"Being so helpful and carrying her bags. Trying to ingratiate yourself with her," Zee said.

"I'm being well-mannered. You know, the thing that you generally aren't."

"You can't fool me. A word of advice—don't embarrass yourself. You are too old for her."

Bailey ignored her and walked back out. Bloody fool. She was being *friendly*, and you were never too old to be friends. Bailey was well aware she was too old for anything else, and she wouldn't want it anyway.

Bailey saw Taylor struggling with a heavy bag and hurried over. "Here, let me."

"You're a lifesaver. I brought too much, I think, but I didn't want to leave anything to chance," Taylor said.

"You're better to be over-prepared than not. That's what I always told my students."

Taylor smiled. "I bet you were a good teacher."

"I don't know about that. I pushed them to always be better, but I didn't have the most approachable qualities."

They gathered all the bags between them and started to walk in. "I imagine you were somewhat scary. You scared me the first time we met," Taylor said.

"Did I? It wasn't meant."

Taylor put her laptop bag down on the function room floor. Bailey did the same with hers.

"You still do—sometimes."

Taylor instantly regretted what she'd said, as a stony look overcame Bailey, and she pulled away.

"Forgive me," Bailey said. "I'll leave you to set up."

"No, Bailey, I didn't mean that…" But Bailey was gone. Taylor watched her leave the function room and walk towards the bar.

"Fool," Taylor chastised herself.

She had meant *scared her* in a good way. That image she had when she closed her eyes at night was of the distinguished woman that Bailey was, sitting in a chair, legs crossed, radiating power, as she had when they'd first met. The look that made her blood run hot and her heart beat faster.

"What's she said to you?" Zee asked.

"Nothing, nothing. Just a misunderstanding," Taylor said.

"Keep out of her way. She'll do nothing but bring down your positivity."

Taylor was about to rebuke Zee when one of the servers came over with a tray of drinks—champagne, orange juice, and lemonade.

"Drink, Ms. Sparks?"

"Just the orange please. I'd better keep a clear head."

"I'll take a champagne. I never pass up a free drink," Zee said.

It wasn't free, of course, it was paid for as everything was tonight, from the business. So that comment annoyed Taylor.

The server said, "We're going to wait at the door with drinks in case there's any early birds."

"Thank you."

Thankfully Zee had moved anyway. It was probably the stress of the event, but she was annoying Taylor tonight.

Taylor got her presentation connected to the smart board and then hung two sample outfits on stands that she had brought with her.

"What next? Music."

Taylor linked her phone to the speaker in the function room and chose her Regency playlist. It was a mixture of orchestral music from the time and soundtracks from her favourite films and TV shows set in the period. Things were starting to gel, now that the music was playing.

She got her mirror out of her bag to check her appearance. Taylor touched up her make-up and jumped when she saw Bailey at her side. Bailey put her iPad on the table next to Taylor's MacBook, ready for her introductory talk.

"Bailey? I didn't mean—"

"Ms. Sparks!"

Taylor turned around and smiled. It was Dani, their first Romantic. He was holding a glass of champagne and smiling broadly.

"Dani." Taylor went to him, and they kissed each other's cheeks. "So nice to meet in person at last."

Taylor had Zoomed each Romantic, and Dani was her favourite. He was flamboyant and already had a Regency-styled head of curly black hair and a thin moustache. His eyes literally sparkled tonight as he wore glittery purple and silver eyeshadow.

"Wonderful to meet you," Dani said. "I know we are going to be the best of friends. I thought I'd get here early and see you. I've been looking forward to meeting you."

"You too, I'm relying on you to keep our group morale high."

"I'll do that, honey, and take any shy pies under my wing," Dani said.

"Thank you. Oh, let me introduce you to our historian. Dani, this is Dr. Bailey," Taylor said.

Bailey and Dani shook hands. "Pleased to meet you."

Dani was looking at Bailey as if he was trying to place her. "Have I seen you in something?"

Taylor cut Bailey off and responded for her. "Oh yes, Bailey's been in lots of history documentaries. BBC, Netflix, lots of others. She's a very eminent historian."

"That's quite an introduction," Dani said.

"Ms. Sparks flatters me, I assure you."

"I'm sure she hasn't. I've definitely seen you on TV." Dani turned to the side and saw Zee walking towards them.

"Now I'm sure I know *that* face. Zee Osman." Then he put on a dramatic voice and said Zee's catchphrase, "*The history, the scandal, the sex...*"

"Hey, I have a fan already," Zee said.

Taylor heard Bailey sigh and walk away. Not only had Taylor upset her, but Zee appeared to be annoying her greatly.

"Bailey—" Taylor was going to go to her but she spotted more Romantics arriving, and she had to go and greet them.

❖

Taylor asked everyone to take their seats so that the evening could begin. It was an excellent, varied bunch, some quieter than others, but true to his word, Dani circulated through some of the quieter group members and brought them into the conversations.

The second most enthusiastic Romantic was Maisie, a gorgeous and elegant woman in her late thirties. Sitting next to Dani was Avery O'Connor, who identified as non-binary. Avery had been extremely quiet when they came in and tried to keep to the back. But Dani spotted Avery and made sure they sat next to him. Now Avery was smiling and not looking worried.

I should have Dani on staff.

One Romantic who didn't need to be taken under Dani's wing was Vida Clifford, a woman in her early fifties with short stylish silver hair, who worked in the fashion industry. It would be important to impress her, as she would have some really good contacts.

Taylor couldn't wait to get to know the rest.

"Good evening, everyone. I'm so happy that all of you made it. This is just a little get-together for us to get to know each other. I'm Taylor Sparks, and this is our historian, Dr. Jaq Bailey."

She then pointed to Zee, who was moving around the room taking pictures. "That is Zee Osman. She is writing a feature on our group, as I emailed you. Just ignore that she is here."

Taylor clicked her mouse to start her PowerPoint presentation.

"Firstly—welcome to the Regency Romance Club," Taylor said excitedly.

Everyone clapped and cheered. It gave Taylor such a buzz to share her own love of this period with others.

"You are all now exclusive members, an elite group of Romantics that have the joy of being able to go back in time. A tourist of an age that fascinated and inspired books, poems, and music. But before we can talk about our time travel, some rules have to be made."

Dani booed theatrically and the others laughed.

"Sorry, Dani, everyone needs rules sometimes."

Taylor cast a glance at Bailey, and she was smiling, but then when Bailey became aware she'd noticed, the smile fell.

Taylor clicked the next slide. "The first rule about Regency Romance Club is…?"

She waited while they all replied in unison, "Don't talk about Regency Romance Club!"

Taylor laughed. "Only kidding. Our first rule above all is be courteous to others in the group, especially at the balls, and respect their pronouns and genders. At the ball please accept any offer of a dance, not only to be polite but because this was a rule back in the Regency period. I know that after meeting you all today, you will all play nice together."

Next was possibly the hardest rule. "Now, one of the things that makes the Regency so alluring to us is that—if you were a gentleman or a lady—relationships were slow-paced, with people getting to know each other before *physically* getting to know each other, if you know what I mean." Taylor winked.

"To that end the next rule is super important. If you meet someone you like in the club, by all means meet up for coffee, a film, a drink between balls, but I ask that there be no physical intimacy."

Again Dani and his new friend Maisie booed.

"I know if you start to have feelings for someone, that will be difficult, but it's part of the experience, and it will intensify your feelings. During the Regency, you wouldn't be together without chaperones, and since I and my staff can't be with you all between balls, I have to ask you to pledge to keep—"

"Our hands off each other?" Maisie said.

"Yeah. Exactly. The point of the club is to build a lasting relationship, and this will strengthen any feelings you will have. Do we pledge? All say *aye*."

"Aye!"

"Thank you. Now for some practicalities. I brought two costumes with me just to give you an idea of the styles on offer. When we meet for our first dance lessons, our costume people will measure you up and then have fittings at dance class when they are near ready. I don't want you to feel constrained in any way by the gender binary. Here we are all queer, and however you wish to present yourself is totally up to you. The costume people will have no problem making something that suits who you feel you truly are. There are no gender or sexuality norms here. This is a safe queer space for you all to enjoy together."

The group broke into cheers and applause, and Taylor launched into the evening's main event.

"Now, finally, I'd like to introduce you to our historian, Dr. Jaq Bailey. You will have seen Jaq on many documentaries and many will know her from her books."

Taylor looked around at Bailey and caught her eye. "We are truly lucky to have her join us for our club weekends. Put your hands together for Jaq Bailey."

Everyone clapped as Bailey stood. Bailey walked past Taylor to get to the table, and as they passed, their hands brushed. Taylor had an intake of breath as a jolt shot up her arm into her chest.

Taylor sat down and tried to calm her breathing.

Bailey began. "Good evening, everyone. My name is Bailey, and I'll be here to help transport you back in time to the Regency period."

She went with it.

Taylor was worried Bailey's approach to their historical experience would be stark, realistic, but so far she had gone with Taylor's time travel analogy.

"The Regency period is one of the most fascinating times in British history. It takes its name from George, Prince of Wales, later to be King George IV. He was created regent when his father, George III, was deemed—unkindly—mad King George. Officially, *Regency* covers the period 1810–1820, from when Prince George was officially named regent for his father, until his father's death. But the era is more widely accepted to range from 1795 to 1837, and that is what makes it so interesting. Industry, architecture, and politics changed radically throughout the period, and that is something we'll discover through our time together."

Taylor hadn't taken her eyes off Bailey. She was so passionate when she spoke. Her eyes sparkled, and her rich honeyed voice drew you in.

She felt a nudge and turned to see Zee had sat beside her. "Boring as hell, isn't she?"

"No." Taylor gave her a pointed look. "I like listening to her."

"But there's no passion, no energy in her talk. It's no wonder I'm on the TV more," Zee said.

"She just has a different style from you." Taylor was surprised Zee couldn't see passion in Bailey's talk because she could, clearly.

"You should have asked me. I would have done it for you."

Taylor just smiled. Zee didn't know that Bailey had been her first choice. She felt Zee's breath in her ear.

"You could have had *The history, the sex, the scandal…*"

Taylor laughed nervously, and at that point Bailey just happened to look around and catch her.

No! Bailey was going to think they were laughing at her.

Bailey continued with her speech.

"All of you have come to this period through the books and films that show you the romantic side of the Regency, the life of the upper class, the landed gentry, but to truly go back in time, you have to understand where that wealth came from and appreciate the lives of the middling sort, and the poor. In the meantime, I hope you will enjoy your dance lessons and costume fittings. Till we meet again in Fairydean, goodbye."

Taylor was first to her feet encouraging everyone to clap. "Thank you, Dr. Bailey. We look forward to hearing more at Fairydean."

Once all of the Romantics left, Bailey got her bag and equipment packed quickly. She wanted to leave as quickly as possible. She'd been a fool to agree to this. Bailey had thought she was doing a good deed for a young person making their way in business. She was hardly taking much of a fee either, as a favour to Margo.

She had gotten to know Taylor and they had a shared goal, but when she turned around and saw Taylor and Zee laughing at her, Bailey knew she had made the wrong decision.

Bailey got her bag and walked over to Taylor, who was just waving the last guest away.

"Taylor, I'm heading off now. I presume you won't need me to help with the bags since you have Zee."

"We're going for a drink. Would you like to come too?" Taylor said.

"Eh, no, thank you. Enjoy your drink."

Bailey walked off, but she heard Taylor saying, "When you saw us laughing…"

But Bailey didn't turn back. She wasn't interested. Now if she could only get out of this pledge to help. Margo would be mad, but not forever. She would head home to her office, her safe place, which she shouldn't have ever left.

❖

Taylor was listening. She had mainly been listening since they'd arrived at the pub. Zee did like to talk about herself. The few times she had tried to add to the conversation, Zee had quickly taken over again. They had covered most of Zee's career from college days to the present, as well as future projects.

Taylor took a sip of her drink while she leaned on her hand. They were sitting in a booth near the back of the pub. While Zee talked, Taylor had been mulling over the differences between Bailey and Zee and her reactions to them.

It was a small thing, but when they arrived at the pub and Zee walked through the door first, Taylor expected her to hold the door, only to have it fly back into her face.

It wasn't out of malice—it was simply Zee was too caught up in her own head. Bailey was nothing if not present when they were together and would never have let that happen, and Bailey would have, no doubt, opened the door and let Taylor go first.

In fact, Bailey anticipated Taylor's needs before she realized them herself—like taking her bags on the train and opening car doors before Taylor thought about it.

Politeness wasn't everything, but it wasn't something Bailey put on. It seemed to be innate to who Bailey was.

Zee moved closer to her as she had done since they got here. Their thighs were now touching. "So, I was in full armour as Richard III, and the stunt guy, who's the expert, comes at me with a sword. I was meant to take the hit and fall as Richard III did. But something just came over me—and this wasn't rehearsed, by the way—and I dodged his blow and swung my sword, and the stunt guy was face down in the mud. They said I was a natural."

"Wow, sounds like it." Taylor humoured her, then moved a few inches over just to create some space. Zee had been flirting since they got here, and Zee was the really good-looking, but when Taylor sat next to Zee, there was nothing, no electricity.

Bailey, on the other hand, didn't even flirt, and the electricity was sparking around them. There was something about Bailey, as if she had everything under control without even trying and if she wanted, she could have Taylor under control too.

Here she was with a woman most lesbians would fawn over, and she was daydreaming about Bailey.

Taylor looked at her watch. "I better think about heading off, Zee. I need to take my mum's car back to her."

"No problem." Zee winked. "We have lots more time to get to know each other over the next few months."

"Sure will."

If only she could get to know Bailey better.

CHAPTER TWELVE

Four days later Taylor had still heard nothing from Bailey. Bailey obviously had thought the worst when she'd seen Taylor laughing during her talk. If only she'd let Taylor explain that she'd been laughing from embarrassment.

Taylor was working at the kitchen table while Gracie had her laptop on the coffee table. Taylor checked her email again, and still nothing. She had tested the water over the last couple of days by sending a few business emails to Bailey, but she hadn't had a response.

"Still nothing?" Gracie asked.

Taylor sighed. "No, nothing."

"Why don't you text her?"

Taylor wrung her hands. "And if she doesn't text back? It'll seem like I'm being pushy. No, I better just leave it."

"Okay, but I can see you turning it over and over in your head. You like her, don't you?"

"Yes, I do. Bailey's kinder than she wants to be, but bloody annoying at the same time. I don't like the idea of her thinking badly of me."

"Then instead of texting, why don't you go and see her?"

"I couldn't just appear out of the blue. Could I?"

Gracie nodded. "Yeah, go surprise her."

Taylor got up and started to pace nervously. "I don't think I could go there with no pretext."

"Invent a pretext then. There must be something to do with the business."

Taylor snapped her fingers. "A welcome pack. I could take her one of the welcome packs, so she has a full itinerary of the weekend."

"Perfect," Gracie said, "take her that and just explain. She'll understand."

Half an hour later she got off the bus in Chelsea. Taylor held out her phone in front of her to follow directions on the map. It said a five minute walk, but with Taylor's pace she should be there more quickly.

As she walked down the street she gazed at the beautiful old houses. She hadn't known professors got paid so well.

True, Bailey was an author too, but she didn't know how well history books sold. But if she was with Margo's publishing company, then they must sell well.

The map showed Bailey's was the next house along. She stopped outside and admired the old Georgian sandstone town house. Somehow Taylor hadn't pictured her in a family home like this—she'd imagined a city centre flat or something similar.

Taylor started to feel nervous at seeing Bailey again, and she knew Bailey would see right through her pretence. Maybe she should just leave.

That idea was starting to sound good when Bailey came to the bay window at the front of the house. Bailey was on her mobile phone but saw Taylor straight away. Taylor smiled and waved but inside felt so embarrassed.

What a stupid idea.

Too late now. She walked up the steps, and just as she was about to press the doorbell, Bailey opened the door.

"Taylor? What are you doing here?"

"There was something I was meaning to give you, and since I was in the area, I thought I might just drop by," Taylor fibbed. "You don't mind, do you?"

"No, no, come in."

As Taylor stepped into the entrance hall, she saw how beautiful the house was, with high ceilings and elaborate plasterwork. The staircase appeared to go on and on, and she couldn't quite see to the top.

"You have a beautiful house, Bailey."

Bailey took her coat and hung it on the coat stand by the door. "It was my parents' house, but they are long dead now."

"Oh, I'm sorry."

"Come through to my office," Bailey said.

Taylor followed Bailey. It wasn't a small office space. It had a large dark wooden desk facing the bay window at the other side of the room. There was a gorgeous fireplace, which was lit, and two leather backed chairs in front of it.

"Would you like tea or a coffee?" Bailey asked.

Taylor would have preferred the coffee, but she knew Bailey liked tea, so she went with that.

"Tea would be lovely, thanks."

"I'll just be back shortly. Take a seat."

Taylor didn't sit when Bailey left. She was nervous and wanted to keep on her feet. She walked over to the bay window and watched as the world went by. It was a very quiet street with a suburban feel, full of the families of bankers, private doctors, and the like.

She turned around and looked at the big, imposing desk. Inside the room the only sounds were of a ticking clock and the crackle of the fire. It reminded her of being called to the headmistress's office when she got into a fight while trying to protect a younger girl from bullying.

Ms. Harlow…the first woman she'd had a crush on and the first to make her heart flutter. Ms. Harlow wasn't your usual headteacher. She wore either a black or navy-blue suit and had an aura of confidence and authority that made Taylor weak at the knees.

Bailey was much sexier than Ms. Harlow.

Taylor sighed. Maybe she had a thing for older women? Bailey certainly didn't share the same opinion of her. Most of the time Taylor felt like she was annoying Bailey.

She heard the rattle of a tea tray, and her nerves returned.

Bailey came through the door with the tea and said, "Here we are. Take a seat." Bailey put the tray on the table next to the fire. Taylor's arrival had been a surprise, but maybe better in the long run. She had been going over how she felt and how to get out of this role as historian to Taylor's company.

She had been angry about catching Taylor and Zee laughing, but then the more she thought about it, the more she realized Taylor probably didn't mean any harm.

It was that Taylor and Bailey didn't match. Taylor needed a younger, more vibrant historian for her company, like Zee except for more credentials. Bailey contemplated emailing her resignation, but that would be cold. Taylor deserved a face to face meeting with her.

She'd put it off for a few days, and then Taylor arrived, so she had to face it, but seeing her again pulled at her heartstrings and made her feel guilty.

"I don't think I've had tea from a proper teapot," Taylor said, "and not in china cups and saucers, that is for sure. We went for big mugs in our house."

"I'm particular about my tea. I suppose it was my mother and father's habit that I picked up."

Bailey lifted the teapot lid and stirred the pot. "I use loose leaves, tea strainer, everything as it should be."

"Like in *Downton Abbey*?"

Bailey smiled. "I suppose, but I didn't really watch it."

"But you're a historian. You would love it."

"I like books and serious documentaries. You like more than just the Regency, then?"

"Yes, although the Regency's my favourite. I love any period drama."

Bailey looked at her watch. "Tea won't be long now."

"Is it not ready yet?" Taylor appeared perplexed since everything appeared ready.

"One more minute. It takes three minutes to brew the tea leaves properly."

"Wouldn't a teabag be quicker?" Taylor asked.

Bailey leaned forward and said softly, "Not everything in life is better done faster. Some things are worth taking your time over."

Taylor's lips parted and her cheeks went pink. Bailey wondered if her turn of phrase had made Taylor think of something far more pleasurable than making tea.

Taylor looked beautiful with the slight pink in her cheeks. Bailey thought about how much she would like to see a look of pleasure, a look of need and want as she took her time touching and kissing her way over Taylor's body.

Bailey quickly chastised herself for her thoughts. She cleared her throat. "The tea is ready now."

"Great, can I steal one of these tasty looking biscuits?"

"Of course."

This was happening too often, the need that Taylor had reawakened in her. It had been a long time since she had enjoyed a sexual relationship or even just an encounter.

Being with Ellis had been all about Ellis, loving a friend, not passion and hunger. But Taylor had switched something on inside her.

But Taylor was so much younger than her. Still, as long as it stayed in her head, it wouldn't be a problem.

"Should I have milk?" Taylor asked.

"Milk? Only if you want it. I don't take milk."

Taylor reached for her cup. "To tell the truth, I don't drink tea, so I'll go with what you do." Taylor took a sip. "Hmm, I think I'll add some sugar."

After two spoonfuls of sugar, Taylor took another sip and hummed. "That's nice now."

Bailey shook her head and smiled. "You have quite the sweet tooth, don't you? Travelling sweets and sugary tea. Your dentist mustn't be happy with you."

"I take very good care of my teeth, thank you. I do love anything sweet. My fav chocolates are Maltesers. Give me them over big expensive boxes of chocolates any day."

Bailey laughed. The little balls of honeycomb covered in chocolate were an everyday children's sweet. Adorable. "You would, wouldn't you?"

"Yeah, I told you I'm a cheap date." Taylor grinned mischievously.

Bailey pointed her finger at Taylor. "We've talked about that. You should never be treated cheaply."

"I wish you'd been around to tell my previous girlfriends that, Professor."

"I would have set them right and instructed them on how to treat such a beautiful girl…woman, sorry."

The atmosphere in the room changed, and Taylor gazed at her with what looked like longing. But then she was so out of practice with reading these signals, she must be wrong. Why would a beautiful young woman look longingly at a middle-aged person like her?

Then it struck her. There was clearly no danger of her attraction going anywhere, so why not enjoy a little flirting if it happened? *Be kind to yourself.*

Bailey decided to change the subject.

"What did you want to talk to me about today?"

Taylor stood up and went behind the armchair she'd been sitting in. She rapped a beat with her fingers as she held on to the back.

"Sorry, I can't sit for that long. I get jumpy. Well, anyway, to come to the point—I wanted to apologize for the other night and explain it wasn't what it looked like. When you turned around and I was laughing with—"

Bailey stopped. "It's okay. I know my presentation style isn't that exciting."

"No, I love your presenting style, your voice. I've been listening to your books on audiobook and just love them."

Bailey was taken by surprise. "You do?"

Taylor nodded then started to pace. "It was Zee, you see. She whispered that catchphrase of hers in my ear, and I laughed out of nervousness. The whole audience of my Romantics were watching, and it was inappropriate. I wasn't laughing at you."

Bailey was delighted to find that out that she wasn't just a boring old professor to her. "Thank you for telling me. That's no doubt what Zee thinks."

"She's wrong."

Bailey didn't know how to respond to that so simply said, "Thank you."

"You are welcome."

"How was your drink after the get-together?" Bailey asked.

She had no right to ask, but Bailey wanted to know if they had grown closer romantically.

Taylor sat back down and drank some more tea. "She's fun and funny. She talked a lot, mostly about herself."

Bailey smiled. There didn't seem to be anything as yet. But there was still something bothering Bailey about that night, and she had to bring it up.

"What about me frightening you?" Bailey asked.

Taylor looked nonplussed. "What?"

"Earlier that evening you were saying I must've frightened my students, and that I frightened you sometimes."

"Oh, that? I didn't mean *frighten* in a bad way." Taylor gave her a shy smile.

Taylor was flirting with her. She was out of practice, but that shy smile said so much.

Bailey smiled back. "That's okay then." She heard Taylor's foot tapping on the floor. Bailey saw Taylor's right leg jumping while Taylor wrapped her fingers on the arm of the chair.

"Are you okay?"

"Just a bit stressed," Taylor confessed. "There's so much work to do in the run up to the first ball. My ADHD makes my mind go a million miles an hour, and it gets overwhelming at times."

"I know it would be useless of me to say calm down when you have ADHD, but have you tried meditation?"

Taylor nodded. "I can't sit still long enough."

"Do you want to try something that might help?"

❖

Taylor had no idea what was about to happen when Bailey asked her to stand up, but she went with it.

"Stand as relaxed as you can, and I'll be right behind you."

Taylor could feel Bailey behind her. There was a pull, an energy between them that Taylor couldn't ignore but had to control.

"I had a…" Bailey hesitated. "A friend, who was very much into meditation to control anxiety and stress, but she meditated standing up because she tended to nod off sitting down. Perhaps standing meditation would be easier than trying to sit still?"

"Maybe."

This was an odd turn of events. Taylor never expected this on her visit today.

"For the moment, try to breathe normally. Do you mind if I put my hands on your shoulders?"

"No, you can put them wherever you like." *Fool! Sounds desperate.*

Taylor wore a little silver camisole vest top, leaving most of her shoulders bare, so when Bailey's hands touched her shoulders, she jumped, feeling every inch of her strong hands.

"Okay?" Bailey asked.

"Yep," Taylor squeaked.

The feel of Bailey's hands on her skin made Taylor shiver.

"Are you all right?" Bailey asked.

Ah, she *had* noticed. "Fine, fine."

Bailey squeezed her shoulders in a simple massage. "This is the way I helped my friend. My hands are your anchor. Close your eyes and only listen to the sounds in the room."

Bailey took a step closer, so that her lips were close behind Taylor's ear. "Listen to the sound of the clock, the crackle of the firewood, the distant sounds of traffic outside." Taylor felt Bailey's lips almost touching her ear, and her hot breath caressing her. "Take a deep breath."

She gulped in a huge lungful of air, and Bailey said, "Hold for five."

Taylor lasted for about two seconds. Far from slowing her breath, Bailey's presence behind her and words at her ear were making her breath shorter.

As she felt Bailey's fingers loosen from her shoulders and trail softly over her exposed skin, goosebumps broke out all over her body, and a deep heavy beat started to pound inside her.

Taylor wasn't used to this kind of intensity. She had to look at Bailey. Taylor turned around quickly and found Bailey gazing at her, with Bailey's hands still loosely gripping her bare shoulders.

Neither said a word but Taylor could see fire in her eyes, a more intense version of the mutual gaze they'd got lost in on the train to Fairydean. Bailey's right hand left Taylor's shoulder and slid up her neck.

Taylor's lips parted, and she moved closer. Her heart was pounding so hard she thought it might burst. Bailey's hand moved from her neck to cup Taylor's cheek, and Taylor gasped when Bailey ran her thumb over her bottom lip.

Bailey's eyes were fixed on her bottom lip as she inched closer. It was really going to happen, Bailey was going to kiss her—

Taylor's phone rang and they jumped apart when Bailey shifted quickly over to the fireplace like a frightened rabbit, which Taylor wasn't pleased about. Why was she so disturbed about kissing her?

Taylor got her phone out of her bag and said, annoyed, "Hello?"

"Eddie's been hit by a car," her mum said, and her stomach fell to her toes. "We're on our way to St. Thomas's Hospital."

Taylor struggled to form words. "I…I'll see you there."

Bailey must have heard the panic in her voice and was over to her in seconds. "What's wrong?"

"I have to go to the hospital. My brother Eddie's been in a car accident."

Taylor's hands shook as she attempted and failed to find the taxi company she used in her address book. Then she felt Bailey's hand cover hers. "I'll take care of it, and you. Which hospital?"

"St. Thomas's."

Bailey took out her phone and ordered the taxi quickly. "Let's get our jackets and wait at the front door. Don't worry. I'll take you."

"You will? You don't have to," Taylor said.

"Just think about your brother and leave everything else to me."

Taylor felt such reassurance. She leaned into Bailey's chest, and Bailey wrapped her arms around her. "Everything will be all right," Bailey said.

But would it be?

❖

In the taxi Taylor had clasped Bailey's hand tightly and never let go. Bailey didn't mind—she wanted to be as comforting as she could be. Taylor was extremely close to her family, and this was hitting her hard.

How much her life had changed. From hiding in the safety of her library to holding hands with a young woman and escorting her to the hospital.

Hospital. A place Bailey had vowed never to enter again. The miserable, heartbreaking hours she'd spent in hospital waiting for news about Ellis were writ large in Bailey's mind, and she'd sworn she would never be back.

Yet here she was. It was simple politeness, Bailey told herself. Yet when she saw the normally confident, lively Taylor overcome with shock and fear for her brother, all she wanted to do was protect her, take care of her.

"Who's looking after Jaden?" Taylor suddenly said.

"Your nephew?"

Taylor nodded.

"I'm sure as soon as your brother-in-law heard there was an accident, he would have found a family member or friend to look after him."

"It's just that Max, my brother-in-law, doesn't have family, or family that wants to know him. He just has us."

"We'll get to the hospital shortly, and you'll find out."

Taylor covered her face with her free hand. "Ed might be my brother, but he's also my best friend. We're the babies of the family. There's five years between Tommy, Luke, Eddie, and me. We've always been so close. I don't know how I could go on—"

Bailey turned quickly and cupped her cheek. "Don't think like that. It could be minor injuries. You don't know the extent of the crash yet."

Taylor nodded. "Thanks for being here. I don't know what I would have done if I'd have been on my own."

Bailey realized she still had her hand on Taylor's cheek and pulled it back quickly. "We're just about there."

The taxi driver stopped outside the accident and emergency, and Bailey quickly paid the driver before helping Taylor out.

Taylor stopped still at the entrance. "I'm frightened at what I might find out."

Bailey was terrified of going inside a hospital, but she put her feelings aside to be strong for Taylor. She put her hand at the small of Taylor's back. "I'm here. You're not alone."

Taylor gazed at her for a moment and then took her hand.

They walked into the A&E reception, and Taylor called out, "Mum."

A tall woman who had been pacing next to the seats turned around, along with who she guessed were Taylor's big brothers, and they were big. The Sparks did breed big boys in the family, compared to Taylor's petite frame.

Taylor ran to her mum's open arms.

Bailey held back but could hear her mum saying, "We don't know anything yet."

As Taylor's mum gave her a hug, she looked directly at Bailey and eyed her suspiciously. An elegant woman joined them, who Bailey assumed was her other mum. Next to her brothers was a younger woman trying to soothe a toddler in her arms.

Taylor had mentioned one of her brothers was married to a woman. This must be her, and the toddler the little boy Taylor was so worried about.

Taylor now slipped into her other mother's arms, while Taylor's mum who'd eyed her suspiciously started to walk towards her.

This felt awkward.

"I'm Kel. You seem familiar."

Bailey offered her hand. "Jaq Bailey. I'm working with your daughter on her new project."

"Yes, I think my wife and I have seen you on TV once or twice. Taylor says you brought her here when I called. Were you having a meeting or…"

Aha. Kel was trying to find out why her daughter had turned up at the hospital, holding hands with this older woman. She was clearly very protective of her family and youngest daughter.

"Taylor came to see me about the project, and when you called she was quite shaken. I thought I should bring her myself."

"Thank you."

Kel continued to stare directly into her eyes. Maybe Bailey wasn't reading the situation rightly—there seemed to be a defensiveness in Kel's demeanour, but there was no reason for it. No one knew the deep thoughts she had been having.

"Taylor has spoken a lot about you, Dr. Bailey."

It made Bailey's heart warm to think that she was in Taylor's thoughts.

"I can't speak more highly of your daughter. Can I ask how your son is doing?"

"We know he's stable, but that's all," Kel replied.

Bailey wanted to make a hasty retreat. The hospital fears and this awkwardness were becoming too much.

This wasn't her place. "I hope he recovers well. I'd better leave you to your family."

"Thank you."

With that, Bailey ran from that place, both physically and mentally.

❖

Taylor walked outside to call her aunt and Gracie, but also to get some fresh air. It was so stuffy and warm inside the hospital, and she would scream if she had to sit or pace any longer.

She took a lungful of the cold, calming night air. Taylor took out her phone and looked at all the messages her aunt and Gracie had sent, desperately wanting to know how Eddie was.

Taylor was just about to press her aunt's number when she looked up and saw Bailey sitting on a bench outside.

"Bailey? I didn't think you'd still be here. Why did you leave without saying goodbye?"

She sat down beside her.

"You were with your family, and I didn't want to intrude. Truth is, I'm not the biggest fan of hospitals. How is your brother?"

"It's good news. He's not in danger. He broke his leg and a couple of ribs, and has a few cuts and bruises. Compared to what it could have been…"

All the fear overcame Taylor. Tears poured from her eyes, and she grasped for Bailey, putting her hands around her neck, and burrowing her head in her chest.

Bailey stiffened. She wasn't used to close contact with people, not since Ellis, and certainly not younger women. Bailey's heart urged her to respond to Taylor's distress, and after a few seconds she placed her arms around her.

"It's okay. He's safe."

Bailey relaxed into the closeness and held Taylor tightly. Bailey inhaled Taylor's scent and closed her eyes. She ran one of her hands up and down her back, trying to soothe Taylor and to protect her from any pain or obstacle that came her way.

She felt Taylor melt into her, and Taylor's lips grazed her neck. Bailey had forgotten that they were outside the hospital and felt the heavy grief that hung around her heart and mind slowly drift, until all that she could feel was Taylor.

With one hand on Taylor's lower back, Bailey's other found its way upward. Bailey's fingertips gently traced Taylor's neck. Her heart pounded with every touch. Taylor's lips touched her neck, and fire erupted and soon would consume her whole body, but a voice interrupted them, and Bailey was brought crashing down to earth.

"Taylor."

They both recognized the voice and jumped apart. It was Kel.

"You can go in and see your brother now."

Kel held her hand out to Taylor but kept her eyes fixed on Bailey. Bailey jumped up from the bench and said, "Taylor was upset."

"I see that. Let's go, sweetheart, Ed is waiting for you," Kel said.

Taylor wiped her eyes quickly. "Okay. Thanks for being there for me, Bailey."

"Yes, thanks, Dr. Bailey. I'll take it from here."

Bailey nodded. She could see Taylor's eyes were awash with emotion. Was it just the situation with her brother, or was it more?

Every time she was with Taylor, Bailey had this gnawing feeling that she wanted Taylor, and she suspected that Taylor's mum saw it too.

She got up and said, "Give your brother my best wishes. I hope he feels better soon. Goodbye."

❖

"You know you're a fool," Gianna said.

"It has been said," Eddie replied.

Max and Eddie's two mums had been in, and now it was Taylor's and Gianna's turns. The two women, as his mums before them, were giving him hell for the cause of the accident.

Anna had been with Thomas so long she was like the older sister they'd all never had, and that gave her the right to give it to Eddie.

"You were so busy engaged with stupid road rage that you walked out onto a junction?"

"The guy was going to clip me he was so close. He said cyclists were a fucking menace on the roads."

"He wasn't wrong in your case, was he?" Taylor said. "You walked out onto upcoming traffic and got hit. You could have been killed."

"I do know all this. Mums have already given this lecture, and the broken leg and cracked ribs have given me a clue."

Anna took his hand. "Seriously, Ed. Think about the effect it would have had on our whole family if you had been killed, and the driver who hit you would have had to live with your death all their life."

Eddie put his head down. "I know. I'm sorry. I apologised to the driver too."

"Just let this be a big lesson, Ed," Anna said. "You've got Jaden now. He needs you."

"Lesson learned. I'm getting out soon once they give me the final once over."

"How's the pain?" Taylor asked.

"The drugs take the edge off. Oh shit!" Eddie suddenly said.

"What is it?" Taylor grasped his free hand.

"Your host for the ball. I can't be your host. I'm not going to be on my feet and dancing for a while."

Taylor scrunched up her face. "Oh yeah. I'll work something out."

"Ask Sexy Prof to be your host."

Taylor shook her head. "She won't do it."

"You've persuaded her this far," Eddie said.

Maybe she could try?

"She is sexy too, Tay," Anna said, "I got a good look in the waiting room."

"Yeah she is," Taylor agreed.

Taylor lay in bed that night unable to sleep. Eddie was safe but the stress of the day made her feel so tired, but her mind would not let her succumb to sleep. When she closed her eyes, she was back in Bailey's arms, her nose pressed into her neck, and then her lips. It took a lot to stop herself from planting the softest of kisses on Bailey's neck and imagined letting her tongue taste her skin.

She grabbed the pillow beside her, placed it over her face, and screamed into it. "Stop, stop thinking that."

Taylor was convinced a sophisticated older woman like Bailey wouldn't be interested in her, yet she was sure she had detected something pulling them together. On the train journey to Fairydean, in the library there, and tonight.

But there always appeared to be a great sense of pain that Bailey was carrying that held her back from engaging with people, engaging with the world, really. Zee did tell her that Bailey gave up teaching for personal reasons, but what those were, she didn't know.

On impulse she lifted her phone and texted Margo: *Margo, do you know why Bailey stopped teaching? I'm trying to get to know her better. She always seems to have this sadness about her.*

It didn't take long till Margo replied, *Hey, I do know, but I feel like it's Bailey's story to tell, if she wants to. I would hate to talk behind her back.*

Taylor felt instant regret. Margo was right of course, and Taylor had no right to ask. She immediately texted back, *You're right. I shouldn't have asked. Speak to you soon. xx*

Taylor let her phone drop onto her chest and let out a long breath. "I've got a million and one things to be worrying about, and I keep thinking of you."

She opened her audiobook app and flicked through her choices of Jane Austen bedtime listening. "*Sense and Sensibility*, I think."

It had been her favourite recently. The narrator started to read, and usually this would lull her to sleep. There was nothing nicer than dreaming of a world where happy endings happened, but she just stared at the ceiling wide awake.

On impulse she changed the audiobook to one of Bailey's, one that she narrated. She smiled as she heard Bailey say, "*Welcome to the world of Restoration Britain. This guide will tell you everything you want to know, and everything you didn't, about the Restoration. Most people's thoughts would turn to the merry monarch, royal mistresses, and the fun of the return of theatre and entertainment in this period. But there was so much more. Black Death, grinding poverty, religious intolerance, to name but a few...*"

Taylor chuckled. Zee's interpretation would be all about the debauchery and mistresses. It was funny to see how much Zee annoyed Bailey and how different they were. There were plenty of Zee's documentaries on YouTube, and yet it was Bailey's voice she wanted to listen to at night.

Bailey's voice was low, rich, and imbued with natural authority. Those three things together made her voice so sexy to Taylor. She closed her eyes and concentrated on Bailey's rich tones, and in her mind's eye found herself in Bailey's study.

She was alone and waiting, she didn't know what for, and pacing restlessly as she usually did. She turned around, and Bailey was suddenly there, half sitting, half standing, with her arms crossed, on the side of her desk.

"Stop pacing."

Taylor stopped immediately. The penetrating steady gaze that Bailey gave her made her forget to breathe.

This fantasy had sneaked up on her and was wrong…wasn't it? Bailey was her friend. Taylor opened her eyes and took a few raspy breaths.

Wrong? Or no harm in it?

She had her answer too quickly.

"Alexa? Turn off light."

The room went dark, and she closed her eyes. Thankfully Taylor got back to the fantasy with no problem.

Bailey sat silently for too long, then finally said, "Come here."

Taylor stood a few paces away, her heart pounding.

"Closer."

A deep heaving pounding was thrumming inside Taylor. She traced her fingers over the outside of the little vest top she had worn to bed. She felt her nipples harden under her touch.

Taylor was now standing between Bailey's legs. Bailey uncrossed her arms and reached out towards her face but never touched her. "You never stop, Ms. Sparks, never slow down and live in the moment."

Taylor leaned in to Bailey's hand, but she took it away. Instead, Bailey stood and moved Taylor's hair from her ear.

"I've seen the way you look at me, Ms. Sparks. Like you want me to touch you."

Bailey then leaned in to her ear and whispered, "Do you want me to touch you?"

Taylor's hand slipped under the hem of her top and cupped her breast gently. She desperately wanted to touch her sex, but not too quickly. She was enjoying this fantasy too much. She couldn't remember anyone ever turning her on like this.

"I said, do you want me to touch you?" Bailey's lips so very nearly grazed her ear.
"Yes, no, yes, I mean—"
Bailey moved to her cheek and caressed her without even touching.
"You don't sound very sure. Do you think this is wrong? Hmm?"
Taylor gulped. She was tongue-tied, unable to form any sort of response.
Bailey moved her lips so achingly close to hers but never touched.
"You shouldn't really be coming on to me, Ms. Sparks. You're twenty-six and I'm forty-five. Do you think that's wrong? What would your parents think?"
"I..." Again, Taylor couldn't speak.
Bailey threaded her fingers through Taylor's hair on both sides of her face and closed her eyes momentarily, inhaling Taylor's scent.
When she opened her eyes, Bailey said, "Do you want it to be wrong?"
Taylor could answer that one straight away. "Yes."
Bailey smiled and then ever so slightly touched her lips to hers.
"Then you are a bad girl, Ms. Sparks."

Taylor was so turned on that she couldn't stop her hand from sneaking under the waistband of her sleep shorts.

Bailey barely touched Taylor's lips.
She breathed. "Please?"
Instead of giving Taylor exactly what she wanted, Bailey licked her way around her lips and then—

Taylor jumped out of her skin when her phone went nuts, chanting *This is Ed, this is Ed, this is Ed.*

She grabbed her phone and fell out of the bed onto the floor and hit her cheek on her bedside cabinet.

"You better have broken the other leg, Ed," Taylor shouted.

Eddie had recorded the annoying custom text tone for whenever he sent a message.

Taylor quickly checked her phone and saw that he had sent her a meme he found hilarious.

"I'm going to kill you," Taylor said.
Her perfect fantasy was gone.

❖

Bailey looked at the time—two o'clock in the morning. She put down the book she was holding and pinched the bridge of her nose. Bailey had gone to bed a few hours ago but was unable to sleep.

She got out her laptop and a few of her research books and started working in bed. Her laptop was balanced on her knee and books surrounded her, all in an effort to distract her.

Distract her from the very reason she couldn't sleep—Taylor.

Since Bailey had got home from the hospital, all she could think about was Taylor. Taylor in her arms, Taylor's breath close to her neck, the way Bailey wanted to hold Taylor and never let any harm come to her.

The feel of Taylor was emblazoned on her mind, and when she closed her eyes to sleep, Taylor was there in her arms, and the scent of Taylor surrounded her.

Bailey tried to immerse herself in work, but it did no good. Flirting was fine. It was a bit of fun, but going any further was asking for trouble, and tonight she'd felt her interest reciprocated by Taylor. God knew what she saw in her, but it was there.

The pain of losing her best friend in the world, the woman she should have been in love with, had destroyed her, and loving a younger woman would just bring more pain.

But then Taylor came into her life and woke her from her slumber.

Bailey rubbed her forehead. "It's just attraction."

An overwhelming attraction to the point that she couldn't think of anything. Every time they met, it was getting stronger.

She's twenty-six.

Although Taylor was an adult, the age gap was way too big. When Bailey had taught at Cambridge, she had plenty of younger students who propositioned her, but even though she had many short-term sexual relationships, Bailey had a strict rule never to become involved with a student.

Taylor reminded her of them, but perhaps more innocent than some of the students that had come on to her. Bailey was a forty-five-year-old with a broken soul who wanted to hide from life till it trudged towards its end—Taylor was too bright, too optimistic about life for her. Taylor believed in happy ever afters and loving someone for the rest of your life.

And it wasn't just her own thoughts making her feel bad, making her sure that these feelings were wrong. Taylor's mum had made it abundantly clear the two times she had seen her today, especially when she caught her comforting Taylor.

The look that bored into Bailey said *Whatever you're thinking about—don't, and if you do, I'll kill you.*

She would just have to try to get through these feelings with hard work and distraction and try not to spend too much time in Taylor's company.

Bailey sighed and got up to put her laptop and books away. She needed sleep. Once everything was away, she came back to bed and switched the bedside lamp off. She closed her eyes, and Taylor walked into her mind and smiled.

CHAPTER THIRTEEN

The music was pounding in Taylor's spare bedroom. She was doing an intensive workout on her spin bike. The screen in front of the handlebars showed a spin instructor taking her through a ride, as well as her stats.

"*You're halfway through this effort, push hard,*" the instructor said.

That was exactly why she wanted to do this—to push her body hard and try to quieten these feelings in her body, this sexual frustration that wasn't leaving her.

She woke up this morning with so much energy and not even her usual early morning walk could use it up.

"*Nearly there. Get ready to lighten the resistance. Five, four, three, two, one.*"

The bike became easier to pedal, and Taylor took the chance to get a drink from her water bottle and wipe down her head and her chest with her gym towel.

Her legs were going at a fast space with the bike at a lower resistance. She didn't want to stop and feel like she had ants under her skin.

"*Okay, get ready,*" the instructor said.

Just as they were about to get going again, Taylor's phone rang. There was a phone holder beside the screen, so when she saw it was her brother Eddie, she turned down the music and answered his video call.

"Hey, big brother. How are you feeling this morning?"

Eddie was sitting on his couch with his leg up on the coffee table. "Much sorer than last night, but that's to be expected. The ribs are the worst."

"Aww. I'm sorry. How is Max looking after you?" Taylor asked.

"Like an angel. He's taken Jaden out to the supermarket to pick up a few things. You're working hard."

"I've got too much energy today." Sexual energy, but she wasn't going to tell him that—she'd never hear the end of it.

"Listen," Eddie said, "I'm sorry I can't be your host for the ball. Have you thought about who you're going to ask?"

"You know who I'd like to ask, but I don't think she'll do it."

"Sexy Prof?" Eddie smiled.

Taylor nodded. "But she hardly wants to be a part of this project as it is. Zee will be taking pictures and video, and there's no one else really that can."

"Zee would do it in a second, I think," Eddie said.

"I know, but she can't. Anyway I think she would ham up the role too much. She does have a tendency to make things about her. I suppose the dance master would do it. He'd get into the part."

Eddie screwed up his face. "The guy you told me had the big bushy sideburns?"

"He's a nice gentleman," Taylor said.

"I'm sure he is, but you're supposed to be playing a part in the spirit of the thing and leaving the outside world at the door. We were going to be brother and sister. Sir Edward Sparks and Miss Sparks. Who are you two going to be to him?"

"Father and daughter? Uncle and niece?"

Again, Eddie screwed up his face. "If you get Sexy Prof to do it, you can be her wife." Eddie winked after that last comment.

"Don't be so ludicrous," Taylor said.

Her heart rate suddenly spiked higher, and not because of the pace of the bike.

"Your cheeks are red." Eddie laughed. "You do fancy her, don't you?"

Flashes of her fantasy from last night entered her mind. "Of course not."

"You do. I know my little sis."

"She's good-looking obviously. Anyone can see that. But..." Taylor pressed stop on her bike and slowly stopped pedalling. She used her towel to wipe her face and then sighed. "All right, I do, but don't tell anyone."

Eddie clapped his hands together. "I knew it, I knew it."

"Aren't big brothers supposed to be pissed if their little sister likes someone much older?"

"Why would I? Max is seven years older than me. As long as she's a good person, I'm okay with it."

"Seven years isn't as big a difference as nineteen. I know how Mum would see it. Mama I think could understand, but Mum gave me this whole talk about someone aged forty-five having different expectations than twenty-six, and I had only started working with her as a colleague."

"You can cross that bridge when you get to it. First you win Sexy Prof's heart," Eddie said.

"What? No. I only said I liked her. It doesn't mean I want to do anything about it. Besides, she wouldn't be interested. She finds most things I do annoying, and I'm sure she has people her own age to date," Taylor said.

"Don't be so defeatist."

"Look, just leave it, Ed. It's not happening. I need to get her to co-host with me, that's all."

Eddie held up his hands. "Okay, touchy. If that's what you want, invite her over, have some nice food, drinks. Schmooze her. I'm sure you can get her to do it," Eddie said.

Taylor took a drink from her bottle. "I'll try."

"I thought it would be Zee you would like, to be honest. She's got that bad boy thing going on."

"I like older women, and when I'm with Bailey, she listens to me. Zee talks about herself. I better go, Ed. I've got lots to do," Taylor said.

"Okay. Good luck, sis."

When Eddie had gone, Taylor held her hands over her face. "Why did I admit that?"

Now she had to persuade Bailey to help her.

❖

The lift door opened onto Taylor's floor, and Bailey stepped out. This was a bad idea. Why had she agreed to come here? She was supposed to be keeping her distance, but when Taylor asked her, she couldn't say no to her.

As she approached the door Bailey said, "Just keep it calm and professional and leave as soon as you can."

Gracie would be there, she was sure, since it was a work meeting. That would keep everything focused on the business of the day.

Bailey rang the doorbell and it didn't take long till Taylor opened the door. "Hi, Bailey, come in."

It was worse than Bailey thought. Not only was she hit with the intense scent of Taylor's perfume, but also Taylor was wearing a beautiful spring dress, a floral print with thin straps on her shoulders, with a low cleavage.

Bailey's eyes couldn't help but be drawn to Taylor's full, pert breasts. She was a breast woman, and Taylor's were perfect. She was already turned on by the scent of her perfume and started to imagine pressing her head and lips into that full bosom.

Bailey felt a steady beat inside her. Even before Ellis's death, she hadn't experienced this level of sexual need with any casual sexual encounters. She had supposed it was age catching up with her, but no, Taylor made age irrelevant. Taylor had rattled her sexual cage and it had come back out with a roar.

Her body might think that, but those who cared about Taylor wouldn't see it that way.

Keep control, Bailey told herself.

Taylor led her into the apartment, and Bailey was struck by more temptation as Taylor's dress was short and her legs were beautiful.

"Take a seat," Taylor said.

The coffee table was set out with all kinds of nibbles and snacks, and she was sure the lights were dimmed.

This was going to be hard.

"What can I get you? Lager, wine, Weird watermelon?" Taylor joked. "I'm sorry, I don't have whiskey."

"Wine is fine."

"Red or white?" Taylor asked.

"You don't like wine."

Taylor smiled. "I got it for you."

Shit.

"You choose. I don't mind," Bailey said.

A short time later Taylor came out with two glasses and one bottle of red wine. "I thought you'd prefer this."

Taylor sat down right beside Bailey, and her heart began to beat faster. Taylor's knee was brushing hers.

This was unbearable.

Taylor was trying to open the bottle of wine and struggling.

Bailey said, "Let me." Anything to distract her from the most beautiful woman sitting right next to her.

"Thank you," Taylor said. "I always have sparkling wine on hand for my mama and sister-in-law Gianna, and it's a nightmare. I'm terrified of the bang and the cork shooting out."

"This is much easier." Bailey pulled out the cork and poured them each a glass.

"Thanks," Taylor said. She took a sip and said, "Wow, that's intense. What will we drink to? Oh, I know." Taylor lifted her glass to Bailey and said, "To a close working relationship."

How close? Bailey asked herself.

"To working together," Bailey said. The adapted wording sounded better.

They clinked glasses and took a long drink. It was then that Bailey noticed light bruising on Taylor's cheekbone.

"What happened to your cheek?"

Taylor went red. "Oh—eh, it's embarrassing, really."

Bailey furrowed her brow, feeling anger start to simmer. She reached out and cupped Taylor's cheek. "No one hurt you, did they?"

"No, no. Okay, I'll tell you the truth. I woke up from a dream a bit disorientated and fell out of bed, hitting my cheek on the bedside cabinet."

"And you're all right?" Bailey said seriously.

"Yes—I expected you to laugh at me."

"I'd never laugh at you."

Taylor locked eyes with her, and Bailey couldn't look away.

It took Taylor to break away from their gaze. "Help yourself to some nibbles."

Bailey ate some nuts one after another, just for something to do with her free hand and so she wasn't looking at Taylor too long.

"Thanks for coming, Bailey. I wanted to talk to you about something."

Bailey froze mid-crunch. Please God, no. Was she going to talk about their attraction?

Tylor continued, "I know you're busy writing your book, but I need to talk to you about the business going forward."

Business? Thank God. Yes, let's talk business.

"Fire away."

"I...uh." Taylor rubbed her hands together nervously. Bailey was going to say no, she knew it.

"Is there something wrong with Fairydean? Has Lady Catherine—"

"No, no. Nothing like that." Taylor felt her whole body twitching with nervous energy. "Sorry, I have to get up." Now on the other side of the coffee table, Taylor started to pace. She stopped briefly and said, "Do you remember me telling you that my brother Eddie was going to be co-host with me at Fairydean?"

"Vaguely."

"Well, a Regency ball needed a host and hostess, usually husband and wife, but sometimes brother and sister or father and daughter. It was acceptable for a sister to keep house for a single brother or a daughter for a widowed father."

"Okay. I can see that, but why is this—"

Taylor went from rubbing her hands to wringing them together. "Eddie was going to be my host and now he's broken his leg. I need someone else to step in for me."

She stared silently at Bailey, hoping for the best response.

"Me, you mean?" Bailey said.

"Yes, you. I wondered if you would help me."

The look on Bailey's face wasn't positive.

"Isn't there anyone else? What about your older brothers?" Bailey asked.

"Tommy and Luke can't spare the time from their jobs."

"Zee—I'm sure she would do it."

"She'll be too busy taking footage of the ball. Why are you trying so hard to find someone else? It's not that bad, is it? You only have to greet the Romantics with me. Welcome them to Fairydean and the ball."

Taylor wasn't going to throw in that they had to dance the first dance together. Get over one hurdle at time.

Bailey sighed. "Right, fine, okay. I'll do it."

"Yes!" Taylor said with joy and did a little celebration dance.

"It wasn't that exciting, was it?" Bailey asked.

"Of course it is. I want my weekend at Fairydean to be perfect, and now it will be."

Bailey smiled for the first time. "I'm glad I made you happy then. But can you stop moving?"

"Yes. Sorry. Let's talk about our roles." Taylor sat down beside her.

"What do you mean roles?"

"The roles the Romantics and all of us are going to play. You know everyone had to chose a name or title that best reflects them inside, and the same for their choice of clothes. On the website everyone has a persona. You chose the Earl of Richmond after Zee chose the Duke of Gloucester."

"That was because Zee was trying to annoy me by taking Richard III's title. That's where our main rivalry comes from. She's a Richard III lover and I'm in the Henry VII camp. His title before he was king was Earl of Richmond."

"Yeah, I still don't understand that whole Richard III thing," Taylor said.

"When we've more time I'll explain, but the quick answer is they fought, Henry, Earl of Richmond, won and took the crown from Richard III, and Ricardians hate that."

"Ricardians?"

"Richard fans, who thought he was a jolly nice man who didn't kill his nephews, and Bad Henry usurped the throne from him," Bailey said.

"He killed his nephews?" Taylor sounded shocked.

"It's too much to go into. I'll tell you another time. You just remember—I'm on Henry's side, and Zee is on Richard's."

"Okay, so that's your part, Henry Earl of Richmond. So who am I? Countess of Richmond?"

Bailey looked tense. "What about my sister, Lady Taylor?"

The thought filled Taylor with horror, and she said seriously, "I could never be your sister. It's going to have to be your countess."

Taylor saw Bailey's jaw tighten with tension. Why was this bothering her? Was it because Bailey had feelings for or attraction to her too, or was she imagining it?

"If it must be, then it must," Bailey said.

Taylor immediately felt hurt. "If it causes you so much distress to think of me as your wife, then just forget about it. I'll get the dance master to host with me. Excuse me."

Taylor got up and went to the bathroom, tears threatening to fall from her eyes.

❖

"Jesus Christ." Bailey rubbed her forehead.

How had she become involved in all this? Ever since agreeing to become Taylor's historian, her well-ordered life had been turned upside down.

Taylor had stormed off to the bathroom, hurt by what Bailey had said. If only Taylor knew the real reason that playing the part of Earl to Taylor's countess would be so difficult for her.

She couldn't stop thinking about Taylor, and it felt so wrong. When Taylor's mum had looked at her with suspicion, Bailey felt all of those nineteen years between them. Bailey couldn't let anything happen, despite the fact that she felt Taylor wanted it too.

What would Ellis say?

She'd probably tell her to follow her feelings. Ellis was a romantic, just like Taylor. She had deserved so much more than Bailey could give her.

The problem was these kind of feelings were new and insupportable. How could Bailey trust her feelings, not having had them before? And anyway, she knew acting on her feelings was wrong.

Bailey had to find a way to make things plain, without upsetting Taylor much. Maybe the answer was to open up and show Taylor that nothing could or ever would happen, before this sexual tension between them got any worse.

She got up and walked to the bathroom door. "Taylor? Could I talk to you? I didn't mean to upset you."

The door burst open, and there was Taylor with a forced smile upon her face. "No need. I don't want to beg someone at every turn to become involved in my project. You do your history chat, and I'll make my own arrangements for a host."

"Taylor, sit down and let me explain," Bailey insisted.

Taylor narrowed her eyes and then walked back to the couch. She sat and crossed her arms defensively. Even worse, when Bailey sat, Taylor crossed her legs, making her dress slip up her thigh.

Bailey's mouth went dry. Why did this have to be so hard?

She sat there for a few seconds unable to think or speak while her eyes were glued to Taylor's knee and thigh. Bailey licked her lips as her mind imagined kissing her way up that thigh, taking her time, and making Taylor moan.

"Well?"

Taylor was speaking, but Bailey hadn't heard the words. "What? Sorry, what did you say?"

"You wanted to talk, and I'm listening."

"Oh yes. Right." Bailey lifted her glass and took a drink of her wine. She tried to shake the arousal away. "Um…I will do what you want—you can be Countess of Richmond. You just caught me by surprise, and the idea of having a role-play wife jarred me. I need to explain why."

"It's just make-believe," Taylor said.

"I know. Just *listen*. About two years ago my wife and best friend in the world died."

Taylor's jaw dropped. "You were married…?"

"Yes. Her name was Ellis. We met at university, but it wasn't until about four years ago that we got married. Ellis was hit by a drunk driver while walking home from the train station. When I arrived at the hospital she could hardly speak. I had a few agonizing hours before she was gone. Internal bleeding."

Taylor moved as close to Bailey as she could and took her hands. Bailey wasn't expecting that.

"I'm so sorry, Bailey. I was jabbering on about playing the role of your wife and…I'm sorry." Taylor pulled up Bailey's hands and kissed them.

Bailey was not used to this kind of close affection.

"It's okay. You didn't know. It jarred me, and maybe I reacted badly, but I never meant to imply that you weren't good enough in some way. You are too good for me. I'm a broken forty-five year old."

"Don't say that," Taylor said squeezing her hands.

"It's true. When I met you, I'd been on my own, in my study at home, with just my books and my research. I didn't intend to come out into the world, but you pulled me out. Once I've helped you with this project, I'll go back to my study, to my books, and live my life quietly."

"You might meet new friends through this. A new social life. Maybe you'll feel different?"

Now Bailey had to make her position clear. "I'm not—I don't want a social life. I'm done with any kind of relationship. I never was searching for one in my life—I'm not like you. Love and romance, it's never been real for me."

"But your wife?"

"Yes, I married Ellis, and that relationship was enough for me. I won't feel hurt or grief like that again," Bailey said.

"Oh, okay."

Taylor looked crestfallen. *She actually did feel something between us.*

"Besides, I'm too old for most in your group."

"Age doesn't matter."

Bailey didn't reply to that. She simply said, "But I will host with you, and we can be the Earl and Countess of Richmond."

"You don't have to," Taylor said.

"No it's okay. I just wanted to explain why your suggestion spooked me. I'm fine with it, and I'll be glad to help."

"Thank you."

There was an atmosphere hanging between them now. Bailey wasn't sure what to say.

"I better go, I suppose." But she made no move to leave.

Taylor was smiling again. Bailey didn't know if she truly understood what she was trying to tell her in not so many words—that anything between them would be unthinkable.

Bailey stood up. "I'll be on my way then."

She walked to the door and Taylor held it open for her. "Thanks for coming. There was just one more thing."

Taylor looked nervous all of a sudden.

"What? You can tell me."

"It doesn't matter. Honestly. Goodnight," Taylor said.

Bailey was unconvinced but walked out the door, and when she was a few paces away from the door, Bailey heard Taylor say, "As host I need you to dance with me."

Bailey's head snapped back around. Taylor had the door half shut, but Bailey was over to it in a second and pushed it open.

"What did you say?"

Taylor cleared her throat nervously. "Dance. The hosts have to lead the first dance at least."

"You think I'm going to prance around like a fool in a silly costume?" She had allowed Taylor to push and push her out of her comfort zone, but this was going too far.

"It's the rules. It's what the hosts do."

"I wanted nothing to do with this dating club. I'm writing a book, but you and Margo persuaded me to be your historian and give a few talks. Then you persuade me to wear the silly Regency costume while I do it. That makes me feel fool enough, and now tonight you want me to host and play a part in a make-believe with all your other Romantics, and as if that wasn't bad enough, you want me to dance? Forget it," Bailey said firmly.

"It's just one dance. You don't have to take part in any others," Taylor said.

"One dance would be too much. Goodnight."

CHAPTER FOURTEEN

Major Bamber knocked his cane on the floor of the dance studio to get the dancers' attention, even though he was hooked up to a microphone.

"Romantics, take a fifteen-minute break and we'll move on to the second dance."

Marcus Fox, one of her Romantics, bowed to Taylor at the end of the dance. "This is such good fun, Taylor. Sorry, Lady Richmond."

"Thank you, Sir Marcus." Taylor curtseyed.

Marcus was only in his mid-thirties but had a head of silver hair. It made him look quite distinguished, Taylor thought.

Ally Okano, another Romantic, joined them. "This is so much harder than it looks in films."

"I know," Taylor said, "and Mr. Bamber has chosen the easiest for us too."

The group had been attending dance lessons with Mr. Bamber's troupe for three weeks now, and they all had bruises on their feet from missteps, but it was all part of the fun. The first week the costumier and her staff came to take measurements and discuss what each Romantic wanted in an outfit. Everyone had great fun except Bailey and Taylor.

After their last argument, Taylor didn't expect Bailey to come, but she sent Bailey the details and was delighted when she turned up.

Her delight didn't last long when Bailey had informed her she was here under duress and did not wish to talk to her. True to her word, Bailey never partnered up with Taylor to practice and ignored Taylor. It was hurting Taylor's heart.

What was worse, after the group had finished the one dance she was taking part in, Bailey would pack up her things and go.

That's just what she was about to do now. Taylor could see her over Marcus's shoulder.

"Marcus, Ally, would you excuse me?"

Marcus bowed. "Of course, Lady Richmond."

Taylor hurried over to the other side of the room where Bailey was packing her bag. "Bailey? Would you talk to me a minute?"

"I'm not interested, Taylor. I've practiced the dance I'm obliged to do, and all the while Zee is walking around taking pictures of me. My fellow historians will find it hilarious."

"You're not obliged to do anything," Taylor said.

Bailey turned around and said angrily, but in a low voice, "Do you think I could say no when you asked me? No, because I can never say no when you ask for help. You know that, and you have taken it too far."

"I think you're blowing this all out of proportion. It's just dancing."

"It is not just dancing. I'm a historian, and you are making me become a dancing fool. I'm going now."

Bailey started to walk away with her bag over her shoulder, and Taylor said, "Don't go, Bailey. I miss you."

Bailey stopped momentarily, giving Taylor hope, but then she just walked out of the room. Taylor had to gulp away her emotion and the frustration that threatened to spill over. *It's just a dance. Why won't she dance with me?*

Her thoughts were interrupted by an overexcited Dani. "Major Bamber says we're doing Mr. Beveridge's Maggot next." It was an odd Regency dance that Dani found hilarious.

"Dance with me, Lady Richmond?"

Taylor put on her best smiling face despite her sadness and said, "My pleasure."

It wasn't long till the first ball of the season, and it was going to be hard coping with her feelings while Bailey was determined to be angry.

She would just concentrate on her Romantics. Bailey could be as angry as she wanted. She was acting like a child.

CHAPTER FIFTEEN

A re you sure you don't mind, my dear?"
Taylor had only just arrived at Fairydean to find Lady Catherine still there.

"Of course not. As long as you don't mind us all trampling about the place," Taylor said.

Lady Catherine had sprained her ankle and was unable to go on her research trip. She had to stay at Fairydean.

"Not a bit of it. It'll be quite exciting to watch if you would allow me to be in your company?"

"We'd be delighted. You will only add to the company, Lady Catherine."

"I think I may have an outfit that would fit in, so don't worry about me sticking out amongst your Romantics," Lady Catherine said.

"I'm sure you'll look wonderful."

Mr. Parrot the butler approached them. "Lady Catherine, Miss Sparks, the costume people have arrived. Jamie and the gardeners are carrying in their baggage."

"Thank you, Parrot," Lady Catherine said. "It's systems go for you now then, young Taylor."

"I'm nervous and excited at the same time," Taylor admitted.

"The weekend will be spectacular—don't worry about that. Where's your handsome historian?"

"We didn't travel together. She's coming down later. We are not the best of friends at the moment," Taylor said.

"Really? I would never have thought you two wouldn't get on," Lady Catherine said. "I'm sure it'll blow over. Ah, here's Jamie with your costume people."

Phillipa—the head designer and owner of the company—and her staff were looking around the entrance hall in awe.

"Would you excuse me, Lady Catherine," Taylor said.

"Of course. I'll retreat to my study so that I don't get under your feet."

"Thank you."

Taylor walked over to Phillipa. They had got on well since they first met. Phillipa got the concept of what she was trying to do, with each costume being tailored to the Romantic's own identity.

"Isn't this perfect, Phillipa?"

"It's just beautiful. So atmospheric. Have you got a room for us to be based in?"

"Yes, it's in the green drawing room. Follow me."

Taylor led them past the main reception room and the ballroom doors, until she stopped outside two large doors and opened them wide.

"This will be your dressing room. Will it fit the bill?"

"It's wonderful. Martin? Jan? look at this," Phillipa said to her two assistants.

"What a wonderful space," Jan said.

Martin replied, "I can't wait to get going. Come on, boys and girls."

Martin directed Jamie and the garden staff to take their bags in.

Taylor looked at her watch. The day seemed to be flying by. "Phillipa? Can I leave you to it? I've got so much to do."

"No problem. When do your guests arrive?"

"Two hours. I've organized tea and cakes on the terrace when they arrive if the weather holds, and then you can call on them one by one," Taylor said.

"Sounds good. Leave it to us then."

Taylor left the new dressing room and walked to the other side of the reception hall, then made her way down the back stairs to the kitchen. She found Mrs. Parrot rolling some dough on the kitchen table.

"Mrs. Parrot, nice to see you again."

She looked up and smiled. Mrs. Parrot was a kindly woman. Anyone else in her position might have been annoyed at the disruption and change in their daily routine.

But Mrs. Parrot had been on board from the beginning.

"Hello there. I hoped you'd be down soon. I've got some samples to show you for the ball tomorrow night."

There were two young women helping in the kitchen that Taylor hadn't seen before.

"Taylor, these are my two nieces, Hannah and Ivy. They've been helping me out with the food. Ivy is going to catering college, so it's a good experience for her," Mrs. Parrot said.

The more help the better, Taylor thought. "Hi, Hannah, Ivy. Thanks for helping out with this."

"It's exciting to take part," Ivy said. "We both think your Regency club is so romantic."

"Thank you. Here's hoping it'll go okay."

"Girls, go and get the samples," Mrs. Parrot said.

The girls laid out some serving dishes, what Taylor assumed were pies, and trays of biscuits.

Taylor moved over beside Mrs. Parrot, who said, "I was able to find some Regency and Victorian serving dishes in Fairydean's old storeroom."

"That's excellent, Mrs. Parrot. I don't know what I would have done without you," Taylor said.

Mrs. Parrot looked very happy with that compliment and stood a little taller. "First of all, we have white soup, a popular dish in your time period. It's made with beef bones, almonds, and double cream. Very decadent."

Taylor bent over and sniffed. It certainly smelled rich and flavourful. She wasn't sure about the beef bones, though.

"Smells lovely," Taylor said.

"As you requested, I've got vegan-friendly options for each dish. Hannah has been my right hand girl in all this, because she's a vegetarian." Mrs. Parrot added in a stage whisper, "Her mum and I think she'll grow out of it."

Hannah and Ivy laughed.

"Hannah and Ivy have sourced the vegan alternative ingredients for me. Instead of white soup, the vegans are getting rich wild mushroom soup."

Mrs. Parrot lifted up the lid and the most wonderful smell hit Taylor. "That smells delicious. I think I'll be having that one."

"Next we've got game pies. The game was shot on the estate by the gamekeepers, so you couldn't get more authentic than that."

Taylor didn't approve of hunting, but it was authentic for the time period and, she supposed, better than buying factory produced meat from a supermarket.

"Again, I have vegan pies, but they aren't quite ready to show you. We have wild goose with orange sauce, Prince of Wales biscuits, Duke of Clarence biscuits, and Duchess of Gloucester biscuits."

Taylor picked one up. It had a stamp on it saying *Prince of Wales*. "Are these like shortbread?"

"No, not as nice as that. These biscuits weren't for having tea— they were part of the dessert course. You'd dip your biscuit into your sweet wine. Mr. Parrot's got the sweet wine in hand. It's something authentic I think your guests will enjoy. There was only one problem with these," Mrs. Parrot said.

"What?"

"The emblems of the Prince of Wales and the Duke of Clarence should be stamped on the biscuits, but I could not find any anywhere. The girls checked on the internet, on eBay. Nothing. So we had to go with a stamper where you can choose the letters and stamp the name."

"That's perfect, Mrs. Parrot. Thank you for going to so much trouble. You've all shown me so much kindness," Taylor said.

"We're like that at Fairydean," Mrs. Parrot said proudly.

And they were. Taylor worried that the next stately home was going to be a let-down compared to this.

❖

Taylor hurried out to the front steps where Mr. Parrot was waiting. She'd just been getting the serving staff up to speed after they had arrived late, when she got a text saying the bus with her Romantics was near the estate.

"Has Dr. Bailey arrived yet?"

"Yes, not long ago. I took her to her room."

"Thanks."

Would it have killed Bailey to come and tell her she was here? They hadn't got on since the night she'd asked her to be host alongside her, and dance of course. That had been the turning point in their relationship. Bailey had shut off from her.

Bailey refusing to be her dance partner at Mr. Bamber's lessons, or talking to her, made Taylor furious. It was so petty. Bailey was making a point, and as she said the last time they spoke, she was doing this under duress.

Taylor didn't even try with her after that. It was too hurtful to think about it too much, so she put all her energies into her Romantics.

Gracie came hurrying out of the ballroom. "I thought I would miss them arriving."

"How are the servers? All ready?"

"Yeah, I took them down to Mrs. Parrot, and she's got them working already."

"Good." Taylor reached out a hand and took Gracie's. "I'm nervous, Gracie. What if this is a disaster? What if no one gets into the make-believe world we're making? What if they stand around not talking?"

"You're just letting your fear talk. You have planned for everything. And at the ball if people are reluctant to ask people to dance at first, Colonel Sideburns's dance troupe will start the ball rolling."

Taylor laughed at Gracie's description of their dance master, with his big, bushy Regency sideburns. He really did live the period. "Don't let him hear you call him that. We need our dancers badly."

"There's the bus," Gracie said.

Taylor looked up and saw the bus come into view. Her stomach was doing flips now. "The musicians have confirmed, haven't they? Everything's okay with the music tomorrow night?"

"Stop worrying. Everything's fine."

It was a few minutes' drive from the gates, and the waiting was making Taylor's nerves worse. Then something made her turn her head. At the window of the library, she saw Bailey looking back at her. Her heart thudded as they held each other's gazes. Then before she knew it, Bailey retreated away from the window.

How could she be like this? Taylor knew Bailey felt like she did.

The bus stopped at the front of the house. "Here we go, Gracie. This is it."

The doors opened, and the first person to jump out was Zee. She'd got the bus with the Romantics so she could take photos and talk to her guests.

"Taylor, Gracie—you look gorgeous," Zee said, before turning her camera towards the bus door.

"She is a charmer, isn't she?" Taylor said.

"And very sexy. Have you gone out with her again?" Gracie said.

"I only went for a drink. Although she does keep asking me. Besides, it's not about me—it's about the Romantics. Have you gotten any clues from the chat room if anyone is coupling up?"

"Yeah, I wrote it down somewhere. Hang on," Gracie said.

While Gracie searched around in her notes on her iPad, her

Romantics started to get off the bus one by one. Dani was first, and ever the organizer. "Come on, gang. Let's step back in time."

He then let out a whoop. Dani was infectious. Taylor was so glad he signed up for their club.

"I've got it," Gracie said. "Okay, I'm not sure about romance, but Dani is very much looking after Avery O'Connor."

Avery was their only non-binary Romantic and extremely shy. "I asked Dani to keep an eye on them."

Next off was Maisie Langford, their bubbly socialite looking for love.

"Maisie has been chatting with the whole group really. She's very sociable, but I noticed Vida Clifford chatting to her more than most."

"There's a bit of an age gap between them," Taylor noted. Vida was ten years older than Maisie.

"No one cares about those things anymore," Gracie said.

"Don't they?"

Bailey did. She'd made that clear.

Vida Clifford came off next. She was certainly a striking woman. She must have been not far off six feet tall, with short silver hair. It didn't make her look any older—Taylor thought it made her look very sexy. She was feminine but had a complete alpha personality.

She watched Vida helping Maisie with her bag and offering her arm. Very courteous. Just like Bailey. Any time they were together, she always made sure doors were opened and bags were carried. Any little thing, Bailey was there for it. Or had been there for it.

"Let's go, Gracie."

They walked down to the group, who were all outside the bus now.

"Welcome, everyone, to Fairydean."

"It's stunning," Dani said.

"I'm glad you think so," Taylor said. "Now I'm going to do a roll call to make sure everyone is here, and Gracie will bring around name badges to remind everyone of who you all are and your pronouns. After that, you'll be shown to your rooms. Then we'll have tea and scones on the terrace, before being called to put on your Regency outfit, and then dinner. Okay…Dani, Vida, Maisie, are all here I can see."

Taylor ran through all thirty names, and everyone was there. They were taken to their rooms and left to settle in for a bit, while Taylor and Gracie rushed around, fixing small last-minute problems.

❖

Bailey held a couple of books in her hands, trying to decide which to borrow first. Lady Catherine had said to make herself at home in the library and borrow what she liked.

She chose a Victorian book called *Britain, A History.*

It would be interesting to read history from a Victorian voice and to contrast it with today's understanding. Bailey left the library and intended to go to her room, but after climbing the stairs she found herself drawn to the window on the side of the long corridor that led to her room.

She could see the terrace from on high. All the guests were enjoying afternoon tea, still in their everyday clothes. They all appeared to be talking well. Having the chat room on the website had given everyone a chance to become at least acquainted with each other.

Then the dance lessons broke the ice even more.

Bailey wondered if Taylor could sense her. She did when she was waiting out front for the bus to arrive. When they'd locked eyes, all Bailey wanted to do was run to her.

But she used all her strength to turn away, just as she did throughout the dance lessons. It was torture not to be near Taylor, and not touch her, talk to her, just enjoy her company. Taylor thought it was a slight to her, but if only she knew.

Bailey was trying to do the right thing. She felt Taylor's attraction, her feelings reeling Bailey in, but a relationship between them was impossible. Bailey was doing the right thing, but the right thing was hard.

Taylor came into view with Lady Catherine and appeared to be introducing her to everyone. It was nice that Lady Catherine was going to be joining in with the festivities. Bailey got the impression she led an isolated life down here and, unlike herself, seemed to enjoy company. Taylor disappeared from view, so she made her way along to her room. It was a pleasant room overlooking the estate.

In the corner was a door connecting her bedroom and the one next door, but Mr. Parrot assured her that it wasn't used any more and well locked up. Bailey's privacy was extremely important to her.

Bailey sat in the seat by the window and opened her book.

There was a knock at the door. "Come in."

The door opened, and Bailey stood up quickly. "Taylor."

"I wondered if you were going to take any part in this weekend or just hide away up here?"

"Of course I will. I'm needed as host at dinner, and then after dinner is my lecture."

"You're not going to mingle and talk to people then?"

"At dinner and at the ball, yes."

"I don't know why you bothered coming if you're not going to enter into the spirit of things," Taylor said.

"Look, I'm here. That's what you wanted."

Taylor walked over to her. "I wanted you to be a part of it. I thought we were friends at least. I thought we had got that far."

"You don't need a friend like me," Bailey said.

Taylor started to pace. She felt a hot burst of anger surge through her. "I don't need a friend like you? What's that supposed to mean?"

"Just as I said."

"I really don't know why you're doing this—no, I take that back. You're hiding," Taylor said.

"Hiding what?"

"Hiding what you feel, what we both feel," Taylor said.

"That's impossible—you must know that."

"I don't know that. Why is it impossible?" Taylor asked.

"Because you are nineteen years younger than me." Bailey turned away towards the window.

Taylor put her hand on Bailey's back. "As Gracie reminded me today, nobody cares about that sort of thing any more."

"She is wrong. If you'll excuse me, I want to rest before dinner," Bailey said coldly.

"That's all you're going to say? Really?" Taylor was so angry.

"Goodbye, Taylor. I'll be down for dinner."

Taylor took a breath. She didn't want to let all her anger rip out of her, or she would never convince Bailey to open up.

"I know your grief has been a struggle, but there's no need to push people away. I don't know anything about your wife, but to gain your love she must have been a special woman. Would she want you to hide away from the world forever? As for the age difference, we're both adults. If anyone thinks it's wrong, including my family, then it doesn't matter. All that matters is us. See you at dinner."

Taylor turned and walked away, hoping that her words would somehow hit home with Bailey. There wasn't any part of Taylor that thought the age gap was wrong, but she was a little nervous as to what her mum, mama, and big brothers would say.

But she was willing to face that if Bailey would only admit the feelings they had for each other.

CHAPTER SIXTEEN

Fairydean was busy for the first time in a long number of years. Taylor and Gracie were waiting at the bottom of the stairs for Bailey. It was nearly time to ring the gong and call everyone to dinner.

"You look beautiful, Taylor," Gracie said.

Taylor looked down at her light green Regency-style dress and hoped Gracie wasn't just saying that.

"Thank you. You do too."

Gracie wore a sky-blue dress and a tiara in her hair. "How does my hair look?"

"Gorgeous."

Taylor had simply put her hair up in a chignon. Tomorrow she planned to have a tiara but was nervous about it. It really suited Gracie, but Taylor didn't have her confidence.

Mr. Parrot walked towards them. "Just a few minutes to the gong, ma'am."

"My other host isn't here yet. Do you think she's not coming, Gracie?"

"She'll come. Bailey won't let you down."

Then Taylor heard footsteps on the stairs. When she looked up, her stomach flipped over.

Bailey was dressed in black boots, cream breeches, a blue tailcoat over a black and blue striped waistcoat, and a white necktie with an attractive pin. She looked every inch the Earl of Richmond, and utterly gorgeous.

When Bailey got to the bottom of the stairs, she fiddled with her cuffs and looked up at her. Her eyes scanned Taylor up and down, and then she gulped. Taylor saw Bailey close her eyes for just a second, but she seemed back in control when she opened them.

Bailey approached them. "Miss Gracie, you look very pretty. Lady Taylor, you look beautiful."

Bailey had started the make-believe. Was this her way of saying what she couldn't as Bailey? Whatever it was, Taylor was going along with it.

"Thank you, My Lord."

Bailey gave her an intense look, then stepped beside her.

"Shall I ring the gong, ma'am?" Mr. Parrot asked.

"Yes, please." Taylor turned to Gracie and said, "Take your place, and fingers crossed this works out."

Gracie took her place by the door and told the waitstaff in the drawing room to be ready with their trays of champagne.

Mr. Parrot hit the gong, and it reverberated throughout the house. Taylor whispered to Bailey, "Thank you for doing this."

"Only for you," Bailey whispered back.

On impulse Taylor took Bailey's arm. Surely, she couldn't deny this, whatever it was between them.

Taylor heard voices and laughter coming from upstairs. *This is it, Taylor.*

As was to be expected, Dani was the first, leading the group downstairs.

He was dressed in gentleman's breeches and a turquoise tailcoat, and his shirt had an extremely large, ruffled neck pierced with an imitation diamond brooch. His outfit was topped off with boots and a cane. He was the perfect flamboyant gentleman. To match his tailcoat, he wore sparkly blue eyeshadow, and some purple lipstick.

Dani whispered to Mr. Parrot, and then he announced, "Mr. Beau Brummell."

Taylor couldn't help but laugh. Beau Brummell? Perfect. The famous dandy who set men's fashion in Regency Britain and ultimately bankrupted himself because of his high standards of fashion.

Bailey shook his hand. "Mr. Brummell, delighted to see you again. My wife, the Countess of Richmond."

Taylor felt a wave of warmth at that introduction. But she had to remind herself that Bailey was play-acting.

"Captain O'Connor."

Avery had told Taylor they'd chosen the title of *captain* as the nearest they could get to a gender-neutral title. The rank might not have been gender-neutral in the Regency, but it was now, and so they went with that.

It worked well, and their outfit was outstanding.

"Captain, you look wonderful," Taylor said.

They lowered their eyes bashfully. "I like it, Countess."

They wore a Regency officer's jacket, with its bright red colour and gold tassels and braiding. Below, Avery wore a straight black skirt, down to their feet.

"It's perfect," Bailey said. "Welcome."

Taylor was getting excited. People's choice of dress was really expressing who they were, and that's what Taylor wanted this to be about.

Maisie was more traditionally dressed in a long flowing blue Regency gown. She really was a beautiful woman, and Vida Clifford who was with her wore a gentleman's tailcoat over a gown.

Marie Johnson had her hair done in feminine style like Taylor's, but she wore a full gentleman's outfit, and Taylor could see the outfit gave her a confidence and swagger that was very attractive.

After that an excitable Zee bounced downstairs. She was also in gentleman's attire. She whispered to Mr. Parrot and he said, "Lord Zee, Duke of Gloucester."

Bailey shook her hand.

"Hmm. Just an earl, Bailey, not quite as good as a duke."

Bailey scowled.

Zee then lifted Taylor's gloved hand and kissed it. "I hope I may be favoured with a few dances with Your Ladyship tomorrow at the ball?"

"If you ask me." Taylor smiled.

"Oh, I will." Then Zee winked at her.

Bailey started fidgeting with her collar, clearly wound up by Zee. She always let her get under her skin.

Once they had welcomed everyone, Bailey offered her arm, and Taylor gladly took it.

"Everyone looks good, don't they?" Bailey said.

"Yeah, I think they're enjoying the freedom of dress. Here's hoping the rest of the night goes well."

They all enjoyed drinks, then went through to dinner.

❖

The dining room at Fairydean was perfect for Taylor's purpose, Bailey thought. Dark wooden table and chairs and wood panelled walls, some with tapestries on them, no doubt made by ladies of the manor in times past.

It wasn't as bad as she'd thought, dressing up in the Regency style. She thought she would feel foolish but only had an initial feeling of worry before heading downstairs.

Bailey would go as far as to say she felt the costume was freeing. It was like leaving the problems of the present day behind and allowing yourself just to be. It also gave her a feeling of power. The gentleman's attire suited how she felt inside and the strap-on that she'd brought to make the outfit complete.

The costume people suggested the strap-on to make the outfit feel natural. Bailey had owned many in the past and enjoyed wearing and using them, but she hadn't for years.

She was glad she did tonight. It gave her confidence and made the male character she played feel her own. Bailey couldn't forget walking downstairs and seeing Taylor for the first time. She'd never seen anyone look so beautiful.

Bailey was at the head of the table, and Taylor, playing her wife, was at the other end. She was too far away.

Bailey took a sip of wine and gazed down the long table to Taylor. Taylor was talking to Zee, who—annoyingly—was sitting to her left.

Taylor's gorgeous hair was perfect, pinned up with a few ringlets falling down on her bare shoulder and neck. Taylor's fingernails were stroking her bare neck, and Bailey's mouth watered. She so wanted her lips to touch where those fingers stroked, her tongue to taste Taylor. Bailey was mesmerized.

Taylor looked up and caught Bailey in her languid gaze. Taylor's lips parted, and she appeared to breathe heavier, almost as if she could feel what Bailey was thinking.

Bailey looked away quickly before she got any more lost. Gracie, who was sitting to Bailey's left, said, "You like Taylor, don't you?"

"Of course I like her," Bailey said.

"No, I mean, *like*-like her. I see the way you look at her."

If Gracie had noticed, then who else had? She didn't want people to think she was some kind of old lech.

Bailey cleared her throat. "Not that way. I'm nineteen years older than her. She needs to find someone her own age."

"Bailey—sorry, Lord Bailey. I keep forgetting we're in character." Gracie laughed. "Anyway, people don't care about age. Live and let live. Lady Taylor likes you too. She goes all gooey when you're around."

Laughter from the other end of the table made Bailey look up. Taylor was laughing at something Zee said, but crucially Zee was holding and kissing her gloved hand.

The sight infuriated Bailey. Without thinking logically, she stood up and said forcefully, "I think everyone's finished, Lady Richmond, and ready for my lecture."

Taylor looked surprised. Then she stood up. "It seems My Lord thinks we're ready to move through."

If I really was yours, you wouldn't be getting pawed by smarmy fools like Zee Osman.

Bailey walked out of the dining room quickly. She had to get away from these feelings. She wasn't used to jealousy. It wasn't something Bailey had ever had for any of the other women she'd had short relationships with.

But seeing Zee with Taylor like that made jealousy erupt in her for the first time. It was bad enough during the weeks at dance practice. Zee was always around Taylor, always offering to be her dance partner, and there was nothing Bailey could do but watch.

She was purposely keeping her distance from Taylor, and she'd just about managed to keep a cool head, but there was no stopping her anger now. Bailey had to stop Zee, and ending dinner quickly was the best way.

Bailey walked behind the staircase and leaned against a marble pillar. She had to take a breath and get a hold of herself.

How can I do this?

Bailey knew it was the right thing to do, to not act on what was so obviously between Taylor and herself, but she didn't want to do the right thing.

She held out her hand and saw it tremor. Her whole body was aching with need, need for Taylor.

Bailey held her hands over her face. She wished she had some cold water. There was a bathroom just along the corridor, she remembered. Bailey hurried along there and locked the door.

She ran the water and splashed some on her face. When Bailey looked up and into the mirror, she saw someone barely hanging on. There were another two days of this—the ball tomorrow, and Sunday there was going to be a whole day of activities before a final dinner.

The only way to cope was to try to keep away from Taylor. And then after this weekend was over, she wouldn't have to see Taylor for a few months before preparation for the next ball.

"Okay, let's go and do this."

The sooner she gave her lecture, the sooner she could slip away from the crowd.

She dried off her face and walked back to the reception hall. Bailey heard her name being called and turned around. Lady Catherine was coming slowly down the stairs in a flouncy cocktail dress.

"Will this do, Dr. Bailey? It was the nearest I could get to Regency wear."

"You look wonderful, Lady Catherine." Bailey offered her arm and Lady Catherine gladly took it.

"Thank you," Lady Catherine said. "How's it all going?"

Apart from slimy faux historian pawing at Taylor? "Very well. Everyone seems to have entered into the spirit of it."

"I'm glad to hear that. Young Taylor deserves it. She's worked so hard for her dream."

"Yes, yes, she has."

Bailey was so wrapped up in her own feelings that she forgot how important this was for Taylor. She had worked hard and didn't need her to create any kind of atmosphere. The way she had ended dinner was abrupt and wrong.

She took a breath and vowed to be on her best behaviour for Taylor.

"You look rather dashing," Lady Catherine said. "Who are you in this fantasy world?"

"The Earl of Richmond."

"Ah Henry VII's famous title."

"You know the woman walking about with the camera?" Bailey asked. Lady Catherine nodded. "*She* is the Duke of Gloucester."

"I see. She's a Richard III fan," Lady Catherine said.

"Yes, so I had to represent the opposition."

"Good for you. I'm not a Richard III lover myself."

Bailey patted Lady Catherine's hand. "We are of like minds then."

She guided Lady Catherine through into the drawing room. Taylor noticed them and came straight over to take Lady Catherine's arm from Bailey. "Come and sit by me. Your Lordship, could you get us a drink?"

"It would be an honour." Bailey bowed her head to them both, playing the part of a gentleman perfectly.

Taylor helped ease Lady Catherine down into the armchair. "Thank you, my dear."

"This is Lady Catherine, everyone. We are delighted she could join us."

"Love your dress," Dani said.

"Thank you. You look wonderful yourself, you all do."

Taylor looked around and saw Bailey was preparing for her lecture. She let out a breath. The longer and longer it had taken for Bailey to appear, the more Taylor thought she wasn't going to turn up.

She didn't understand what had happened at dinner, but something had upset Bailey to make her end dinner so abruptly. Hopefully the rest of the evening would run smoothly.

Bailey walked over and whispered in her ear, "I'm ready to start."

Taylor got shivers all over her body. It took her back to her fantasy in Bailey's study, when Bailey had leaned forward and whispered. She could never get that out of her head.

Bailey was the one her body and her heart yearned for.

❖

Most the party had gone upstairs to bed, Bailey being the first to run off as quickly as she could after her lecture, followed by Lady Catherine. The last two to leave were Dani and Avery. Avery wasn't used to drinking champagne and it had gone to their head.

Dani was being such a good sport looking after them and keeping an eye on everyone in the group. If anyone appeared shy or fading into the background, he made it his mission to talk to them and give them confidence.

"Come on, Captain Avery."

Taylor and Gracie went over to help Dani lift them to their feet. "It was so much fun, Miss…"

Avery struggled trying to remember Taylor's fantasy name through the fog champagne.

"The Countess of Richmond."

"Richmond, yes, that's it. It was so much fun."

"I'm so glad you had a great time, and there's more to come tomorrow at the ball, so you need some rest."

Taylor turned to Dani, "Do you want us to help you get Avery upstairs?"

"No, we'll be fine. Come on, Captain, to bed."

Dani had his arms around Avery's middle and supported them as they walked.

"Thank you, Dani."

He raised his hand in acknowledgement as they left.

Once they were alone, Taylor and Gracie kicked off their shoes and flopped onto the couch. Taylor lifted her feet onto Gracie's lap.

"We did it, Gracie. Day one in the bag."

Gracie let out a big breath. "It was perfect. Everyone was loving it."

"Do you think so?"

"Oh yeah. The Romantics were chatting and laughing. They loved it."

"We've been so lucky with Fairydean. All the help Lady Catherine and her staff have given us is more than I could have hoped for, and at such a cheap price. It makes me worry our next ball won't be as good at Pardale Abbey. There'll be no Mr. and Mrs. Parrot there."

Gracie chuckled. "They are sweet."

"Bed, then?" Taylor asked.

"Bed."

They gathered themselves together and headed upstairs. When they reached Gracie's room, Taylor hugged her and kissed her cheek. "Thank you for being a part of this with me."

"Are you kidding? This is the best job ever."

After Gracie entered her room, Taylor made her way along the corridor. On her way to her room, she slowed as she got to Bailey's door. She so wanted to talk to Bailey, but she didn't know if she had the courage.

Taylor walked up to Bailey's door. She listened for sounds of Bailey moving about. She heard footsteps.

Knock, Taylor told herself.

She lifted her hand but instead of knocking placed her palm on the door and closed her eyes.

Taylor's heart was pounding. *Just knock.*

Before she could change her mind, Taylor rapped on the door. In a few seconds Bailey opened up.

"Taylor? Is something wrong?"

"Uh…no, not…"

Taylor couldn't take her eyes off Bailey. She had dispensed with the tailcoat and had her waistcoat hanging open, with her shirt loose and open to her chest. She looked so sexily dishevelled.

Then she cast her eyes down and noticed something she hadn't noticed all evening—the bulge in her Regency trousers.

Oh God. She was playing the role to the full.

Taylor was hit with the heavy beat of sexual arousal. Much more intense than before. She'd never been with someone who used a strap-on before, but the thought of the much older, experienced Bailey introducing her to it made her body feel all kinds of out of control.

It was hard enough that Bailey looked so gorgeous in her Regency gentleman's outfit, but she had to add that didn't she? This was definitely going to make its way into her fantasy.

"Taylor? Taylor?"

"What?"

"Did you need something?" Bailey asked.

Yes, you.

"I just wanted to thank you for your lecture. Everyone enjoyed it," Taylor said.

"I'm glad. I was worried it would be too academic for your Romantics. It's not something Zee would have done."

"If I'd wanted Zee, I would have asked her."

Taylor was fully aware of this double meaning and hoped it would get through to Bailey, but if it did, she never said.

They gazed into each other's eyes until Bailey closed her eyes for a second, then said, "It's getting late."

There it was. Pushing her away yet again. "I suppose it is. A big day tomorrow."

"The ball," Bailey said.

"Yeah, you ready to dance?"

"No, but I'll have to go through with it anyway."

That comment made Taylor mad. "It's just one dance."

"Goodnight, Taylor."

"Fine, then. If you want to be like that about it. Goodnight."

CHAPTER SEVENTEEN

B ailey was dreading today. The day of the ball. She was going to have to dance, not something she was comfortable about in the first place, but to dance with Taylor, the woman she wanted more than anything in the world, would be torture.

After waking up early, Bailey went for a walk around the grounds, hoping to get some air outside before any of the Romantics would be out taking part in today's pursuits. She went over last night in her mind for the millionth time.

It was so out of character for her to show jealousy. To make matters worse, Bailey had to play the bad guy yet again and rebuff Taylor at her bedroom door. Taylor appeared to be determined to explore this attraction between them. Why could she not see how impossible it would be?

Bailey could only imagine what her two mums would think of it.

"Dr. Bailey? Sorry, it should be *My Lord*, shouldn't it?" Lady Catherine said.

"I'll answer to either, Lady Catherine. You're out early."

"Yes, I like to have a walk before breakfast, despite my wonky ankle. Blow out the old cobwebs."

Bailey smiled. "Indeed."

"Shall we walk back together?"

Bailey nodded. "I would be delighted."

"I must say, it's like a breath of fresh air having all you young people at Fairydean," Lady Catherine said.

"I hardly think I qualify, Lady Catherine."

"It's all comparative. Believe me, from where I'm standing, you qualify as a young person."

"It doesn't feel like that when I'm around some of the young people on this weekend," Bailey said.

"I noticed—what's her name, the journalist?"

"Zee? Zee Osman."

"That's the one. I notice she pays Taylor a lot of attention. You should act fast, or you'll risk losing her."

Bailey was shocked. How did she know? What did she think? "I'm not in any race for Taylor. I'm nineteen years older than her, Lady Catherine."

"Taylor doesn't seem to mind. I've seen the way she looks at you, and if you don't mind me saying, the way you look at her. I worked it out the first time I met you both. When you came to visit me? You bickered like an old married couple. Your chemistry was so well matched."

Bailey hated being caught. First Gracie, and now Lady Catherine. "It's irrelevant how I feel about Taylor. What is relevant is what is best for her, and that's not me. She has a lifetime ahead of her. She should be falling in love, falling out of love, meeting that special someone. Getting married, having children, growing old with a partner who she doesn't need to end up caring for."

Lady Catherine stopped. "You are assuming too much. We don't know what life is going to throw at us. You could live to be a spritely ninety-five year old, and her health could fail at forty, and you would be nursing her. I lost the love of my life by not telling her how I felt. Don't lose your chance at happiness."

Bailey thought about Ellis. She had been in love with Bailey since they were at university, and even though her life had ended early, she got to spend it with the person she loved. That was what was important to her. Not the duration.

Bailey didn't deserve Ellis's love or Taylor's.

"No, I can't, Lady Catherine. It's just not right. If Zee can give her excitement and—"

"You can't finish that sentence, can you?" Lady Catherine said.

"Whether I can or not doesn't alter the facts."

Bailey had to change the subject, and fortunately there was something she had been planning to ask. "Lady Catherine, I notice you have fine stables. May I take one of your horses out?"

"Of course, do you ride?"

"Not for many years now, but I rode to county championship level as a youngster and a teenager," Bailey said.

"Then fire away. You'll probably find Jamie around the stables. He has an office there. Just chap his door, and he'll be happy to help."

"Thank you."

Lady Catherine looked over her shoulder and suddenly said, "I think I'll leave you here and take the path by the pond."

Bailey turned around and saw Taylor striding across the grass towards her. She wore the green dress from yesterday but today had her hair down, tumbling across her bare shoulders.

With the sun shining behind her, Taylor Sparks was like a vision, a dream sent to steal her heart. It was at that moment that Bailey fell in love with her completely, and unreservedly.

Bailey dug her nails into her palm to check this wasn't a dream. With both their dress and surroundings, it was as if they had truly stepped back in time.

But it wasn't a dream—it was real life. Bailey had truly fallen in love with the most impossible woman.

"Have you been hiding from me, My Lord?"

If only I was her lord and she my lady.

"Quite clearly not, since you have found me. I thought I'd have an early walk before breakfast," Bailey said.

"I thought you might join me today for some of the activities. There's clay pigeon shooting, and Jamie's brother is bringing birds of prey to show us how to hunt with them."

These overwhelming feelings made Bailey want to run. She was scared.

"No, I won't be available." Bailey started to walk off leaving Taylor behind.

Taylor walked fast to try to keep up with her. "You won't be available? Why are you speaking like you've just met me?"

"I have plans, then. Does that sound better?"

"Please stop and just talk to me for one second. Please?" Taylor said.

Bailey couldn't help but stop. "I've stopped."

"What are these important plans?"

"Lady Catherine is allowing me to use one of her horses to go for a ride."

"Wait, you ride horses?" Taylor asked.

"I did up until my late teens. I rode at school and in competition," Bailey said.

Taylor put her hands on her hips. "What school has riding as part of the curriculum?"

"Boarding school."

"You went to boarding school? You were a posh kid then?" Taylor joked.

"So, the rest of my day…after riding, I'm going to spend the afternoon in Lady Catherine's library reading. She has some excellent books that can help with my research. Then I'll be getting a shower and ready for your ball, to make a fool of myself dancing. Is that enough detail for you?"

Taylor looked at her silently, with sadness on her face. "Why do you always have to be so harsh with me? I try to be nothing but nice, but it's never enough. You push and push me away."

Bailey had to purposely keep her mouth shut so she didn't say *I'm sorry. It's because I love you, and I'm terrified of these feelings.*

"I hope your day goes well." Bailey bowed her head and walked away. It was one of the hardest things she had to do.

Bailey could imagine the sadness on Taylor's face, and it killed Bailey that she was the cause of it. But it was for Taylor's own good. Once this was over, they could part ways, and Taylor could enjoy her young life.

Taylor poured herself into her work to try to blot out the hurt from this morning. Bailey was so changeable. One minute they were something approaching friends, and the next, Bailey was as cold as ice.

It had been hurtful enough at the time, but she didn't want to dwell on it. While her Romantics were enjoying a buffet lunch in the picture gallery, Taylor was keeping busy, helping the Fairydean staff decorate the ballroom for tonight.

She didn't have to try too hard to keep busy. There was so much to do. In the run-up to the weekend, Taylor had arranged for flowers to be delivered by a local florist. They hadn't long been delivered, and now came the hard bit of decorating the room.

"Taylor? Is this okay?"

Jamie and some of the gardeners were up on ladders putting up garlands of flowers and foliage.

"Perfect. Thank you."

She couldn't be luckier than having the Fairydean staff to help her. What Taylor had realized was that she had woefully underestimated the staff she needed to put on one of these weekends.

But she supposed that's what this trial of the business was about. Next time Taylor would be better prepared because she knew she wouldn't find the kindness that Lady Catherine had shown her everywhere the business went.

Taylor was pinning garlands to the orchestra stand in the corner of the ballroom when Gracie came in clutching her iPad and talking into an earbud. "I'll see what I can do. Leave it with me."

"Everything all right, Gracie?" Taylor asked.

"The orchestra needs overnight accommodation. The bus they had ordered for after the ball has cancelled on them."

"Shit. The serving staff are in the only free staff rooms at Fairydean. Lady Catherine said there are lots of rooms, but they've never been kept up over the years, no beds or anything in them, and the Rose and Crown pub is fully booked with Mr. Bamber and his dancing troupe. What are we going to do?"

"I don't know. There's lots of space here, but we can't ask them to sleep on the floor," Grace said.

Taylor began to pace up and down frantically. "What can we do?"

Jamie climbed down the ladder and walked over to Taylor. "How many are there in this orchestra?"

"Six."

"If they don't mind doubling up, they can stay at my cottage. I've got a cabin in the woodland that I stay at when I'm taking care of the tree felling. That'll give them a whole cottage to themselves."

"Really?" Taylor said excitedly. "You don't mind? You're sure?"

"Of course. I'll take them there when they arrive and give them a lift up to the big house when they're ready," Jamie said.

Taylor threw her arms around Jamie. "Thank you so much. You're so kind here."

Jamie bowed his head. "No trouble at all."

Once he walked back to his task, Taylor let out a long breath. "That was a close one."

"The people here couldn't be nicer," Gracie agreed.

"How is everyone getting on through there?" Taylor asked.

"Really well. They've been filling out the dance cards I handed out, and there's a lot of laughter," Gracie said.

"They're a good mix, aren't they? Any more simmering romances?"

"Vida and Maisie are getting even closer, and Avery seems to be developing a crush on Dani," Gracie said.

"Aww. Dani is taking care of Avery. Sweet. What about the others?" Taylor asked.

"I think they are all enjoying each other's company at the moment. I guess it'll be Pardale Abbey before we see any hot and heavy romances."

"You're probably right. Even if the Romantics just enjoy the balls and make some great friends, that'll make me happy. Speaking of hot and heavy, I better remind everyone we're in the Regency, and they have to refrain from any hot and heavy business." Taylor winked.

Gracie chuckled. "I think Vida and Maisie might need reminding of that. The hall is looking great, by the way."

Taylor looked up at the high painted ceilings and twirled. "It's going to be like a dream."

"There's quite a few asking to get on your dance card as well." Gracie looked to the door and saw Zee coming towards them. "Here's one of them. I'd better leave you to it."

"I'll see you outside for the clay pigeon shoot, Gracie."

Zee bowed to Gracie as they passed each other. "Taylor, I've been looking for you everywhere."

"I see you're enjoying the costume."

"I love it, but it's what I do. Every documentary I do, I dress up as a person of the time period."

"I know, I remember. How are the photos and videos coming along?" Taylor asked.

"Excellent. It's going to be a great story for me. I think the pictures from the ball tonight will be the best. All the vivid colours, people laughing and dancing. Speaking of the ball, can I reserve three dances at least—with you?"

Taylor liked Zee a lot, but she was going to be the perfect hostess and dance with everyone, she hoped. "I haven't got a dance card."

Zee produced one from behind her back. "I came prepared."

Taylor took it and the pencil Zee handed her and filled up three dances. "I have to dance the first with Bailey."

"Ah yes, the Earl of Richmond. It'll be utterly boring for you, but if you must."

Zee had no idea how exciting Bailey could be, and she felt defensive of her. Although why she should when Bailey was nothing but dismissive to her, Taylor had no idea.

"Bailey isn't boring. Intense and passionate, maybe, about things you aren't."

"She doesn't make her history interesting. I make dry history jump off the page," Zee said.

She was a nice person but was also completely full of herself. "You both have your good qualities."

"If you say so. I tell you what, Taylor. When this story goes out in the Sunday papers, you are going to be overbooked for your next season."

"Fingers crossed."

Taylor had to remember to be very grateful to Zee. She was really lucky that such a well-known figure had chosen to write about her.

"Thank you, Zee, for covering my club. I am grateful."

Zee winked. "No problem, sweetheart. I'll see you out at the clay pigeon shoot?"

Taylor smiled. "See you there."

❖

It would have been a strange sight to any stranger to walk into the library that afternoon—Bailey in full Regency dress, tapping away at her laptop at the library table.

Bailey was enjoying distracting herself from her emotions by taking notes from some of Lady Catherine's wonderful books. She found several Victorian volumes of the history of the medieval and early modern period that she hadn't known existed.

Victorian history books could not all be relied upon for the strict facts, as they tended to let their own moral judgements cloud their view. But as she always used to tell her students, it was good to study how a previous generation saw historical events. You learned more about them, and you could better understand your own biases.

It was only when she heard voices and laughter or a shotgun from outside that she left her safe academic world and was brought down to reality. Reality was a confusing place, full of feelings and want. Anxiety too for being attracted to someone outside her age group, and whose family would probably want to kill her.

A barrage of shotgun fire disturbed Bailey yet again. She shut her laptop and rubbed her face with her hands.

She got up and walked over to the open window. Outside on the front lawn she saw one group of the Romantics. They were clay pigeon shooting, and Gracie had told her the other group was around the back of the house learning falconry, so the birds weren't frightened by the guns.

Taylor was with the clay pigeon shoot. Bailey could find her anywhere in a crowd, and of course, wherever Taylor was, Zee was right next to her. Bailey was unsure whether Zee actually liked Taylor or whether she had noticed Bailey's regard for her, and it was a competitive thing.

Bailey was going to find out, though. Tonight, at the ball, she would have a word with her. Bailey might not be able to own up to her feelings, but she'd be damned if she'd let Zee use Taylor.

It was Taylor's turn with the gun. Jamie showed her how to use it, but Taylor didn't look confident. Zee stood behind Taylor and tried to guide her. The sight infuriated Bailey. She wanted to march down there and tell Zee to take her hands off Taylor, but of course she didn't.

To do so would be to open up a can of worms, where everyone could get hurt.

Taylor let off her shot and recoiled in from the noise. She handed her gun back to Jamie and laughed along with her group.

"You're not a hunter, Taylor." Mind you, she had captured Bailey's heart.

Bailey couldn't watch any longer and went back to the safety of the books.

CHAPTER EIGHTEEN

Taylor had a notepad in hand and ran downstairs to the kitchen. It was full of servers and Mrs. Parrot's nieces putting food onto platters, and some of the team were organizing the alcohol to pour in the punchbowls upstairs.

"Mrs. Parrot? Is everything in hand? Do you need anything?"

"Tickety-boo and a half, Miss Taylor."

Taylor smiled. What a quaint phrase. The people out here in Fairydean did feel like they came from a bygone age.

"Great. If you need me, I'll be in the ballroom."

"Right you are," Mrs. Parrot said.

Taylor ran back upstairs to the entrance hall. She was going to lose weight by the time she got back to London, with all the running about she was doing.

She could hear the musicians tuning their instruments in the ballroom. It was getting very real. The ball she had always dreamed about was going to be reality in an hour. Gracie was helping get things ready in the ballroom, and Taylor was on her way there too when she noticed Mr. Bamber and his dancers arriving.

"Mr. Bamber, so nice to see you."

He walked up to her and bowed his head. "*Major* Bamber. We're all in character now."

"Quite right. Nice to see you again, Major."

"It's a pleasure, My Lady."

"Let me show you to the ballroom, Major," Taylor said.

She led him and his dancers into the decorated ballroom. Gracie was talking to the musicians, and the room was busy, with the servers going back and forth from the side room where the buffet would be laid to the tables with drinks in the main ballroom.

She heard the dancers gasp. Some said, "Beautiful, magical."

"My Lady, this is a wonderful room. It will be a pleasure for us to dance in here," Mr. Bamber said.

"I hope so. I've asked my Romantics not to come down until I've sent for them. I would like them to come down and find the ball, the dancing, and the music already started. I think it'll add to the magic of going back in time," Taylor said.

"Marvellous idea. Now, if you'll excuse me, I'd like to go and introduce myself to the musicians. Make sure we're on the same page with dances, and then we'll do a few warm-up dances."

"Good idea. Thank you, Major."

Once he had walked away, Gracie came over to her. "What did Major Sideburns have to say?"

Taylor laughed. "You are going to get caught."

"I think he would take it in good spirit," Gracie said.

"You're probably right."

Gracie clapped her hands together excitedly. "This is it, what you've been waiting for—the ball."

"I know—I'm so nervous," Taylor said.

"Don't be, just enjoy. You created this because you wished it was the way you could fall in love."

"You know, you're very insightful for a younger cousin."

Gracie twirled on the spot. "I like to think so. Now to capture the heart of Bailey. She is your Mr. Darcy, or Colonel Brandon, or Mr.— Who else is there?"

Colonel Brandon. It came to Taylor in a flash. Older, constant, there in the background being gentlemanly. Yes, that's why she'd been listening to her *Sense and Sensibility* audiobook every night.

All the little things Bailey had done since they met that had annoyed her at first—opening doors, carrying bags, insisting on paying for drinks on the train. All of it was done without thought of currying favour. It was just naturally who Bailey was. Zee, on the other hand, pushed through the door first and let it swing back to hit Taylor.

There wasn't any malice in it. Zee was simply too caught up in her own head. Bailey was thinking about Taylor's comfort before her own.

I love her.

This wasn't just a physical attraction or need. Taylor loved her. But Bailey was never going to love her back.

"She's not, Gracie. Let's keep concentrated on the business," Taylor said firmly.

Gracie held her hands up. "Okay, okay, we better go and get ready. I can't wait to see your ballgown."

She would keep her mind on her Romantics. This wasn't about her.

❖

Bailey dusted down her black tailcoat and then made sure her cravat was sitting just right. Taylor hadn't been expecting it, but Bailey texted and asked when she would be ready, as she intended to walk Taylor downstairs to her ball.

Bailey knew how much this night meant to her, and she was determined to do the right thing and be the co-host Taylor needed.

She couldn't put it off any longer. It was time to escort her lady like the gentleman she was pretending to be.

Bailey left her room and walked along the corridor to Taylor's room. She was passed by several excitable ladies going in and out of each other's rooms, to help each other get ready, no doubt.

She was slightly embarrassed when Maisie came out of someone else's room half dressed. Bailey tried to look everywhere but at her. Maisie just laughed at her embarrassment.

"Good evening, My Lord."

Thankfully Maisie went back inside her room. If someone had told Bailey she'd be in this situation, striding to a young woman's bedroom, dressed in Regency fashion to go to a ball, she'd have questioned their sanity.

But here she was. Bit by bit, Taylor Sparks had worn her down and captured her heart. When they got back to London, she would give Taylor a list of former colleagues who could help her going forward, and Bailey could retreat into her study to try to mend her broken heart. It was the right thing to do.

Bailey chapped Taylor's bedroom door. When the door opened, Bailey wasn't quite prepared for the vision that was before her. Taylor wore a duck-egg-blue dress with a lace overlay decorated with flowers and a blue sash around her waist. On her pinned-up hair was a diamond tiara, and even though the stones were imitation, they seemed to sparkle in the light just the same.

"Is there something wrong?" Taylor said.

Bailley bowed her head and took Taylor's hand. "Good evening, My Lady. You look astonishingly beautiful."

Taylor narrowed her eyes. "A compliment? Who are you, and what have you done with the Earl of Richmond I know?"

"I speak nothing but the truth." Bailey smiled and offered her arm.

Taylor took her arm, and they began to walk down the corridor. "I must admit that I thought I'd have to drag you kicking and screaming from your room."

"I said I would play host with you and give you one dance, and I'm happy to do it," Bailey said.

Taylor stopped and pulled her to the side of the corridor. "Look, I'd rather you be bad-tempered than treat this as a sarcastic joke. This is my dream. That ball downstairs is my dream."

"I know that. I'm not treating it like a joke. I want you to enjoy this special night."

Bailey took Taylor's hand and placed it on her chest. "Cross my heart. I'm telling the truth."

Taylor felt connected to Bailey's heart as she looked into her eyes. She wanted to pull Bailey towards her, tell her she loved her, and kiss Bailey until she could feel the same.

But Bailey wouldn't, no matter how long she waited.

"We better go down."

Bailey nodded, and they walked arm in arm downstairs. Taylor gasped when she saw the servers dressed in traditional servants' livery—green and gold tailcoats, knee breeches and tights, and white wigs.

Gracie was at the bottom of the stairs taking a video of her reaction.

"Gracie? How?"

"My little surprise. I know you thought the budget couldn't stretch, so I thought I'd make it my present to you, and the servers love it."

Taylor hopped down the last few steps and hugged her cousin. "Thank you so much. They look wonderful, don't they, Bailey—My Lord."

"They do. Great idea, Gracie."

"Wait till you see the ballroom. Major Sideburns and his crew are dancing just as you wanted," Gracie said.

Taylor heard the music playing and took Bailey's arm. "Let's go and see."

She walked through the ballroom doors and gasped. It was exactly like her dream. A big, bright ballroom full of couples dancing. Taylor felt like Elizabeth Bennet, Marianne Dashwood, and all of Austen's other heroines.

"It's perfect. Just perfect." Taylor spun around in a circle out of pure joy.

Bailey laughed. "Careful you don't fall, My Lady."

"I did it, My Lord, I made my dream come true," Taylor said.

"Shall I get the Romantics down now?" Gracie asked.

"Yes, let's start our ball."

❖

Bailey escorted Lady Catherine into the ballroom. "Oh my. This is—it's taken my breath away. Taylor has made this like a dream."

Bailey looked across the room to where Taylor was talking to Vida and Marcus. "Yes, she has."

Taylor had taken a dream and turned it into reality in such a short time. She really was a remarkable and beautiful person.

She guided Lady Catherine over to the seats at the side of the room. "I believe these are called the chaperones' chairs, Lady Catherine. You can make sure everyone behaves appropriately."

"Don't you worry, My Lord. They'll be no hanky-panky on my watch."

"If you'll excuse me, Lady Catherine, I have to go dance."

"Good luck."

"I'll need it." Bailey bowed to her, then fiddled with her cuffs nervously and went to Taylor.

"My Lady? I am the first on your dance card, I believe."

Taylor smiled. "You are indeed."

Taylor took Bailey's hand, and she led her to the dance floor. Major Bamber noticed they were ready and stood up on the orchestra platform.

He smacked his staff on the ground and called out the dance. "Romantics, we are ready for the first dance. It will be a country dance, so get into your groups of six."

Bailey and Taylor were joined by Dani and Avery, plus a couple from the dance troupe, and the other Romantics made up groups of six all over the ballroom.

"Are you ready for this?" Bailey asked.

"Are you?"

Bailey didn't answer before the music started. They turned to each other and bowed and curtsied. This was it, and Bailey prayed she could get this right, for Taylor's sake.

The group turned back to the circle and held hands. On cue they began to circle, once one way, then the other.

They did that a few times and then crossed their opposite number in a figure eight. Once Bailey had completed hers, the others did the same, returning to their partners. This pattern was repeated and repeated, until the last part of the dance. Bailey put her hand around Taylor's waist and saw her inhale sharply.

They gazed into each other's eyes as they twirled in a circle one way, then the other. Bailey could feel the electricity pulling them together, and each time they parted in the dance, Bailey felt such a great loss.

For the final phase of the dance, Bailey moved behind Taylor, with one hand on Taylor's waist again, while her other held Taylor's hand as Taylor's arm was across her chest, and they spun.

Bailey was so close to Taylor's body, so close to her neck, that her nostrils were filled with Taylor's scent. It was intoxicating. Whatever the scent was, Bailey had been dreaming of it for a long time now.

The spin ended as did the dance, but neither dancer moved. Bailey didn't want to let go and evidently neither did Taylor. In fact, she leaned her head back towards Bailey.

They could have kissed right there and then, but the clapping of the dancers made them jump apart. The first dance was done. Bailey's obligation was done. So she bowed quickly to her partner and walked off as quickly as she could.

CHAPTER NINETEEN

Bailey stalked around the edge of the room. She had been watching too many people dancing with Taylor, especially Zee.

Zee had danced the last three dances with Taylor, and not just dancing—making her laugh, leaning in close, and whispering in her ear. It was torture.

It was her own fault. If she hadn't been so stubborn and had learned some more dances, she could have had Taylor on the floor more herself or cut in when she needed to.

Their opening dance had been *perfect*. Bailey didn't know why she'd been so worried. Everything was so natural about it, and the way they moved together was like they were meant for each other.

Bailey poured out a glass of punch for herself and watched as the couples on the dance floor laughed as someone took a misstep or stood on each other's toes. In between dances, she could see a few couples were already showing an interest in each other.

There had been no stepping on toes where she and Taylor were concerned. Bailey remembered locking eyes with Taylor and never looking away. The dance steps just happened.

In fact it had been like there was no one else in the room. They were dancing just for each other. It was like nothing she'd ever experienced, and then she had to hand Taylor over to others—like Zee Osman.

The current dance finished, and Zee made a great scene of kissing all the way up Taylor's arm. Bailey gulped down her punch and longed for a real drink. Zee walked in her direction, full of swagger and arrogance.

Zee filled a glass of punch and gulped it down, before filling it again.

"Thirsty work."

"I'm sure," Bailey said with annoyance.

"Taylor is a wonderful dancer. You would never have known she hadn't done this kind of dancing before."

"It is the period she loves. Taylor adores everything Jane Austen. It's her world."

"Yeah, we've been talking about that a lot as we danced together. We've had really deep conversations about her life and her childhood. She told me how many times she'd read and re-read the books."

"Quite obviously bullshit," Bailey said.

"Excuse me?"

"Taylor doesn't like to read novels," Bailey said flatly.

"What? Why?"

Bailey took a sip of punch. "That is not my confidence to divulge."

"Anyway, I must have misheard. She meant TV and films," Zee blustered.

This was Bailey's chance to have the quiet word she'd wanted to. "Zee, what exactly are your plans towards Taylor?"

Zee looked around to her sharply and laughed. "You are seriously asking my intentions?"

"If that's how you want to take it. You are what I would call, in Regency terms, a rake. We both know you aren't the settling-down type."

Zee pointed her finger at her. "You know nothing about me. You're just jealous that I am winning the race. I know how much you want her, anyone can see it, but face it, you're too old, and I am the perfect age."

Zee began to walk away, and Bailey caught her arm. "Taylor is not a prize to be won in a race."

Zee pulled her arm away. "Good evening, My Lord. I'll go and spend some time with your wife."

Bailey slammed her cup down and walked briskly out of the ballroom to the library. She slammed the door shut and pulled off her tailcoat. Lady Catherine had drinks decanters in the corner of the room, and that's where she headed to pour herself a drink.

She hoped the burning liquid would numb the torrent of feelings inside her. Anger, jealousy, hate, and love. A love that was tearing her soul apart.

How could she survive this?

❖

Taylor finished the dance, Mr. Beveridge's Maggot, with her group and clapped in applause. It was a popular dance that made everyone laugh, due to its funny name. She looked over at Gracie who signalled it was time for the buffet to start in the adjoining room.

"Everyone? If you can follow Gracie through next door, the food is served."

"Yes, I'm famished," Dani said.

"Off you go then. I'll just get His Lordship." Taylor was enjoying her little joke. It made her laugh, and it also kind of felt nice that they were married in this elaborate fantasy.

As the room emptied, Taylor looked all around for Bailey but didn't see her. Lady Catherine was being escorted through to the buffet by Avery.

She stopped them and asked, "Have you seen Bailey, Lady Catherine?"

"No, my dear. I haven't seen her in quite a while."

"I'll find her. Thanks."

I bet she's in that bloody library, hiding.

Taylor marched out of the ballroom straight across the entrance hall and burst into the library.

There was no light in the room except from the fireplace. Bailey was leaning against the mantel, shirt and waistcoat undone, just like last night, with a glass of something in her hand.

"This is where you've been hiding," Taylor said.

"I have not been hiding."

Taylor walked over to her. "Of course you have. You've been hiding in here all weekend."

Bailey moved over to the drinks table and poured out a top up to her whiskey.

"I escorted you in, took part in the first dance as I promised. My job was done, and I wanted a real drink. The punch is like a child's drink."

Bailey hadn't turned back around to face her.

"What is your problem? One dance was all I asked, and you've made such a big deal out of it. Everyone else has been making a fool of themselves, standing on toes, falling down in a few cases, but it was all in good fun. Why couldn't you have just taken part and had fun?"

Bailey spun around and said with what appeared to be a mixture of passion and anger, "Because just one dance would never be enough. That's why I didn't want to do it. I didn't want to be close to the woman who has captured my heart, body, and soul."

Taylor was shocked to hear Bailey opening up about her feelings. She'd hoped Bailey might be attracted to her or falling for her, but this was not what she had hoped for. Why was Bailey so angry?

Bailey started to pace. "You captured a heart I didn't want to give away. The heart I couldn't give to Ellis."

"What? What do you mean? She was your wife—you must have loved her."

Bailey stopped pacing and covered her face with her hands. "As my best friend, not as a lover, a partner, a true wife. When we were young students, we made a pact that we'd get married if we were both single by the time we were forty. I was a couple of years older than Ellis and had forgotten all about it, but when she turned forty, she reminded me of our pact. I was happy being single. I saw no need for marriage or commitment. It never worked for my parents, but when I saw the pain in Ellis's eyes—I had to do the right thing."

"Why was she in pain?"

"Because she told me that she'd been in love with me since we were teenagers, and that was why her relationships never turned out well. I wasn't in love with her, but I loved her with the deepest friendship, and I wanted to make her happy."

Taylor brought her hand to her mouth. She was shocked by what she heard. The kindness and the care Bailey had shown her friend was remarkable. Tears started to well up in her eyes.

"I tried to love her the way she wanted. I tried every time I kissed her, every time I made love to her, but then you came along and just took my heart without even trying. I feel guilt because of that. I fell in love with the one person I can't," Bailey said.

Taylor grasped Bailey's loose shirt and pulled her towards her. "Why can't you? And don't say because of the age thing."

"Of course it's the age thing. Everyone, including your family, would think I was lecherous and old."

Taylor was getting annoyed and angry at Bailey now. It should be a happy thing that Bailey had fallen for her.

"I'm not seventeen. I'm twenty-six. You do realize I could be married with four kids by this age."

Bailey pulled Taylor's head to hers, so their foreheads were leaning on each other. "I want you so much. I love the way you smell. I want to taste you, become lost in you."

Bailey's breathing was heavy.

"Yes, I want you too," Taylor said. "You've always known that."

But Bailey pulled away quickly and said, "No, it's impossible."

Taylor replied, "Stop trying to be so fucking noble and trying to say what's best for me."

Baily turned and gave her a searing hot look, and then before Taylor could think, Bailey's lips were on hers. Taylor grasped at her neck and dug her fingernails in. It was as if they had held their passion at bay so long, it now was pouring out like a tidal wave.

Bailey's hand was pulling up Taylor's dress, so she could touch her thigh. Bailey squeezed Taylor's thigh and moaned when she felt Taylor only wore a G-string. She then grasped hold of Taylor's buttock.

Taylor was soaking wet. Bailey's touch was so much better than her fantasy. She reached down and grasped Bailey's strap-on. Bailey stopped her frantic kissing.

"How did you know?"

"I couldn't miss it, and I'm sure others haven't either. It made me so hot."

Taylor leaned forward to whisper in Bailey's ear, "Feel what it does to me."

She guided Bailey's hand to her sex, and Bailey groaned. "Jesus Christ."

Bailey lifted Taylor around her waist and carried her over to the library table, while continuing to kiss her frantically.

It was akin to being denied water for years and suddenly being able to drink from a fresh, clear waterfall. She allowed herself to inhale the scent of Taylor's neck and finally taste it.

She first kissed her neck, and then licked the sweet, sweet taste of her skin. Taylor moaned and pulled Bailey's trousers closer to her and began fiddling with the infuriatingly difficult to undo buttons.

Bailey kissed from Taylor's neck down to her cleavage. She'd dreamed about this dress no longer being a barrier between them and her lips loving Taylor's breasts.

But cold water was poured on her dreams when Taylor suddenly said, "Stop."

Bailey took a step back immediately. She was breathing hard. "What's wrong? Did I do something?"

Taylor grasped her hand. "No, no. Remember the rule of Regency Romance Club—no sexual intimacy."

"Seriously? But you're not one of the Romantics, you're the organizer, the boss of this business."

Taylor's hand was shaking. It had been so hard to stop. "But we're taking part, we're both part of it. How would it look if I fell at the first hurdle?"

"Okay, okay."

Taylor grasped Bailey's shirt again and let one hand slip under and touch her skin. "We mustn't, *mustn't* let ourselves succumb to this need for each other. It's against the rules."

Bailey lifted Taylor's free hand and placed soft, tender kisses over it. "You don't want to break the rules now, do you?"

The question in Bailey's voice matched the question inside Taylor. Not only did she want Bailey so much, but the fact that it was against the rules made her want her all the more.

Taylor pulled Bailey close again. "It would be wrong."

"Terrible, impossible."

"Yes, impossible. Definitely out of the question."

Taylor's words did not match the aching want inside her. All of a sudden she pulled Bailey towards her and kissed her deeply.

Then Taylor pulled away again. "I'm sorry, I'm sorry."

Bailey cupped her cheeks and said, "Don't be sorry. This way of doing things is important to you, so let's just go back to the ball and be with your Romantics."

"Thank you for understanding," Taylor said.

Bailey began buttoning her shirt and waistcoat. "Don't be silly. I got to tell the woman of my dreams how I felt about her."

Taylor helped retie her cravat and put her tailcoat back on.

"You meant it?" Taylor asked.

"You know I did." Bailey offered her arm and said, "Shall we return to your ball?"

Taylor took it, and from then on it was like she floated on air right through to the ballroom.

The room was filled with happiness and laughter. Major Bamber's dancers really did create a good atmosphere and hold the event together.

They stopped beside Gracie, and Bailey said, "Would you excuse me a moment, My Lady?"

"Yes, hurry back."

Once she was away, Gracie said, "Wow, there's a change in you both. Have you gotten it together finally?"

For some reason Taylor didn't want to share it with anyone yet. Not when they weren't on any kind of firm ground yet.

"No, we're just enjoying each other's company."

Gracie chuckled. "Yeah, I believe you—thousands wouldn't."

Bailey arrived back just as the orchestra started to play.

"Would you have room on your dance card for one more, My Lady?"

"If there isn't, there is now. You're in charge, Gracie."

Taylor couldn't take her eyes of Bailey as they took their positions, bowed, and curtsied. Major Bamber couldn't have picked a nicer dance for the last dance of the event.

It allowed couples to be quite close, and at the moment that was all that Taylor wanted.

CHAPTER TWENTY

Taylor was pleased to see Vida and Maisie hand in hand, as they walked up the stairs in front of her and Bailey.

She held Bailey's arm tightly. Taylor was still on the cloud of air that she had been earlier. Bailey loved her, and she loved Bailey, although she hadn't told Bailey that yet. Not that she was holding back—there just hadn't been the right moment. They had been pretty busy kissing at the time.

Vida and Maisie were the last Romantics downstairs. They were eager for the evening not to end, but the intimacy rules meant they couldn't join each other in their rooms.

Taylor had so very nearly broken those rules. In fact, she had broken them. Kissing, licking, and biting would qualify as intimacy, even by the most generous of judges. But she had stopped it before it went too far.

"Goodnight, Earl and Countess of Richmond," Vida said.

"Goodnight to both of you," Taylor said.

Bailey said her goodnights and watched as Vida kissed Maisie's hand and went to her own room.

"That's the way we should be handling things," Taylor said.

Bailey walked Taylor to her door. "We were overcome with emotion, and we stopped. It was just a raw emotional event."

"But I'm trying to create the Regency. They couldn't have become overcome with emotion. Reputation was everything."

Bailey rolled her eyes. "Do you honestly think people, young people, didn't get overcome with emotion? There were hastily arranged marriages, babies being adopted to local families, women and girls being sent away to Europe for a year, and being forced to come back, and act as if nothing had happened. It wasn't just the poor who had to give up unplanned babies, but whether the high or the low end of society, it was women who bore the cost of becoming overcome with emotion."

"I suppose you're right. I have to keep reminding myself that my precious Jane Austen stories put on an idealized version of the Regency. But"—Taylor poked her finger into Bailey's chest and then pointed down—"at least we wouldn't have those problems, unless that thing has magical powers."

Bailey laughed. "No, not quite. Well, I better say goodnight, My Lady."

She kissed her hand.

"Goodnight, My Lord."

Taylor had to watch Bailey walk away. She wanted to shout *Stop, don't go*, but she couldn't.

She went into her room and locked the door. The room felt so empty without Bailey there. Taylor had been through the wringer of emotions tonight, and her head was a mess.

Just get ready for bed. One thing at time.

Taylor sat at the dressing table and started to unpin her hair. It came down in lovely ringlets, because of the way it had been pinned up.

She began to brush her hair out when she noticed a big, old fashioned key on her dressing table. It had a label attached to string on it.

It read: *To be used if needed. True love should be nurtured and cherished.*

"What?"

Then she looked up at the interconnecting door behind the chair. It led to Bailey's room. "Lady Catherine, you're not making this easy."

She was such a sweet older woman. But Taylor couldn't use the key. The rules would be broken if she went through with it. "Just go to bed."

❖

Bailey kicked off her boots and took off her tailcoat, then went to lie on her bed. She was thinking, overthinking really, about what had come between her and Taylor. She had let the genie out of the bottle and told Taylor she loved her, and there was no going back on that.

Down here, in this fantasy, away from the harsh realities of London, the problems of any relationship seemed less intense. In any case, Bailey had tried and tried to repress her feelings, but she just couldn't do it any longer.

But somewhere deep inside, she had the feeling she was going to be broken-hearted in the end, perhaps when Taylor realized she needed someone her own age. But there was no changing how she felt, especially now that she had tasted Taylor's lips and her neck.

Bailey had dreamed of kissing Taylor's neck ever since they had first shared a hug. She touched her fingers to her lips and remembered how soft Taylor's lips were, how good her perfume smelled. It was intoxicating.

She jumped when she heard the noise of a key in a lock, but it wasn't coming from her door, it was coming from the other side of the room, from the interconnecting door Mr. Parrot said had been locked for years.

Bailey walked over a few steps and waited for the door to open. It couldn't be Taylor. How would she have a key?

The door slowly opened to reveal a nervous looking Taylor.

"Taylor? How—"

"Lady Catherine left a key on my dressing table. Seems like she wants to help us be together."

"Is that what you want?" Bailey's heart thudded, waiting for her response.

"I was thinking about it, and technically we are playing a married couple, aren't we?" Taylor said nervously.

Bailey crooked her finger and beckoned Taylor over. Taylor closed the door and followed Bailey's lead. Bailey could visibly tell how nervous Taylor was. Her lips were parted, and her breathing was harder than normal.

Bailey turned Taylor around and pulled her as close as possible. Bailey leaned in to her ear whispered, "Is this what you want, My Lady?"

Taylor shivered at the touch of Bailey's breath in her ear. Taylor rubbed her arm when it erupted in goosebumps, which turned Bailey on so much. Her body wanted to love Taylor everywhere and quickly.

But Bailey was going to take her time and make Taylor feel totally loved. She whispered again, "Is this what you want?"

Taylor reached up and softly scratched her nails on Bailey's neck. "This isn't an overcome with emotion thing, is it? Like downstairs?"

Bailey let her breath graze Taylor's ear, and she said, "You have to make the decision. It is all kinds of wrong. It's breaking your rules, we're sneaking behind everyone's backs, and your family will go wild probably. So tell me what you want, My Lady?"

"I want you, My Lord."

Bailey's sex was pounding as the same rate as her heart. Staying in this fantasy was a turn on for her. "You do?"

"Yes."

Bailey wrapped her arms around Taylor's waist and untied her silky dressing gown. She slowly slipped it off and threw it on the bed. Now Taylor's shoulders were bare, just how Bailey liked them.

She threaded her fingers into Taylor's hair and pulled it back in a bunch. "I love your hair, and I adore your neck."

Bailey kissed Taylor, and she gasped.

"Do you like breaking rules, Taylor?"

"No, I never do, but I like breaking the rules with you."

Taylor began to turn around, but Bailey stopped her. "Not yet. Remember the concept of the boiled sweet?"

Taylor nodded.

"Slow," Bailey breathed in her ear.

She pulled up Taylor's nightie inch by inch. When it was past her buttocks, Taylor pushed back against her crotch and her strap-on.

That made Bailey pull the nightdress more quickly, and she threw it to the floor.

"Don't turn around, not yet."

Taylor moaned as Bailey grazed her neck with her teeth. Bailey couldn't believe she had Taylor naked in her harms, something she had fought for so long. She wanted to enjoy every moment.

Bailey put her hands on Taylor's hips and indulged herself with grinding into her buttocks.

"God, you feel so good. I want you in every way."

Taylor turned her head to the side and pulled Bailey into a kiss.

Bailey's hands moved around from her hips and swept up her stomach. Taylor took Bailey's hands and guided them up to her breasts. They both moaned when Bailey cupped and squeezed them.

They were just the right size for Bailey's hands. "You are perfect. I can't wait to taste them with my tongue."

"Yes, yes."

"Turn around." Bailey finally had to see all of her.

Bailey was enraptured when Taylor turned around. She trailed her fingers between her breasts and down to her stomach.

"You are so beautiful."

Taylor kissed hard and started to pull at her shirt.

"No, not yet. Go and lie on the bed."

Taylor did as she asked and lay down. Bailey couldn't take her eyes off Taylor. She was simply the most beautiful woman she had ever seen.

Bailey popped the buttons on her shirt and took it off. Bailey always kept fit, and was in good condition for her age, but she hoped Taylor wasn't disappointed.

Taylor made all fears disappear in an instant when she looked at her and said, "I love you, Bailey."

Bailey kept her loosened trousers on and walked over to the bed. She lay on top of Taylor and with her mouth inches from Taylor's whispered, "I don't know what I've done to deserve that love."

Taylor reached up and stroked Bailey's face. "You are you, Bailey. You are courteous, kind, thoughtful, and the sexiest woman I have ever met. Do you know how many times I've thought about this moment? Fantasized about it?"

"You have?" Bailey lowered her lips to a hair's breadth from Taylor's. "What did you do when you thought about us together?"

Bailey was surprised when, without hesitation, Taylor circled her own nipples with the tips of her fingers. They went rock-hard, and Bailey had to force herself to stop being impulsive and closing her lips around one of Taylor's hard nipples.

Taylor then palmed her breast. "This is what I wanted you to do, and this." She reached down and slipped her two fingers into her own wet sex. At the first touch of her clit, Taylor groaned.

"You've been thinking about us like this?"

Taylor looked into Bailey's eyes and said honestly, "Every time I close my eyes."

That answer broke Bailey's resilience. She pulled Taylor's hand away from her sex and held it above her head, before Bailey's lips met hers in a deep and passionate kiss.

Through the kiss, Bailey mumbled, "I'm…going to make…you come." Bailey's kiss moved onto her breast, and Bailey sucked her nipple into her mouth.

"Oh God," Taylor gasped.

She gripped Bailey's short hair and dug her fingers into her scalp. If she was being too rough, Bailey never said. In fact, it spurred her on.

Bailey released her nipple with a pop. "Every time I closed my eyes, you were in my head too. It was so hard to resist you."

Taylor cupped her cheek. "You don't have to any more."

"I'm going to have you every way I can, and never stop touching you."

Bailey slipped her fingers into her wetness and split her fingers around Taylor's clit. Taylor's nerves were jumping, and she was frightened of losing control She pulled Bailey into a kiss, while Bailey moved her fingers up and down around her clit.

Her excitement was running away with her, but the dull ache she had lower down needed to be filled.

"Inside, Bailey, I'm desperate for you to be inside."

Bailey teased her by circling her opening with her fingers.

"Don't tease me. I need it."

"Patience, My Lady."

"No, no. I can't. I'm shaking," Taylor said.

After calling for patience, Taylor was taken by surprise when Bailey slipped two fingers deep inside her.

"Bailey, yes."

Bailey went from rubbing the tips of her fingers on the inside of her walls, to long deep thrusts. Both satisfied that deep ache. When Taylor came, she knew it was going to be deep and overwhelming.

She held on to Bailey's shoulders and kept trying in some way to pull Bailey in deeper. Taylor knew what she wanted.

Taylor reached down to the bulge in Bailey's crotch. "Bailey, can you come with this?"

"Yeah," Bailey said. "Do you want to try it?"

"Yes." Taylor placed desperate kisses all over Bailey's face. "I want to feel filled, and I want you as close as possible, My Lord."

Bailey groaned and pulled her strap-on free from her britches. "You are such a bad girl."

Taylor gazed up into her eyes and whispered, "I know. We shouldn't even be doing this."

Taylor knew the breaking of the rules was making them both hot. "I know."

Bailey placed her strap-on at Taylor's entrance and pushed it in, inch by inch. "Jesus, you've taken it all."

Taylor pulled Bailey's head down and whispered, "Fuck me, My Lord."

Bailey gave her an instant gaze of fiery passion. Bailey held Taylor's wrists loosely over her head and began to thrust long and slow.

Taylor loved the look of utter pleasure and losing control on Bailey's face.

It was becoming too much for Taylor. She needed to come. Taylor pulled her wrist free from Bailey's and reached for her clit.

"No, come with me," Bailey moaned.

Bailey sat up more and put Taylor's legs over her shoulders. Taylor was not expecting that, but immediately understood why Bailey chose this position.

"It's so deep."

Bailey held her thighs and thrust her hips faster and faster. All that could be heard in the room, apart from their moans, was slapping flesh. It was so intense Taylor couldn't do anything apart from throwing her arms back and allowing the torrent of her orgasm crash through her body.

She grasped one of the brass bars at the headboard and held on tightly, as if she was in danger of being washed away.

Taylor gave a deep moan and closed her eyes tight, as she let go of all the pent-up tension in her body. It was all she could do to breathe properly.

When she opened her eyes, she saw Bailey throwing back her head, while she thrust faster, and then let out a guttural groan.

They fell together in a tangle of limbs, until Bailey laid her head across Tylor's chest, trying to get her breathing back.

Taylor stroked her hair. "I love you, sweetheart."

Bailey threaded her fingers through Taylor's. "I love you, no matter what."

No matter what.

CHAPTER TWENTY-ONE

Bailey started to wake from her sleep to the sound of banging. She smiled when she remembered what she and Taylor had shared last night. Bailey reached out and found a cold side of the bed.

She's gone. She knew it was a mistake.

The banging noise continued to echo in the room. She raised herself up on her elbow and saw Taylor. She hadn't left. And she was the source of the banging.

But what was she doing?

She was bouncing up and down into a press up and continuing one after another.

"What the hell are you doing?"

Taylor stopped immediately, and her face was wreathed in smiles.

"You're awake! Finally." Taylor smiled.

Bailey beckoned her over. "Come here."

Taylor jumped onto the bed, grasped Bailey's face, and placed kisses all over.

"You're lively in the morning." Bailey rolled Taylor onto her back.

"Once I'm awake, I'm awake. I can't lie in bed, and I didn't want to wake you. I usually go on my spin bike in the morning."

"How on earth am I going to keep up with an energetic twenty-six year old, with ADHD?"

"I'll keep you young." Taylor stroked her cheek. "You haven't changed your mind, have you?"

"Would I be lying here like this if I had? Do you have any concerns? You can, you know," Bailey said.

"I do, but I don't know if it'll upset you."

"You can ask me anything."

Taylor pushed her onto her back and leaned over her. "Can I ask about Ellis?"

Bailey pursed her lips and nodded.

"What was she like?"

"Kindness itself. We met on our first day at university. I was lost, and she helped me find where I was going. We were best friends since then. I never realized she was in love with me. When she told me, everything in me wanted to say the same, but I had to lie."

"You didn't lie. You did love her. You showed so much love in caring for her the way you did."

"Not the right kind of love," Bailey said.

"There is no right kind. We love every person differently. I've loved girlfriends before, but nothing like this." Taylor put her hand on Bailey's chest "This love is a deep, passionate, all-consuming love. Something I've never felt in my life."

Bailey put her hand on top of Taylor's. "Ellis would have liked you. You both love without fear. You know, near the end, when she was still conscious, she told me to find someone who would make me happy, love me—and I've found her."

Taylor pressed her lips to Bailey's, opened her mouth, and ever so softly ran her tongue around Bailey's lips.

"Ah," Bailey flipped her on her back again. "You have intoxicated me, you know."

"Me?" Taylor pretended to be innocent.

"Yes, you. I thought my sex drive had packed up for good, and now I'm hungry for you. I feel like I'm twenty-one again."

Taylor laughed. "Good. I've dreamed of this for months and had fantasies for months."

"Oh you have, have you? Tell me more." Bailey gave her kisses over her face and neck as she spoke.

"Well, we're in your study, you see, and…"

❖

Taylor glanced up to the top of the table and caught Bailey's eye. They shared a secret smile as they had since they'd arrived down to breakfast.

Upstairs they'd agreed to play the married couple to the full, so as to hopefully cover any signs that they had been up to anything.

It added some extra excitement to be breaking the intimacy rules and share in the secret of their love. Bailey stood up and announced to the table, "Excuse me, Romantics all. I'm just going for a morning ride. I'm sure my wife will keep you very well entertained."

There was laughter from around the table. Bailey winked at her before leaving the room. Taylor was so caught up in watching her that she hadn't heard Maisie ask a question.

"Sorry?"

"It's supper and cards tonight, isn't it?" Masie asked.

"Yes, and perhaps a few poetry readings. Zee has promised to give us a reading, haven't you, Zee?"

Zee who was sitting a few chairs down said, "Yes, My Lady. Always happy to perform."

"How are you enjoying it so far, Maisie?"

"I'm loving it. Such a wonderful idea. It's like stepping into a happy world of my dreams. Manners, dancing, Regency pastimes. It's been wonderful, and I...no, it doesn't matter," Masie said.

"You like Vida, don't you?"

"Is it obvious?"

They both looked down the table to where Vida was chatting with Marcus. "Just a bit. She likes you very much, I think."

"I was hoping. Vida's so tough, mentally strong, but so caring and sweet. She always thinks of me and makes sure I have everything I need. When I danced with her, it felt like a dream."

Taylor knew that feeling. She clasped her hand. "Enjoy your time and have fun together."

"I will."

Zee came to sit beside Taylor. "Bailey seems happier this morning."

"She does, doesn't she? Maybe Bailey's mellowing."

"Bailey? Mellow? Let's see if it lasts the day."

Taylor loved having their little secret. It was theirs and it was special.

❖

Taylor needed to see Bailey. Really needed to see her. They had been apart since after breakfast, and now her Romantics were occupied, enjoying a walk in the forest, led by Dani, of course. Taylor took a chance to try and find Bailey.

She checked her room, her favourite place in the library—nothing.

It was a few hours since Bailey'd gone horse riding. She couldn't still be out, so Taylor decided to go and ask Jamie. He had an office at the stables and might have seen where she went.

As she entered the stable yard, she saw Jamie hurrying out of his office. "Jamie, have you seen Bailey?"

"Yeah, she's just stabled her horse. Excuse me but I'll have to run. There's a young deer caught in a fence out in the grounds."

"Oh no. I hope it's all right."

"We'll get it out. John!" He shouted over to a man who was sweeping up in the stable yard. "Let's go."

"Good luck, Jamie."

The two men jumped into a Jeep and drove off quickly.

Taylor walked over to the stable and popped her head in. She saw Bailey patting the nose of a brown horse.

"There you are."

Bailey looked around and smiled. "Hi, I thought you'd still be busy."

Taylor walked up beside Bailey and stroked the horse's neck. "Dani's taken them all out on a ramble."

"Good old Dani." Bailey pulled Taylor by the hand to a stall. The floor was covered in straw, and a thick wooden pole crossed the centre of the stall and had a saddle sitting over it.

Taylor smiled as Bailey manoeuvred her up against the wall. "You were out riding for a long time."

Bailey kissed her and in between kisses said, "I couldn't get you, or what you told me this morning, out of my head. I wasn't going to sit in the library with thoughts of what I wanted to do to you in my head."

Taylor clasped her hands around Bailey's neck. "Jamie and the stable guy left, but what if someone else comes in here? We shouldn't."

Bailey kissed her neck. "I want you."

"But we could be caught."

Bailey grinned, and then Taylor did too. "Hmm, I love the way you think."

"I love you in these dresses." Bailey pulled up the hem of Taylor's dress so she could grasp her thigh.

Taylor tried to undo Bailey's britches, but Bailey pushed her hand away and fell to her knees.

"What are you doing?"

Bailey smiled and bunched up the hem of her dress. "Hold this."

"Someone will catch us."

Bailey handed her the dress and Taylor took it. The look of want and nervousness on Taylor's face turned Bailey on so much, and she couldn't wait to taste her.

Bailey pulled down Taylor's underwear and saw how wet Taylor was. She kissed around Taylor's thighs and sex before opening her up and teasing Taylor's clit with the tip of her tongue.

Taylor's hands came down and held onto her head.

"Don't tease me. Please? Anyone could come in."

Bailey lapped at her clit in rhythm, occasionally running her tongue around Taylor's opening.

Taylor's orgasm was building up quickly, and Bailey chuckled to herself as Taylor tried to keep her moaning from becoming too loud.

"I'm going to come, going to come," Taylor moaned anxiously.

Just before Taylor did, Bailey slipped two fingers inside while she continued to lick her clit.

Taylor grabbed Bailey's hair, and her body went stiff. Then she let go and tried to regain her breath. Bailey stood up and kissed her deeply.

"You are bad, My Lord."

"Extremely, My Lady."

❖

"Okay, everyone," Taylor said, "if you all have a drink in hand, then we'll begin. Zee has kindly offered to give us our first reading from Shakespeare's sonnets."

This evening after a light supper, the Romantics played some cards and enjoyed good conversation. Everyone was full of chat about the deer that was rescued from a fence this afternoon.

The ramble had come across Jamie, and everyone helped to get the deer out and running away happily. The whole group had been quite uplifted and excited by the whole thing.

Taylor came to sit beside Lady Catherine, as Zee began to recite her sonnet.

"You look happy tonight, Taylor."

"I am happy. Everything's gone perfectly this weekend," Taylor said.

Lady Catherine glanced back to where Bailey was sitting quietly with a book. Bailey smiled at them.

"I think you know what I mean."

Taylor leaned in and whispered to Lady Catherine, "I wonder who could have left a certain key on my dressing table?"

Lady Catherine acted surprised. "A key? Maybe it was the fairies? They do have the run of the house."

Taylor laughed softly. "Thank you for everything. We are very happy, but it's top secret."

"Mum's the word."

CHAPTER TWENTY-TWO

It was so strange to be back in London, back in real life. The taxi dropped Taylor off first, and Bailey promised they could see each other tomorrow. Taylor dropped her bag on her bedroom floor, then flopped onto her bed.

What a weekend it had been. She and her Romantics had stepped back in time, and everything had gone like a dream. There were even a few couples starting to form.

Then there was Bailey. She couldn't have dared to dream that Bailey would admit there was something between them or, even more remarkable, that she would act on it.

Taylor let out a sigh of happy contentment. She had never felt like this in a relationship before, never so easily compatible with a partner, physically most of all.

Sex had always been just all right, mostly awkward and clumsy. But with Bailey, everything just flowed. It was passionate, needy, and Bailey had made her come like she never had before.

Was it because Bailey was older, or that they were just so compatible? Whatever it was, Taylor was happy, happier than she could remember.

Her phone rang, and she assumed that it was Bailey, but it was Eddie. Taylor answered the video call.

"Hello?"

"You sound disappointed. Were you expecting someone else?"

"Don't be silly. How's the leg?"

"Sore, annoying. Max is being an angel, doing everything for me, and I'm secretly lapping it up."

"So you're sitting on the couch like a king, and he's running around getting you everything and making you comfortable?" Taylor said.

"Yes. So, how did the weekend go?"

"It went perfectly. It was my dream ball and everyone enjoyed it. Lady Catherine made it special."

"She sounds like a nice lady who's helped you out a lot," Eddie said.

"Oh, she is. Charged us next to nothing and gave us the use of her staff. She's told us to come back next year, she enjoyed it so much."

"Excellent, and Sexy Prof?"

Taylor could feel her cheeks heat up. She was never embarrassed telling Ed anything, but she was this time. Maybe it was that she was so serious about Bailey. And maybe she was worried about what her brothers would say about the age gap. Her brothers had always been protective of her and were bound to have some concerns.

"Yeah, Bailey was fine."

"I know that look."

"What look?" Taylor asked.

"The I'm so much in love and have just had brilliant sex look."

Taylor giggled nervously. She couldn't speak too openly about relationships and sex with her other two brothers. But she and Eddie had a special kind of relationship where they could tell each other anything.

"Okay, yes. We talked about our feelings while we were away, and we're together."

Eddie clapped his hands fast in excitement. "I knew it. Is she everything you'd hoped she'd be?"

"Yes, and then some."

At that point little Jaden walked into the camera. "Jaden, it's Auntie Taylor."

He waved and shouted, "Tay-Tay."

"Hi, sweetheart. I miss you."

Eddie pulled him up onto the couch beside him. "What was it like? I want every detail."

"Not in front of my sweet little nephew. But are you okay about it? I thought you, Luke, and Tommy would be worried about the age difference."

"They might, but not me. As long as you're happy, and she makes you happy, that's all that I care about."

Taylor smiled. "I wish I could hug you."

"Why don't you bring her for dinner on Friday night if you're free."

"That would be lovely, but don't tell Mum and Mama. I think they're going to need some time to get used to the idea. Oh, and don't tell Luke or Tommy yet."

"I won't, and don't worry. It'll just take our mums time to get used to it, but they'll get there."

"Fingers crossed."

Secretly Taylor was dreading it.

❖

The days dragged on until Bailey saw Taylor again. Bailey had thought of nothing apart from Taylor the whole time they were parted. But tonight was the night.

Bailey had invited Taylor over for dinner, and Bailey was cooking. She hadn't cooked a meal for someone since Ellis was alive. She hoped that Ellis had been telling truth and this wasn't going to be a big let-down for Taylor.

Bailey looked into the oven to check her piece of roast beef. It was doing nicely. Then she heard the doorbell and her heart began to thud. Bailey hurried to the door and opened it to find Taylor with a bottle of wine and something in her shopping bag.

"Hi." Bailey was nervous and felt a little tongue-tied, like she was a teenager on her first date.

"Hi, can I come in?" Taylor asked.

"Oh yes, sorry. Come in. Here, let me take that." Bailey took the wine and the bag so that Taylor could take her jacket off. Taylor hung it on the coat rack by the door.

"I've missed you so much." Taylor threw her arms around her and kissed her deeply.

Bailey forgot just how good Taylor's kisses were, but if she let herself enjoy the kiss too much, they'd go straight to bed and miss out on everything else, like the romance she knew Taylor wanted so much.

She pulled out of the kiss and whispered into Taylor's ear, "Not yet. Later, naughty girl."

"You make it so very hard." Taylor kissed along Bailey's jawline.

She was so close to giving in, but she resisted. "Be good."

"If you insist. Mmm. Something smells nice."

"I hope you'll like it."

"I like it already. Nobody's ever made me dinner before. I mean, this will be the first meal a girlfriend's made me."

"Girlfriend?" Bailey laughed. "I'm too old to be a girlfriend."

"No one's too old to be a girlfriend. What should I refer to you as then? Because there's no way I'm referring to you as a friend. Partner? Partner sounds like we've been together a long time. What about my latest squeeze, my woman of the moment?"

"Okay, okay, girlfriend then. Come through to the kitchen."

"The wine is for you, by the way. I brought some Weird watermelon."

"Thank you for the wine. You should try some—you might like it as much as Weird watermelon. You never know." Bailey put Taylor's bottles in the fridge.

"I'm always up for trying something new," Taylor said.

Bailey chuckled. "Good to know."

Taylor sat down at the kitchen table. It was a warm, modern kitchen. It looked as if it had been decorated recently.

"The kitchen's lovely. Did you have it done recently?" Taylor asked.

"Last year. After I lost Ellis it took me a while to even think about these kinds of things. But once I did, I wanted to do everything I'd put off over the years, because I realized you never know what's around the corner. I did the kitchen first. Then I did the bedrooms and the drawing room and the TV room. I wanted everything new."

"I can understand that." Taylor's heart ached for what Bailey had been through.

"The only thing that's the same is my study. It's just as my father left it. It's always been my place of sanctuary, where I've spent time with my books and writing. I didn't want to change that."

Bailey brought over the bottle of red wine Taylor brought and two glasses.

"So what's for dinner?" Taylor asked.

"Roast beef and all the trimmings."

"Wow, you didn't have to go to all that trouble during the week, and for me."

"It's a pleasure to have someone to cook for. Now, take a drink," Bailey said.

Bailey handed her a wine glass, and she sniffed it suspiciously, then took a sip. Taylor screwed up her face, and Bailey laughed.

"That bad was it?"

"I'm going to reserve judgement until I finish the glass," Taylor said.

"Very fair-minded. Now I'll go and get dinner together."

"Can't wait."

❖

Taylor put down her knife and fork and rubbed her stomach. "That was amazing."

Bailey had finished her plate a while ago, but Taylor had gone back a few times for second helpings of meat, roast potatoes, and Yorkshire puddings.

She could only smile as Taylor wolfed down her food. It felt nice to share a meal again with someone, and someone who was so appreciative of the food.

"Don't tell my mum, but that might be on par or slightly nicer than my mama's roast beef dinner."

"That's high praise indeed, I'm sure."

"It is, believe me. You might have to give me some time before I can move again," Taylor said.

"I don't know where you put it all. You have a great figure."

"I use up a lot of energy. Exercising, walking, my spin bike."

"Why don't we leave the dishes and take our drinks through to the drawing room. There's a big comfortable couch there you can lie back on."

"Sounds perfect."

"Can I get you another watermelon?" Bailey asked.

"Yes, please."

Bailey led her through to the drawing room, and Taylor gasped.

"You have a real fire."

"Yes, I thought you'd like it. I lit it before you arrived so that there would be a good blaze for you."

Taylor walked straight to the fire and warmed her hands in front of it. "It's perfect."

Bailey was quite proud of the room. It was a mixture of the old and the modern. On the main wall was a huge TV. Bailey loved to watch documentaries and films while relaxing on the couch.

The couch was L-shaped and ran the length of the wall facing the

TV, and around the corner. It was as comfortable as a bed, and many times Bailey had fallen asleep here.

Bailey sat and patted the seat. "Come and sit down."

She put on some music and they just enjoyed each other's company for a while.

Taylor sat beside Bailey and folded her legs up under her. She was nervous. She was going to ask Bailey if she would come to dinner with her brother, and she was frightened she'd say no. This had been going around and around her head since they sat down.

Just ask.

"Bailey? I..."

"What?" Bailey stroked her hair away from her face.

Instead of asking, she leaned closer and said, "I've missed you so much, My Lord, since we got home."

"I've missed you, My Lady."

Bailey's lips touched hers so softly. Taylor moaned. She'd forgotten just how perfect it felt when Bailey kissed her.

Bailey was so tender, so in control that Taylor felt free to let go. "I want you to touch me."

Taylor swung her leg so that she was sitting on Bailey's knee. Bailey's hands gripped around her waist. She smiled as Taylor pulled off her little midriff-baring T-shirt and revealed the lacy black bra she was wearing.

"You are beautiful, My Lady." They had just fallen into their Regency names for each other. It gave an element of role-play, where everything they did together was exciting. They could do anything as the Earl and Countess of Richmond.

Her hands squeezed Taylor's breasts, and then she unhooked her bra. As soon as Taylor's bra was off, Bailey pressed her face between Taylor's breasts.

Taylor put her hands around Bailey's neck and hugged her tightly. "Take your shirt off. I want to feel you skin to skin."

Bailey quickly unbuttoned her shirt while kissing Taylor and pulled it off, together with her sports bra.

"You feel so good," Taylor said.

Bailey couldn't wait to get even closer, so she eased them both off the couch and onto the floor. She could feel the heat from the fire at the same time as the heat they were both generating.

Taylor unbuttoned Bailey's jeans and tried to push them off her hips. Bailey pushed them and her underwear off, then took Taylor's off.

Their lips didn't leave each other as the firelight danced across their bodies. Tonight was about connecting back in the real world and feeling closer than skin. Their bodies came together quite naturally, Bailey thrusting her hips steadily.

Bailey could feel Taylor's wetness on her own sex as they moved together. It was a long slow ride, and when they both came to the peak of orgasm, Bailey had never felt closer to another human being in her life.

This woman had utterly stolen her heart, and come what might, there was no going back.

❖

Taylor woke up and saw Bailey standing by the bedroom window in only her boxers. Taylor loved Bailey's build, her strong back and shoulders. She took care of herself well. "Sweetheart? Is everything all right?"

"Yes, I'm just thinking."

"About what?" Taylor got up and pulled on one of Bailey's T-shirts and walked over to her.

"It's the first time I've been with another woman in this house."

Taylor worried that Bailey was having second thoughts, that her grief was making her feel guilty again.

"Did you live here together?"

"Sometimes, but most of the time at her house, where Ellis was most comfortable. I still have the house. Ellis had no other family, so it came to me. I haven't been able to make myself sell it," Bailey said sadly.

"You don't ever have to if you don't want to. Don't put a time limit on your grief. You might sell it in a year or never—just go with what feels right."

Bailey turned to her, and to Taylor's surprise, Bailey had tears in her eyes. Taylor's heart ached.

"Oh, sweetheart, it's okay."

Bailey held Taylor's head in her hands and caressed her cheekbones with her thumbs. "I've never had anyone to talk to about this, to share my grief with—I'm so grateful you came into my life, and I'm sorry I fought it for so long."

"Come here."

Taylor put her arms around Bailey's neck and pulled her into a hug. Bailey sobbed on her shoulder for a few minutes, then pulled away and wiped her tears away quickly.

"I'm sorry," Bailey said, "for crying. It's not something I do."

"There's nothing wrong with crying, sweetheart. It a natural thing to do. It'll help if you open up when you're with me. I'll never betray what happens in private between us."

"Come to bed. I just want to hold you close."

Bailey led them to the bedroom, and they both took off what little clothes they had left and climbed into bed. Bailey spooned behind Taylor, and Taylor held Bailey's hands to her heart.

CHAPTER TWENTY-THREE

I t's just along the street," Taylor said.

They were nearly at Eddie and Max's house, and Bailey was nervous.

"Do I look okay?"

"You look gorgeous." Taylor kissed her.

When Taylor had asked her to meet her brother and his husband, Bailey had been nervous. She became even more anxious as they were about to arrive at his house. But they had to tell people sometime, and Eddie was Taylor's closest brother, so she prayed he'd be okay with their relationship.

When they arrived at the house, Bailey paid the driver and got out to hold open the door for Taylor.

Once she got out Taylor said, "You don't have to pay for the taxis all the time."

"I do, My Lady."

That made Taylor smile. She took Bailey's hand and said, "Come on, they'll be perfectly nice."

Taylor knocked at the door, and Max opened it up. "Hi, Taylor, and you must be Bailey. Come in."

"Thank you," Bailey said.

Max was nice so far. He led them into the living room where Eddie was on the couch with Taylor's nephew.

"Hello, Bailey, it's nice to meet you."

Eddie started to get up, but Bailey said, "Don't get up with your leg. I'll come to you."

They shook hands and Jaden ran across to his auntie. "Hi, sweetie, I missed you."

Taylor was so good with him.

"Jaden," Taylor said, "this is Bailey. Say hi."

Jaden waved and said, "Hi."

"Max, will you put Jaden to bed?" Eddie asked. "We just kept him up so he could see you."

"Tay-Tay, story?" Jaden asked.

"Not tonight," Max said.

"It's okay. I'll go and read him a quick story, and I'll be back in no time. Gives you a chance to talk."

Oh God, Taylor was leaving her alone. *Don't?* Bailey pleaded with her eyes.

But Taylor wasn't listening. "I won't be long, sweetheart."

When Taylor left the room, Bailey waited for the inevitable questions. After a few seconds of silence, Bailey thought she would just get it all out there.

"Are you okay with this? Taylor and me."

"If my sister is happy and you're treating her right, then I'm fine with it. You seem like you didn't jump into this blindly, from what my sister's told me."

"Far from it. I thought it was wrong to even think about it. But I couldn't fight love. No one has ever stolen my heart in my whole life. Love was never something that I was looking for, but now it's here, and I never want to lose it."

"I've never seen Taylor this in love, and I'm happy for her," Eddie said. "My two older brothers and my parents might be harder to win over, but I'm sure when they see how happy you are, they'll be fine."

"Here's hoping."

One family member down, a few to go.

❖

"Are you sure you don't want to stay?" Taylor asked Bailey.

They got a taxi back from Eddie and Max's and were nearing Taylor's flat.

"It's okay. You've got work, and I'm well behind with my book. I'll call you in the morning." The taxi stopped and Bailey said, "If you can just wait here, driver, I'll be back in a minute."

Bailey helped Taylor out and escorted her to the door.

"You are a gentleman, My Lord."

"I know the way to take care of a lady."

"I'm going to miss you so much," Taylor said.

"I'll miss you too, darling. Oh, I forgot—I got you something."

Bailey fished around in her jacket pocket and pulled out a paper bag with a label saying *Burt's Sweets, Fudge, and Toffee.*

"You got me sweets?" Taylor beamed.

"It's a little traditional sweet shop near my house. I thought you'd like them, and you can crunch them as loud as you like."

Taylor had never felt more in love than she did at that minute. "I love you."

Bailey cupped her face and kissed her tenderly. "I love you, I adore you. Don't ever doubt it."

❖

The next morning, Bailey was hard at work in her office when her phone rang. It was Taylor on FaceTime, so she answered straight away. "Good morning, darling."

When the call connected, all Bailey could see were flowers filling the screen.

"You got them then?"

Yesterday afternoon Bailey had ordered flowers to be delivered to Taylor that morning, one of the reasons she wanted Taylor to stay at her own house last night.

Taylor's beautiful face came on screen. "Thank you, sweetheart. This is so special."

"I'm glad you like them," Bailey said.

"No one has ever made me feel special like this."

"Then they were fools. So have you been busy working?"

"Yeah, I was in the chatroom this morning to see how everyone liked the weekend, and they loved it. People have been telling their friends and family—oh, and there's some lovely photos. You should go on and look when you can," Taylor said.

"I will. I've got another couple thousand words to do, and I'll have a look. I'm so happy everything is going so well for you. You deserve it, and I'm proud of you."

Taylor gave her the biggest smile. "Thanks. I've got so much to organize. Next is the assembly room event, which mostly takes care of itself. I've hired a room in the town hall. It's only a one-night thing.

It's the weekend at Pardale I'm worried about. It's going to be a lot of work."

"But Fairydean was spectacular. You've got nothing to worry about," Bailey said.

"I had a lot of help from Lady Catherine and the staff at Fairydean. This time I'll be on my own. The owner didn't sound the friendliest on the phone."

"You'll have me and Gracie. With that team we can make it work."

Taylor blew her a kiss. "I'm lucky to have you."

Bailey laughed. "I think anyone could see I'm the lucky one. You sure you don't want a lecture for the assembly room event?"

"No, it's okay. They won't be enough time that evening. Save your best for our last weekend at Pardale."

"I'll start my research on the history soon and then help you any way I can. Have you thought about when to talk to your parents about us?"

"I thought we could just enjoy being together for a little while longer before I tell them," Taylor said.

"I was thinking about it, and I don't want them to think we've been sneaking around. I always like to be straightforward with people," Bailey said.

"Just a little while longer? Oh, hang on. There's another call—can I call you back? I'll just be a minute."

"On you go."

It was more than a minute. More like ten when Taylor called back. "Hello?"

Bailey knew something was wrong as soon as she saw Taylor's face. It was utter panic.

"Pardale's cancelled. I don't know what to do. I'll never get anywhere else at this late stage."

"Slow down, okay. Why have they cancelled? What happened?"

Bailey could see Taylor was pacing up and down frantically while holding the phone.

"They've had a fire. The kitchen and most of the bottom floor went up. No one was injured, but the rooms aren't usable. Things were going so well, and now I can't give my Romantics a second weekend."

"Just wait a second. When you booked Fairydean and Pardale, were there any others you could have chosen? Maybe they would still be available," Bailey said.

"No, I was lucky to get those two. These houses are booked up a few years in advance for weddings and parties. It's all over. I'm going to need to cancel and refund my Romantics."

"Look, I know this seems like a disaster, but there will be a solution. Just let me think."

Bailey pinched the bridge of her nose. *Come on. Think.* Then it hit her. Yes, yes. That would be perfect.

"Right, okay. Now I'm not promising anything, but I have a contact who may be able to help. I'll call them and get back to you."

"Who is it?" Taylor asked.

CHAPTER TWENTY-FOUR

H arry Knight! Come and take your child."
   "I'm coming, I'm on my way."
"You said you were on your way an hour ago," Annie Knight said.

Annie was standing in the large Axedale Hall kitchen with her eighteen-month-old son Oliver in her arms and Riley's Great Dane, Caesar, cuddling in at her side, all whilst surrounded by cakes and breads at different stages of preparedness.

Harry came running downstairs. "I'm here."

"You promised you'd have Olly. It is baking day you know, and it's the vicar's baking sale this weekend."

"I have an excuse."

Harry walked over to her and held her arms out to take Oliver. "Come here, my little Olly."

He wriggled in Annie's arms, eager to get to his other mum. "Mum, Mum."

Harry took him in her arms. "That's my big boy."

Annie went to the cupboard and got one of Caesar's favourite chewy bones. He happily took it and went off to his dog bed in the corner of the kitchen.

"What's the good excuse?" Annie asked.

Harry was bouncing Oliver on her hip and singing a nursery rhyme to him with singular attention.

"Harry?" Annie said more loudly.

"What?"

"Your excuse?"

"Oh yes, I got a phone call from an old friend from Cambridge, Jaq Bailey," Harry said.

Annie stopped still. "You're not going away on a dig are you?"

Although Harry was retired from lecturing on archaeology at Cambridge, she did sometimes take consultancy jobs on digs all across the world. They had always gone together, with Riley, their oldest child, but since Oliver was born, they didn't think it fair to drag him around.

"No, no. She was professor of history, but her specialty is early modern, so we sat on a good few interdepartmental committees."

"Early modern?"

"About 1450 to 1800ish," Harry explained.

"History, not archaeology like you, got it. What did she want?"

Harry launched into the story of the Regency Romance Club. "They've had their first ball, but the next one was supposed to be at Pardale Abbey."

"Didn't I see on the news they had a fire?" Annie asked.

"Yes, all their events have been cancelled, and Bailey's partner is stuck. If she doesn't get a venue, then it will be a disaster for her. Bailey asked if we could do her a favour," Harry said.

Annie picked up her iPad and said, "What's the date? If that weekend is free, then I'll be only too happy to help."

"I wrote it down. Hang on."

Annie had arrived at Axedale with her daughter Riley as house-keeper to the new Countess of Axedale, Harry. She had not only taken Harry in hand, bewitching the confirmed bachelor, but made Axedale a business that was profitable, making the house pay for itself.

Harry, Annie, and the children lived in one wing of the large house, and the other wing, including the ballroom, was dedicated to hospitality and catering—weddings, special events, and family anniversaries.

"It's the third weekend of September," Harry said.

Annie flicked through her calendar on screen, then sighed. "No, we have a wedding that weekend. Wait—if they could postpone it by a week, we could do it."

"Thanks, Annie. It sounded as if her partner was in complete dire straits."

"No wonder. But ask them to come down on Sunday and we can have a proper chat," Annie said.

"Excellent." Harry kissed her wife's head. "You are a treasure."

"I know that." Annie smiled and kissed Olly on his chubby cheek. "Now out of my kitchen. Scoot."

"Come on, Olly. We're not wanted. I'll call Bailey."

❖

The sun was shining that Sunday lunchtime as Taylor and Bailey took the cut-off for Axedale village. Bailey had hired a car for the weekend, so they didn't have to worry about catching a train, as Taylor wanted to make a day of it.

Taylor had been singing and dancing from the waist up for most of the journey.

Bailey chuckled to herself.

"What?" Taylor asked.

"Nothing."

"It's something, so get telling me, Dr. Bailey, or you'll be sorry."

"Oh, really?"

"Really."

"I'm laughing because I've never met anyone as alive as you. You've shimmied the whole way from London, while crunching your way through your travelling sweets."

"What's the point of being alive and not enjoying every second? And you can't go anywhere without some travelling sweets."

"Of course not."

Taylor put her hand on Bailey's thigh and squeezed it a few times. "I can't believe you got us Axedale Hall. You are the best."

"I know. Aren't I wonderful? Here's the car park."

Bailey turned into a piece of land just outside Axedale village.

"It's busy, isn't it?" Taylor said.

"Got one, over on the right." Bailey reversed into the space. "The grounds are open to the public at weekends. I think they have some family attractions."

"This is going to be a fun day. Let's go."

They walked into the village hand in hand. As they did Bailey saw a couple of people looking at her, then at her hand holding Taylor's. Only a few older people, but it niggled her.

Bailey forgot about their age difference when they were together, but when they were out in public, she had become hyper-aware of any looks she got.

Just forget it.

But the niggles were building up. Taylor still hadn't told her parents or oldest brothers about her. She thought they should have done, but Taylor kept asking for a few more weeks.

"What's wrong?" Taylor asked.

"Nothing. It's beautiful village, isn't it?"

"Perfect. This is going to be so much better than Pardale Abbey.

I've been poring over the website. The pictures of the grounds are gorgeous. There's a herd of alpacas. I love alpacas."

"You would." Bailey rolled her eyes.

"There are two celebrities that live in Axedale. Penny Huntingdon-Stewart-McQuade—she's a social media influencer and cook, and I follow her on YouTube and Instagram, and then there's Finnian Kane, the illusionist."

"I've heard of the magician but not Penny..."

"Huntingdon-Stewart-McQuade. She's famous and has a range of her own food in supermarkets. Do you even have Instagram?"

"Of course I do. I'm not that old, but I follow history accounts, not celebrity influencers."

"I never meant to imply you were old," Taylor said.

"No, just older."

"Don't be grumpy—you're my sexy, experienced, older woman." Taylor gave her a peck on the cheek.

"All right then." Bailey smiled.

They walked on and came upon a church. "That's a beautiful church," Bailey said.

"It is."

A vicar walked out the front doors of the church and shouted, "Good afternoon."

"Good afternoon," Bailey replied.

The vicar then went back to locking up her church.

Once they were out of earshot, Taylor whispered, "Did you see the vicar? She looked amazing. Did you see her leather jacket and heels?"

"I wasn't really looking."

"Liar." Taylor play-hit her.

Bailey stopped and turned to Taylor. "Why would I look anywhere else when I have a woman I desire by my side?"

Taylor stroked her cheek. "You are the sweetest and most romantic soul I've ever known."

Bailey saw an older lady glare as they went past. Bailey pulled away from Taylor's hand. "Let's go then."

"Okay, sweetheart."

After a few seconds Bailey said, "I will admit she was a striking-looking woman. Not someone you would guess was a vicar."

"It's a wonderful village. Like the kind of thing you'd see on an old style chocolate box. Oh, look." Taylor pointed down the street. "There's a river that cuts through the village down the street there, and a stone bridge. I saw it on the website, and there's swans and ducks to feed. We have to go there."

"Why don't we do that afterwards? Harry and Annie will be waiting for us."

"Okay, but you have to promise," Taylor said.

Bailey put her hand on her chest. "Cross my heart."

That was one thing Taylor had brought to her life, a joyful view that every new experience was exciting. The few women she had short relationships with before Ellis were accomplished, serious women of her own age. They would talk about politics, business, their areas of intellectual interest, but not feeding ducks and swans. It made Bailey's heart feel younger even if not in years.

"Here's the gates to the estate."

They turned in and began walking up to the entrance to the estate, but they couldn't see the house yet. Couples, families, and walkers passed them, coming and going.

"It's a popular place," Bailey said.

"I love it."

They turned the corner, and the house came into view. "Wow, that's much bigger than Fairydean."

"It is." Bailey was just delighted to see Taylor happy. It would have been such a disaster for Taylor if they hadn't found another house to use.

Before long they came to the alpaca enclosure.

Taylor sprinted off to the fence. Around it many people, adults and children, were gathered around the fence, laughing at the animals bouncing around with their funny expressions.

Bailey joined her and took her phone out. "I'll just text Harry and tell her we're here."

"Look at them, sweetheart. They're so funny."

"Very ugly," Bailey joked.

"They are not. They have their own beauty."

Bailey's phone buzzed. "They're going to meet us at the front door, so we better get going."

Taylor waved to the alpacas, and they made their way to the front door. When they arrived, Harry, her wife Annie, two children, and a very large dog sat waiting for them.

"Bailey, welcome to our home." Harry walked down the steps and shook Bailey's hand.

"Good to see you, Harry. Married life seems to suit you."

"It certainly does. This must be Taylor."

"Hi, Lady Harry. Nice to meet you."

"It's just Harry. Let me introduce you to my family." Harry led them up the steps.

"This is my wife, Annie, and in her arms there is our son Olly, and next to them our daughter Riley."

"Great to meet you," Taylor said.

Riley was taller than Annie already. She must be fifteen or sixteen.

"Come in, everyone," Annie said, "and we can have a good chat."

"Who's a good boy?" Taylor was down on her hands and knees making a fuss over Riley's dog Caesar.

"He's so handsome, Riley. You're really lucky."

"He's the best boy," Riley agreed.

They were standing in the Axedale entrance hall. Bailey was chatting to Harry next to them.

"Mum, you said another hour." Riley pointed at her watch.

Annie sighed. "Riley's best friend Sophie has just got back from holiday today, and she's desperate to go and see her. They've hardly been home two hours, Riley. Go, but if her parents aren't happy, you come right back."

"Okay, come on, Caesar."

When they ran off, Annie said, "Let's show you the ballroom first, and then we can have some tea. Follow me."

Taylor followed Annie into the ballroom. "Wow, this must be twice the size of Fairydean's. That was the last house we had a ball in."

"It was refurbished not long after I arrived at Axedale. It needed a lot of work, but Harry and her workmen have done an amazing job with it, and the whole house."

"It's beautiful. Perfect for a Regency ball. Isn't it, Bailey?"

"Perfect. Really stunning."

Olly reached out to Taylor. "I see you, sweetie. He's adorable. How old is he?"

"One and a half, and a little terror," Annie said.

"Can I hold him?"

"I'd be glad if you would. He's a heavy weight."

Taylor took him in her arms and then tickled him, and Olly giggled.

"You're good with him. Have you got little brothers or sisters?" Annie asked.

"No, I've got three big brothers, but they have kids, and I love them to pieces."

Across the room Bailey watched Taylor bounce Olly on her hip with a growing sense of trepidation. This worry had been building up bit by bit since they came back to London, back to reality, and it was gnawing away in her stomach.

Taylor was a natural with kids. She had seen her with Jaden, and as she saw Annie and Taylor laugh at something Olly had done, another barrier between them went up.

"Bailey?"

Bailey just realized Harry had been talking to her.

"Sorry?"

"I heard about your wife, Bailey. I'm sorry."

"Thank you."

"You've found happiness again, though. Taylor seems like a great woman," Harry said.

"A lot younger than me, you probably want to say."

"Me? How could I? I had more than one liaison with one of my twentysomething students at Cambridge. Probably don't mention that to my wife," Harry joked. "But this looks like more than that. You appear happy together."

"It is. I love her, but is love enough?" Bailey said.

"I'm not one to give advice. I avoided love like the plague, but I know it's worth fighting for. There are obstacles in every relationship, but if you face them together, then there's nothing that can't be overcome."

Annie turned to them and said, "Time for some tea or coffee. I have Super Duper cookies just for the occasion."

They began to walk out of the ballroom and Bailey said, "What are Super Duper cookies?"

"A thing Dionysus himself would kill for." Harry grinned.

"Really? Lead on then."

CHAPTER TWENTY-FIVE

Taylor and Bailey were driving back to London, and Taylor was so excited, she'd probably talked the whole way. She was going to have a sore head tonight. Taylor always did when her mind raced as fast as it had today.

"The ballroom was just perfect, and Annie said we could book up each year for the club. I'm so glad you introduced us. This will be miles better than Pardale, don't you think?"

Bailey didn't reply. She just stared at the road ahead. Bailey had been really quiet today. The day had started off great, but she'd grown quieter as the day went on.

"Bailey?"

"What? Sorry, my head was elsewhere."

"Thinking about your book?"

"Yes, that's it," Bailey said.

"I was saying how much better Axedale will be than Pardale."

"It will. Much better," Bailey said.

"Is there anything wrong? You've been quiet."

"No, not at all. Probably just worrying about my book. I'm fine."

Taylor wasn't sure she believed her.

Not long later, Bailey parked outside Taylor's building. "Are you sure you won't stay?"

Bailey rubbed the back of her head. "No, because the car hire place is closer to me, so I've just got a short walk back to my house."

"Okay. Weren't Olly and Riley adorable? Oh, and Caesar. What a gentle giant. I'd love a dog, sometime in the future, would you?"

"I hadn't really thought about it, to be honest."

There was something worrying Bailey for sure, but she couldn't make her talk.

"I better go." Taylor leaned in and gave Bailey a kiss. It wasn't the most incendiary kiss they'd ever had but would have to do.

Taylor got out of the car and walked up to her building's door. Bailey always waited until she was safely in the building.

My knight in shining armour, are you happy?

❖

"Hello?" Bailey answered her phone. It was Margo.

"Hi, Bailey. How are things?"

"The book's nearly done. Don't worry."

"Good, and Taylor?"

Taylor. The name that was never off her mind. It had been a month since their visit to Axedale, and despite promise after promise, she hadn't told her parents about her yet. Every time Taylor delayed telling them, the more Bailey thought this relationship was wrong.

Taylor's latest excuse was that it was her parents' anniversary party next week, and she didn't want her news to overshadow it if they reacted badly.

The romance of Fairydean seemed so long ago.

"Taylor's fine," Bailey said quickly. "How's the family?"

"Running rings around us as usual. I don't know how I keep up."

Yet again a reminder of how she would struggle to cope if Taylor wanted children. When she ended her call with Margo, she got up and walked over to the window and gazed out at the rainy day that matched her mood.

Her mind had been going back and forth over the right thing to do, and the painful truth was that losing Taylor would break her heart.

She took out her phone and gazed at one of the pictures she had taken of Taylor. Taylor was so full of life and its possibilities, and she deserved to experience every one of them.

What should she do?

❖

Taylor and Bailey were cuddled up on the couch watching one of Taylor's favourite films—Emma Thompson's *Sense and Sensibility*.

Bailey had told her to choose their film for the evening, which was always dangerous. She'd never had a girlfriend that she could share her love of Jane Austen with, and watching the films with Bailey made them extra special.

Taylor had chosen *Sense and Sensibility* to hopefully assure Bailey that age gap romances weren't totally abnormal. The heroine was a good bit younger than her, but Bailey was her Colonel Brandon. She pulled Bailey's arm tighter around her.

"This is so nice. Can you stay?"

"If you like," Bailey said.

"No, it's if you like. Is everything okay? You've been quiet."

Bailey kissed her head. "There's nothing wrong, and I'd like to stay."

"Good." Taylor snuggled her head closer into Bailey's chest. This was perfect—her dream woman at her side, some Jane Austen on the screen, and the only light in the room coming from the candles that were dotted about.

The cosy romantic feel was harshly interrupted by the buzz of the flat's intercom. Taylor clutched her hand to her chest. "I got such a fright."

"You're not expecting anyone, are you?" Bailey asked.

"No. Hang on and I'll check. It might just be a neighbour that's forgotten their fob."

Taylor hurried over to the intercom and said, "Hello?"

"Taylor, it's us."

That was Mama's voice. *Shit!*

"We thought we'd drop in."

"Sure…eh…come up."

Taylor slammed down the handset and said in utter panic. "It's my mums! Shit, shit, shit."

"It's okay, don't panic." Bailey got up and pressed off the TV.

Taylor was running around the room, blowing out the candles and putting the lights back on. "It'll look like they've stepped into a romantic evening."

"It *was* a romantic evening," Bailey said with annoyance.

"Look, they don't know about us yet, and this…I'm not ready for them to find out like this."

Taylor grabbed her laptop from the walking treadmill and put it on the table, and added a pen and paper.

They heard a knock at the door. "Quick, sit down. It looks like we were doing some work now."

Bailey just sighed and shook her head. Taylor knew that she was making Bailey angry. Bailey had been pressing her to come clean about their relationship, but she could just imagine her mums' reaction.

Mum would blow it out of all proportion, and it would cause trouble between her and Bailey, and she wanted nothing to come between them. Kel had always been overprotective of her, much more so than of her brothers. She had pointed out that this was sexist. But Kel just said it was realistic. She was a lot more vulnerable than her brothers. They'd had that argument since she was a girl, wanting to go out and have some independence. No matter the time of night, or wherever the party or club was, Kel would get out of bed and come pick her up.

Taylor opened the door and put a big smile on her face. "Hi, this is a surprise."

Vicky walked in first. "We were having dinner at a restaurant nearby. They've just started getting their fruit and veg from us and offered us dinner. So we thought we'd drop in and say hello."

Taylor gave each of her mums a kiss and took their coats. She saw Kel looking suspiciously at Bailey.

"You know my historian Bailey—we were just working on some things for the Axedale ball."

Mama seemed to buy it and walked over to shake Bailey's hand. "Hello, Dr. Bailey. I never met you that night at the hospital. I believe you've helped our daughter a great deal with her business project."

"I hope I've been useful, and please call me Bailey."

It was Kel whose turn it was to shake hands next. "Hello, Bailey." When Kel looked into her eyes, she was sure she knew.

"Sit down, Mum. Can I get you a drink?"

Kel looked at the wine bottle on the table with two glasses. "Bailey, I can see you've expanded my daughter's horizons"—she waited a beat—"from watermelon alcopops to wine."

Bailey felt very uncomfortable. "I brought some wine with me, and she wanted to try it."

"It was nice," Taylor said. "I think I might be growing up at last." Taylor laughed nervously.

Bailey felt like the cause of the discomfort in the room, and her anger was growing. Taylor described her as her historian. Not lover, not love.

She stood up and said, "I'll leave you and your family to it."

"Oh no, please don't for our sake," Vicky said. "We were just going to stay for five minutes and call for a taxi."

"Yes, stay, Bailey," Taylor said. "We've still got some work to do."

Bailey couldn't really say no now. So she sat there, feeling awkward, and her anger brewing, until their taxi arrived.

Once Taylor saw them out and shut the door, Taylor said, "That was a close one."

That comment just sent Bailey over the edge. "A close one? We're not having a clandestine affair."

"What? No I didn't mean—"

"I'm your historian? Your historian? You couldn't even go for friend?"

"Why are you so angry?" Taylor asked.

"Because I've had enough of being hidden away. You were the one who kept telling me this age difference wasn't wrong. I believed you, but you're too ashamed to admit to loving me."

Taylor marched over to Bailey angrily. "I am not ashamed of you."

"Well, why do you not tell your mums and your older brothers?"

"I told Ed."

"That's because he's your best friend, and you knew he'd be fine about it. I asked you and asked you to tell your parents, but you just keep pushing it back. I'm forty-five years old. I'm not a child. I will not hide like one."

"Look, I'll tell them after their anniversary party. I promise."

Bailey let out a breath. In this moment she had come to her decision. "It's too late."

"What do you mean it's too late?"

"Just what it says. I don't want to be the cause of strife in a family, and over the last few weeks I've come to the conclusion that I was right from the start."

"Right about what?" Taylor asked.

"Any relationship between us is impossible."

Taylor's eyes went wide, and she grasped at Bailey's hand. "No, it's not."

"Did you know that sometimes people look at me when we're walking down the street, hand in hand. Not everyone but enough that got me thinking this wasn't right. Then I saw you with Olly at Axedale. You deserve to enjoy your young life, then get married and have children like Harry and Annie, or Ed and Max, or your mums, even."

"You don't even know if I want children," Taylor said.

"You do. When I saw you with Jaden and Olly, I knew. By the time you were ready, I'd be in my sixties."

"What? Does life end at sixty now?"

"No, but I wouldn't be kicking a ball about in a park."

"Sure you would. You keep healthy and fit, and what if I never had any?" Taylor said angrily.

"Then you'd be nursing me when you should be living life."

"You're going to get some sort of disease or have a mental decline now? Okay, when I want to go and live this life you think I want, I'll chuck you in the basement and lock you in."

"Don't be childish."

"Me, childish? You're determined you are going to need a nursing home by sixty. No one knows what lies ahead—you could end up caring for me, or we could actually have a nice life together for however long that lasts."

"If that's what you think, then why don't you tell your parents." Bailey left her a beat to answer. "That's what I thought. More likely is that we would get some years together, and you would yearn for a younger lover and break my heart. I've already lost someone I love, and I'm not doing it again. This is over."

Bailey grabbed her jacket and walked to the door.

"Fine, if that's the way you want it, go." Bailey could hear Taylor was crying and distressed. "If you think I'd leave you for the first younger woman that came my way, then you obviously don't know me the way you should, because I never would."

Bailey hesitated as she clutched the door handle, and Taylor said, "You are my Colonel Brandon."

It was the hardest thing Bailey ever had to do, but she walked out the door, and she didn't look back.

❖

"You need to tell our mums," Eddie said.

He hobbled back into the living room with a plateful of sandwiches. Eddie was now in a lighter cast and walking with only one stick, so it was easier for him to look after his heartbroken sister. Taylor had been staying with Max and Eddie for the past week since her breakup with Bailey.

"I don't want to talk about it." Taylor cuddled her blanket tighter under her chin.

"You can't keep putting off seeing them. They think you're ill. Mama keeps texting me. Here."

Eddie handed her the giant plate of sandwiches he made. Unlike most women who craved ice cream when they were heartbroken, Taylor craved sandwiches.

"Max is going to bring more bread when he picks up Jaden from Mum's."

She started consuming the sandwiches like she hadn't eaten for two weeks. Taylor wanted to hide from the world under her blanket and use food to try to fill the pain inside her.

The day after their argument, she'd called and called Bailey's phone, but it just went to voicemail. Then she went around to her house for a few days in a row, but there was no sign of her. In the end, Taylor gave up. She had ruined the best thing in her life.

"She won't see me, Ed."

"Give her time," Eddie said, sitting down beside her.

"I was a coward, and I let her believe that what we had was wrong. I promised her that it wasn't, and then I behaved like it did. She was my Colonel Brandon, Ed."

They could hear a key in the front door. "That'll be Max and Jaden. Hang on."

Taylor put her plate on the coffee table and wiped the tears from her eyes. When the living room door opened, Taylor was shocked to see Mum, Mama, and Max.

"I'm sorry, Taylor. They made me tell them the truth. I'll just take Jaden in the bedroom."

"Oh, my poor baby." Vicky rushed to the couch and took Taylor in her arms.

Taylor started to cry again. "I wanted to tell you but—"

Kel sat on her other side and joined the hug. She kissed Taylor's brow. "You should have told us, princess." Then Kel pointed her finger at Eddie. "You and I will be having words. You don't keep secrets from your parents."

"I didn't even do anything." Eddie gesticulated in frustration.

After five minutes Taylor began to calm.

"Tell us what happened, Tay-Tay," Vicky said.

"I fell in love—we fell in love, Bailey, I mean."

"I knew there was something, but your mama told me to leave it," Kel said.

"I've never felt like this before about anyone. She has my heart, Mama, and I ruined it."

Vicky rubbed her back. "How did you?"

Taylor wiped her nose. "There was something between us from the start, an electricity that drew us together, but Bailey wouldn't do anything about it. She thought the age gap was too much, that you and the boys wouldn't accept it."

"Not too far from the truth," Kel said under her breath.

Vicky glared at her.

"What? She's nineteen years older than our baby girl."

"She's not a baby any more, Kel. Taylor is a young woman with her own business, and it sounds like Bailey did the right thing at the start. She didn't take this lightly."

"At the start."

"Carry on," Vicky said.

"Then as time went on what we had just grew and grew until the ball at Fairydean. We were in love, but still Bailey tried to hold us back from acting on our feelings. She kept saying that I should live my life and that I would end up becoming her nursemaid or something ridiculous like that. I said that it could be me, how did she know what the future might bring?"

"You began a relationship then?" Vicky asked.

"Yes."

Kel stood up quickly and started pacing, no doubt uncomfortable about what she was hearing.

"Bailey wanted to tell you both from the start. She wanted no secrets, but I just kept putting her off week after week. I was frightened that you would be so angry and that it would frighten Bailey away and I'd lose her. That night you dropped in, we were just having a romantic night watching a film. I panicked, tried to hide it from you, and totally dismissed and hurt her. I told you she was my historian, not even my friend."

Kel sat down on the coffee table. "I was sure there was something."

"After you left, she was angry I didn't come clean with you, that I obviously thought there was something wrong with us being together, deep down, like Bailey had feared. She told me that she didn't want to hold me back from having children, having fun living life. She walked away from me, even though she loved me."

"Maybe that's the right outcome," Kel said.

"The right outcome, Mum? Bailey is the love of my life, and now she won't even speak to me. You always told me I'd find the one, just like you did with Mama. You didn't say what age she'd have to be. What if my one chance at living a happy life is Bailey, and I've destroyed it?"

Kel clasped her hands together and sighed.

Taylor hugged Vicky. "She was my Colonel Brandon."

Chapter Twenty-six

B ailey had forced herself outside to pick up a few bits of shopping. She was staying at Ellis's house, where she knew Taylor wouldn't know where to find her. For four weeks she had avoided talking to or seeing Taylor, because if she did, Bailey knew she would crumble.

That was something she was determined not to do. All the worries Bailley had about the age gap had come true, and that was proven by the fact that Taylor tried to hide her relationship from her parents.

After her shopping, Bailey found herself sitting on a bench in a park across from the house.

It had taken everything in her to walk away from Taylor and ignore her phone calls, but she was doing the right thing for her, for them both, in the long run. Bailey, on the other hand, felt like she was carrying around a dagger plunged in her heart.

She could hardly sleep or eat and found herself staring at the four walls until she thought she might scream. But if Taylor felt like she had to hide, then they were wrong together, and sooner or later heartbreak would destroy them both.

Tonight was going to be the hardest yet. It was the evening of Taylor's assembly room event, where the Romantics would get together for one night of dancing at Taylor's local town hall, and she wouldn't be there.

Was Taylor going to be angry Bailey wasn't there, or would she be sad? Or a bit of both?

Bailey put her head into her hands. "Why did I let this happen?" Why didn't she follow her instincts and stop this thing before it hurt both of them so much?

She reached into her pocket and brought out her phone. She had only recently turned it back on, knowing that Taylor would call. Bailey couldn't bring herself to listen to the voicemails.

But she did open the picture that Dani had taken of them at the ball. They looked so happy. Bailey couldn't remember a time when she had smiled as much as her time with Taylor.

Darling Taylor.

Bailey's phone came alive, displaying a number she didn't know. It couldn't be Taylor with someone else's phone, could it? But it could be a business thing, so she answered with trepidation.

"Hello?"

"Hi, is that Dr. Bailey?"

"Yes, speaking."

"This is Taylor's mum, Kel."

Shit.

"Oh." Bailey didn't know quite what to say.

"I'd like to come and talk to you, if that's okay?"

Her mum must've have found out and either wanted to kill her or warn her off. The only decent thing to do was to meet her.

"Yes, can you give me an hour? I'm out of the house at the moment. I'll text you my address."

"Thanks."

Once Kel hung up, she hurried back over to Ellis's house and shut it up, before heading home. From there she waited, playing over everything she might say to Taylor's mum.

The doorbell rang. "Right then. Time to face the music."

She opened the door to Kel and said, "Hello, please come through to the kitchen. Can I get you a tea, coffee, cold drink?"

"No, I'm fine."

They sat down at the table. "Before you say anything, I just want you to rest assured I will not be seeing Taylor again."

"So she tells me."

Kel didn't add to her reply, making Bailey feel quite uncomfortable. Perhaps this was her aim.

"I'm only sorry it went as far as it did."

"Let's put that to one side for the moment. Taylor tells me you're a widow."

"Yes, my wife Ellis and I were married for a few years before she was killed by a drunk driver."

"I'm sorry to hear that. Taylor said you gave up teaching at Cambridge after her death. You must have loved her very much."

"Ellis was my best friend in the world, and I loved her as my friend. Ellis felt more, but I gave everything to make her happy. When she died, I felt pain and guilt, and I didn't want to be in the world any more, so I came back here and began writing full-time," Bailey said.

"I see. So back to why you let things with Taylor go on as far as they did…Working with Taylor on her business, you would know her romanticized view of love?"

"She is a true romantic."

"My wife tells me that's my fault for telling her and my boys how Vicky and I met and how it was love at first sight. I told them—when you know, you know, and don't ever give up on the person you love," Kel said.

Bailey had no idea where this was going. Kel was so cool and collected it was unnerving.

"Why did you hold out so long?" Kel asked again.

"Because she's a young woman with her life in front of her. She shouldn't be tied down to someone older like me. Nineteen years is a big difference, and I knew what people would think, including yourself and your wife."

"Yeah, you're right. I thought I saw a closeness between you when I first saw you, and to be honest it made me angry, but there's two things I want to know. Be honest. One, why did you eventually give in to a relationship? And two, what finally made you walk away?"

Bailey could answer simply. "Love is the answer to both. Taylor brought me out of my grief and made me look at life again. She made me believe that love could conquer any barriers to a relationship. And I walked away because I thought the greatest act of love I could show Taylor was to let her go and let her live her life."

Kel went quiet and appeared to be thinking hard.

"I did insist we tell you, but Taylor was worried about it and kept putting it off," Bailey said.

"Taylor told me. It makes me feel like I've failed as a parent, to know that she was worried about telling us."

"You have every right to be angry. I would be if I had a daughter in that situation."

"Taylor is heartbroken. She was staying with Eddie, but she's home with us now. She needs her mama looking after her," Kel said.

"I'm sorry to have caused so much pain, but I can only say that I feel the same, and my love for Taylor will never diminish," Bailey said.

"Hmm. There was something Taylor said to me. She said, what if this happy life I'm meant to live is with Bailey?" Kel tapped her fingers on the kitchen table. "I found out about the relationship weeks ago, and I've been mulling it over in my mind, while watching Taylor's heart crumble."

"I understand, and I am as hurt as Taylor, especially today when I won't be at her club event tonight. But it's the right thing to do."

Kel was silent for a few seconds. "I came here today not knowing much about you. I wanted to assess your character. I've found a person that was very honourable to her late wife, and honourable to my daughter, by walking away despite your feelings. I looked back at the other girlfriends she's brought home and thought, would they do that? The answer was no."

Bailey was confused. What was Kel trying to say?

"I can't believe I'm going to say this, but if you want to pursue this relationship with my daughter, then you have my blessing."

"What?" Bailey was dumbfounded.

"I trust you to look after my daughter and to love her."

"But the age—"

"You're not eighty years old. You're a lot younger than me, and I don't like to think of myself as a pensioner with one foot in the grave."

Bailey's heart was thudding, and her mind was swirling with emotions. "I don't know if I can. Taylor could change her mind as we both grew older, and to lose her would break my heart."

"You told me you were in pain without her," Kel said. "All I can say is this—I know my daughter, and I know that when she gives her heart, it will be for good. Vicky and I are having an anniversary party next Saturday. Have a think about everything we've talked about and if…Well, you're invited to meet the extended family. If you come, I think we'll know the answer about Taylor. I'll see myself out."

Bailey leaned her elbows on the table and covered her face.

"What the hell just happened?"

❖

The music filled the assembly room in the town hall, along with the sounds of merriment from Taylor's Romantics. The room hadn't heard such sounds of joy for years, and yet Taylor was standing by the punchbowl feeling bereft.

It had taken everything to get Taylor to dress up and come out to her own ball. She had lost all appetite for her business, for happiness, and for encouraging her Romantics to believe in love and find it.

Instead, she was drinking punch and trying to look as if she was not broken-hearted. Gracie had pushed her along at every step and was taking Taylor's place, talking to the guests and making sure they had everything they needed. She didn't know where she'd be without her.

The current dance came to an end. Taylor realized everyone would be making their way to the drinks table after such a vigorous dance, so she moved further down the room, not wanting to get involved in any of the chitchat.

There was a small part of Taylor, the part that believed in happy ever afters, that thought Bailey might turn up and profess her undying love, and they would all live happy ever after.

But she didn't come. Because Bailey was right when she tried to tell her that romance like in Jane Austen didn't exist in real life.

Taylor took a sip of her punch. This was a fine time to realize that romance didn't exist when she was trying to sell it to these people.

A voice beside her said, "Hey, beautiful. You're quiet tonight."

It was Zee. She couldn't be bothered with her competitiveness tonight.

"I'm taking it all in, that's all," Taylor said.

"You haven't had a dance at all. That's not like you."

"I just don't feel like the life and soul of the party. Gracie is making sure she brings the energy to the evening."

Zee nodded. "She has. Another beautiful girl." There was a long silence. "I thought Bailey would be here tonight."

The question she was dreading.

"She had a clash of engagements, and Bailey wasn't due to give a lecture tonight anyway."

"Yeah I heard you telling people that earlier. I don't believe it. You've fallen for each other, haven't you?" Zee said. "I could see it that last day at Fairydean. As much as she and I have a professional rivalry, steady, reliable Bailey wouldn't hurt you. There's something else keeping you apart."

Tears started to well up in Taylor's eyes. She'd been trying so hard to keep them at bay.

"Hey," Zee said, "come and dance with me and take your mind off it."

Taylor dabbed her eyes and shook her head. She just wanted to run away.

Zee took her hand. "Come on. You don't want your Romantics to see you upset. A dance around the hall will calm you down. Trust me."

Taylor found herself taking Zee's hand. Zee had a kindness and sensitivity that she kept well hidden under all that bravado.

When they got onto the floor, Taylor whispered, "Thank you."

"Always happy to help a lady in distress."

❖

Taylor was determined to try hard and not look like the heartbroken woman she was. It was her parents' anniversary party. All their friends and everyone from their extended family was here.

Her parents' house was big, but people spilled out from the living room into the conservatory and into the garden. Kel had put up a gazebo in case it rained, but it had turned out to be a nice sunny day and a warmish evening.

Taylor had tried to hide in the corner of the room with her Weird watermelon, but her great aunt Joyce had found her. Aunt Joyce always had the knack of making you feel like you were failing at life even if things were going brilliantly. In Taylor's current state, it was going to be easy.

"Your mother told me that you left your PR job to start a dating business, is that true?" Joyce asked.

"Yes, Aunt Joyce."

She leaned in and whispered, "Were you pushed from your job? No one in their right mind would leave a secure job like that to run a dating thing where everyone dresses up in silly clothes."

Taylor didn't have the energy to bat back with a sarcastic comment as she usually did. "No, it was a disaster, clearly."

Her brother Luke and Gracie suddenly appeared at her side. Luke put his hands on her shoulders. "I need to steal Taylor for a family photo, but Gracie wanted to tell you about her new boyfriend."

"Yeah he's a cage fighter," Gracie said dramatically.

As Luke walked her away, she could hear Joyce say, "He's called Mad Dog?"

Luke laughed. "Gracie is good at winding people up. You'll need to thank her later."

"I think I'll just go upstairs, Luke."

Eddie and Thomas joined them. "No, you're not. Come out to the garden."

"Okay, you don't need to push. It's just a photograph."

"No it's not, sweet pea," Eddie said.

When she stepped out, Taylor got the shock of her life. There standing with her two mums was Bailey.

"What is this all about?"

Her brother's smiled. "Mum will tell you."

When Kel spotted Taylor, she left Bailey and walked over to her. "I'm sorry you didn't feel able to tell us, princess, but if Bailey is your choice, I don't think you could find a better woman to love you."

This wasn't happening. It must be a dream. "I don't understand."

"I went to have a talk with Bailey. I wasn't sure what to expect, but she is a good, honourable person, much like the heroes in your books. If you love her, don't let her go. She'll be a welcome addition to our family, and someone I know will take care of my best girl. Give me that silly watermelon drink and go speak to her."

"Thanks, Mum." Tears were already forming in her eyes.

Taylor took a breath and walked over to Bailey. Vicky squeezed her shoulder as she passed.

When she got to Bailey, she was lost for words.

"Your mum invited me. You've got a good family," Bailey said.

"I know."

Bailey reached out for her hands. "I've missed you."

"I'm sorry how I handled everything with my family. I let you down," Taylor said.

Bailey wiped away her tears with her thumb. "It was a confusing situation for you. I understand."

"No, I should have been stronger."

Bailey clasped her hands and pulled them to her chest. "I love you, Taylor, and if there's one thing I've learned, it's that life is too short to worry about what might happen. If we did, I would be giving up the greatest love of my life, and Ellis would kick my arse for it if she could. That is if you want there to be an us?"

"With all my heart."

Bailey pulled Taylor to her and kissed her. It had been so long since they'd touched, and they'd both felt so much pain, that they poured every feeling they had into that one kiss.

Taylor heard clapping. She looked around and saw Mum, Mama, and her three brothers grinning like Cheshire cats.

"I think my heart might burst."

"No, it won't, because I'm going to look after it from now on. Come here, My Lady."

"As you wish, My Lord."

Their lips met again, and Taylor ran her fingers through Bailey's short hair. With each touch and kiss Bailey gave her, it mended her heart just a little bit more.

In the background Taylor could hear a lone voice.

"She's how much older than Taylor? Good God."

Then Eddie said, "Inside, Aunt Joyce, and we'll get you a drink to smooth the shock."

Taylor laughed inside. Aunt Joyce was going to have enough gossip to last a lifetime, but she didn't care because love, when it's right, can get across any obstacle.

EPILOGUE

N o, no, leave it on," Taylor gasped.
Bailey was trying to shrug off her white shirt, but she stopped, confused at Taylor's request. Taylor pushed her on the chest to stop her.

"All the best romantic Regency heroes have either wet shirts or unbuttoned and rumpled ones. I want you unbuttoned and rumpled."

Taylor grinned and kissed her way down Bailey's exposed chest and slid down onto her knees.

Bailey groaned. "You were just supposed to be helping with my tie."

Taylor untied the fastenings at the front of her breeches and giggled. "I will help you get dressed again."

She and Taylor arrived at Axedale for the last big ball of the season, promising each other that they wouldn't be intimate, to at least show some adherence to the no-sex rule.

That lasted all of five hours. They had both been dressing, and Taylor sneaked into her room under the pretext of helping Bailey with her costume, and moments later they were kissing passionately and losing control.

Taylor pulled out Bailey's strap-on while kissing all around her thighs. Bailey loved to use her strap-on while making love to Taylor. It had become such a big part of their Earl and Countess of Richmond role-play, that both of them became so turned on by it.

Taylor loved Bailey to be her older, more experienced, in control Regency lord and husband, and Bailey loved giving it to her. Bailey wanted Lady Taylor just as much as Taylor wanted her. After Bailey's libido had deserted her for so long, Taylor had brought it back with a bang, which was lucky because she had to keep up with her much younger lover.

Bailey groaned when she watched Taylor take her strap-on into her hot wet mouth. It was pure bliss. She threaded her fingers through Taylor's hair and encouraged her rhythm. As long as Bailey was in the right headspace, which she was always was with Taylor, she could come this way.

Just as Bailey's orgasm was starting to build, there was a knock at the door. They both stopped dead. They looked at each other in panic.

"Hello? Who is it? I'm not dressed yet," Bailey said.

Taylor put her hand over her own mouth to stop her from laughing so hard.

"Oh sorry, it's Gracie. I was looking for Taylor. There's been a mix up with the band and the music they've prepared for this evening."

Taylor mouthed, *Oh shit, oh shit.*

"She told me she was going downstairs, last I heard, Gracie," Bailey said.

"Okay, I'll have another look. See you later."

Once they heard the footsteps disappear, Taylor got up and sighed. "I better go."

"Oh no, you don't."

Bailey lifted Taylor into her arms and kissed her hard. "Let Gracie do her job. We need each other now."

"Yes," Taylor gasped.

She kissed Bailey back with equal passion, and Bailey carried her over to the nearest surface, while trying not to get tangled in her breeches that had now fallen down.

Taylor laughed into the kiss as Bailey nearly tripped. Everything was a joy being with Bailey. Making love, being caught out, nearly falling while trying to carry your lover—Taylor thought her heart would burst.

Bailey set her down on a chest of drawers that was just the right height. "I want to be inside you, My Lady."

"Yes," Taylor breathed.

Bailey pulled up her dress and still couldn't get to where she longed to be. "How many bloody petticoats does this thing have?"

Taylor laughed at Bailey's frustration and helped to pull up the many undergarments, until Bailey was near the wet heat of Taylor's sex.

"Do you want this, My Lady?" Bailey whispered.

"Yes, go inside."

"Hold on to my neck."

Taylor felt the hardness of Bailey's strap-on near her entrance and gasped as Bailey eased her way in.

"Jesus." Bailey moaned.

Bailey rocked her hips slowly at first, allowing Taylor to get used to the size. To have Bailey so close and filling her up so well was pure bliss. As Bailey's hips rocked faster, the deeper she went.

Taylor ran her hands up and down the back of Bailey's head and neck, her body starting to get desperate for a release. The chest of drawers began to move and shake as Bailey's thrusts got more intense.

"Yes, baby." Taylor's voice got louder and louder.

Bailey's voice was breathy. "We can't let anyone hear us."

Even more restriction turned Taylor on all the more. "Faster, baby."

Taylor's orgasm was on the edge of crashing on her, and she leaned all the way back on the chest of drawers and watched as Bailey was thrusting hard and losing control.

Bailey pulled her hips forward, and Taylor was overcome with a deep, deep orgasm and couldn't help but cry out. Bailey thrust a few more times and groaned hard and loud.

"Fuck, fuck."

She fell onto Taylor, and Taylor wrapped her arms around her.

"That was so good," Bailey said.

Taylor kissed her head, her body still shaking from the orgasm. "Don't leave me again, please? I love you."

"I never will. I love you. Do you think anyone heard us?" Bailey asked.

"Probably. We were loud enough."

Both of them chuckled with laughter.

Bailey and Taylor moved around in a circle, their palms touching and huge smiles on their faces.

The dancing at Axedale Hall was in full flow. Every one of Taylor's Romantics had been delighted with Axedale, and especially the ballroom.

"You're getting better at this, you know," Taylor said.

Bailey had to move in a figure eight with another dancer before getting back to Taylor. "Yes, I think I've missed my calling. Perhaps I should join Major Bamber and his troupe?"

"I wouldn't go that far, My Lord. You just stay here with me," Taylor said.

They continued to dance, and Bailey twirled Taylor around in a circle. "It's been a good weekend, hasn't it. I mean, everyone has enjoyed it, haven't they?"

"It's been a triumph," Bailey said. "Annie and her staff have made everything run perfectly, leaving you more time to spend with your Romantics and me."

"That has been the best bit. Your lecture was wonderful, and you even got involved with everything. The shooting, the fencing."

Bailey laughed. "And put Zee on her backside a few times while doing it."

The group held hands and spun together. "Don't. You enjoyed that too much."

"Well, she needed to be put down a peg or two," Bailey said.

"Now, now—she's giving me good publicity, and she was so good to me at the assembly room event. She was kind when I was upset. There's a good person under her flash personality."

"I suppose. But I think it's the thrill of the chase that Zee likes best."

"And you, My Lord?"

The music stopped and the dancers curtsied and bowed. "I'm in for the very long haul."

The dancers all applauded. Taylor watched Dani kiss Avery's hand.

"You know, I think Dani and Avery might be our season's next lovers," Taylor said.

"I think you're right. I don't think Dani was expecting it, but he's fallen for Avery. Let's go and talk to our hosts."

Taylor took Bailey's arm, and they walked over to Harry, Annie, and their friends. Taylor insisted they come to the ball and enjoy it with them.

"That must take a lot of practice," Harry said.

"You both looked wonderful up there," Annie added.

Taylor smiled. "Thank you. It was wonderful that you all could come."

The vicar and her partner Finn were there, and Quade and her wife Penny. They all had Regency clothes on and looked like they enjoyed wearing them.

Taylor loved that Finn wore her signature top hat that she used on stage.

"I wish we could dance with you all," Penny said. "Wouldn't you like to dance like that, Quade?"

"As long as it is with you," Quade said.

"Why not next year?" Bailey said. "Major Bamber could send you the instructions and you could practice together."

"Perfect idea, darling. Wouldn't you say, Annie?" Bridge asked.

"Perfect."

They were interrupted by Major Bamber banging his staff on the ground. "Romantics, can I have your attention please?"

Taylor looked at Bailey. "What's this about?"

Bailey shrugged.

"Lady Vida would like to say something."

All eyes went to Vida. She held Maisie's hand and led her into the middle of the dance floor. Taylor gasped when Vida went down on one knee. "She isn't, is she?"

Bailey smiled and put her arms around her from the back and pulled her close.

"Lady Maisie, you light up my life and fill it with love. Would you do me the honour of becoming my wife?"

"She is, she is," Taylor said.

There was a silence, and everyone held their breath.

Then Maisie said, "Yes, Vida. I'd love to be your wife."

Everyone burst into a round of applause. Vida stood up and kissed Maisie before twirling her around.

"Yes," Taylor said excitedly, "I've got my first happy ever after."

Bailey turned her around in her arms and said, "You already had your first happy ever after. It's right here."

Taylor grinned happily. "Yes." Then she put her hand on Bailey's chest. "It's right here."

Bailey placed her hand on Taylor's cheek. "I think that will be us next. What do you think? Why waste time?"

"I think so, My Lord."

"My Lady, you have brought life and sparkle to my life, and I will love you till the day I die and beyond."

Bailey kissed Taylor with more love than she had ever known. *Thanks, Jane Austen, for making me believe in true love.*

Zee chose that moment to catch them on camera. She snapped the perfect picture and said, "Gotcha."

About the Author

Jenny Frame is from the small town of Motherwell in Scotland, where she lives with her partner, Lou, and their well-loved and very spoiled dog.

She has a diverse range of qualifications, including a BA in public management and a diploma in acting and performance. Nowadays she likes to put her creative energies into writing rather than treading the boards.

When not writing or reading, Jenny loves cheering on her local football team, cooking, and spending time with her family.

Books Available From Bold Strokes Books

A Degree to Die For by Karis Walsh. A murder at the University of Washington's Classics Department brings Professor Antigone Weston and Sergeant Adriana Kent together—first as opposing forces and then as allies as they fight together to protect their campus from a killer. (978-1-63679-365-8)

Finders Keepers by Radclyffe. Roman Ashcroft's past, it seems, is not so easily forgotten when fate brings her and Tally Dewilde together—along with an attraction neither welcomes. (978-1-63679-428-0)

Homeland by Kristin Keppler and Allisa Bahney. Dani and Kate have finally found themselves on the same side of the war, but a new threat from the inside jeopardizes the future of the wasteland. (978-1-63679-405-1)

Just One Dance by Jenny Frame. Will Taylor Sparks and her new business to make dating special—the Regency Romance Club—bring sparkle back to Jaq Bailey's lonely world? (978-1-63679-457-0)

On My Way There by Jaycie Morrison. As Max traverses the open road, her journey of impossible love, loss, and courage mirrors her voyage of self-discovery leading to the ultimate question: If she can't have the woman of her dreams, will the woman of real life be enough? (978-1-63679-392-4)

A Talent Within by Suzanne Lenoir. Evelyne, born into nobility, and Annika, a peasant girl with a deadly secret, struggle to change their destinies in Valmora, a medieval world controlled by religion, magic, and men. (978-1-63679-423-5)

Transitioning Home by Heather K O'Malley. An injured soldier realizes they need to transition to really heal. (978-1-63679-424-2)

Truly Enough by J.J. Hale. Chasing the spark of creativity may ignite a burning romance or send a friendship up in flames. (978-1-63679-442-6)

Vintage and Vogue by Kelly and Tana Fireside. When tech whiz Sena Abrigo marches into small-town Owen Station, she turns librarian Hazel Butler's life upside down in the most wonderful of ways, setting off an explosive series of events, threatening their chance at love...and their very lives. (978-1-63679-448-8)

The Accidental Bride by Jane Walsh. Spinsters Miss Grace Linfield and Miss Thea Martin travel to Gretna Green to prevent a wedding, only to discover a scandalous passion—for each other. (978-1-63679-345-0)

Broken Fences by Jo Hemmingwood. Former army sergeant Seneca Twist has difficulty adjusting to civilian life until she meets psychologist Robyn Mason and has a place to call home. (978-1-63679-414-3)

Never Kiss a Cowgirl by Ali Vali. Asher Evans dreams of winning the National Finals Rodeo in Vegas, and Reagan Wilson wants no part of something that brings back the memory of what killed her father. (978-1-63679-106-7)

Pantheon Girls by Jean Copeland. Cassie Burke never anticipated the detour life is about to take when a meeting with a prospective client reunites her with a past love and reignites the star-crossed passion they shared twenty years earlier. (978-1-63679-337-5)

Roux for Two by Aurora Rey. For TV chef Chelsea Boudreaux and hometown boy Bryce Cormier, love proves as tricky as making a good pot of gumbo. (978-1-63679-376-4)

Starting Over by Nance Sparks. Jennifer has no idea if she can mend Sam's broken soul after the sudden loss of her wife, but it's never too late for starting over. (978-1-63679-409-9)

Three Wishes by Anne Shade. A magic lamp, a beautiful Jinni, and a cursed princess make for one unbelievable story. (978-1-63679-349-8)

Undiscovered Treasures by MJ Williamz. For Cyl and her friends Luna and Martinique, life's best treasures often appear when they're not looking. (978-1-63679-449-5)